She Was As Old As
Earth

She has no name, no p[...]
black, and though she has been seen by many men, she
is known only to a handful of them. You'll see her—if
you see her at all—just after you've taken your last
breath.

Then before you exhale for the final time, she'll
appear, silent and sad-eyed, and beckon to you.

She is the Dark Lady, and this is her story.

Also in Legend by Mike Resnick

**SANTIAGO
STALKING THE UNICORN**

THE
DARK LADY

A Romance of the Far Future

Mike Resnick

A Legend Book

Published by Arrow Books Limited
62–65 Chandos Place, London WC2N 4NW

An imprint of Century Hutchinson Limited

London Melbourne Sydney Auckland
Johannesburg and agencies throughout
the world

First published 1987 by Tom Doherty Associates Inc.
Legend edition 1988

Printed and bound in Great Britain by
Anchor Brendon Limited, Tiptree, Essex

ISBN 0 09 958190 6

To Carol, as always,

And to Tom Doherty and Beth Meacham,
who kept every one of their promises.

Table of Contents

Prologue

SHE WAS OLD WHEN THE Earth was young.

She stood atop Cemetery Ridge when Pickett made his charge, and she was there when the six hundred rode into the Valley of Death. She was at Pompeii when Mount Vesuvius blew, and she was in the forests of Siberia when the comet hit.

She hunted elephant with Selous and buffalo with Cody, and she was there the night the high wire broke beneath the Flying Wallendas. She was at the fall of Troy and the Little Bighorn, and she watched Manolete and Dominguez face the brave bulls in the bloodstained arenas of Madrid.

She was there when Man went out to the stars. She saw the Battle of Spica and the Siege of Sirius V, and she sat in Jimmy McSwain's corner the fatal night he fought Skullcracker Murchison. She rode the spaceways with the Angel, watched Billybuck Dancer die beneath the red sun of a distant world, and stood beside Santiago when Johnny One-Note gunned him down.

She has no name, no past, no present, no future. She wears only black, and though she has been seen by many men, she is known to only a handful of them. You'll see her—if you see her at all—just after you've taken your last breath. Then, before you exhale for the final time, she'll appear, silent and sad-eyed, and beckon to you.

She is the Dark Lady, and this is her story.

PART 1

The Man Who Had It All

1.

Where am I to begin?

This is not an epic saga, though it spans both millennia and star systems. Nor is it a story of passion and romance, though it was passion and romance that drove several of the participants to their doom. It is not even a tale of high adventure, though without high adventure there would be no tale to tell.

This is simply a true chronicle of events, and as such should be presented in the Language of Formal Narration. Were I to do so, however, I would be required to relate to you, in elegant order, all of my life experiences from the day of my birth, and this would give you a distorted view of my importance, since in truth I am little more than an onlooker who nonetheless managed to bring dishonor to his name, his House, and his race.

Therefore, I choose to speak to you in the Language of Informal Recital, and according to its rules, I shall begin my story at the last possible moment, which was, in fact, the first moment of my personal involvement.

That moment occurred as I climbed the broad titanium stairs of the Odysseus Art Gallery and, panting from my exertion in the thick, humid air, approached the front door of the vast, angular building. There were two attendants standing there, both clad in muted purple uniforms with glaring red stripes on their trouser legs, and I deemed it proper to address them in the Dialect of Honored Guests.

"Attention, my good man," I said formally. "I must have directions to the site of the forthcoming auction."

"Well, I'll be damned!" said the taller of the two attendants. "It not only wears shoes, but it talks, too!"

I immediately realized that I had chosen the incorrect form of address, and quickly changed to the Dialect of Supplication.

"Please, good sir," I said, dimming my color and lowering my head in a gesture of submission. "A thousand pardons if I have offended. I humbly entreat you to aid me in reaching my destination."

"That's a little more like it," he grunted, and I relaxed somewhat as it became apparent that he had forgiven my social error. "Let's see your papers."

I handed him my passport, invitation, and credentials, and waited in silence while he and his companion examined them.

Suddenly he looked up and stared at me.

"Leonardo?" he said dubiously.

"Yes, good sir."

"What's someone like you doing with a human name?"

I pointed to my passport. "If you will notice, good sir, Leonardo is not my real name. I am a member of the House of Crsthionn."

He looked where I indicated, tried twice to pronounce my Bjornn name, and finally gave up.

"Then what are you doing with an invitation for a Leonardo?"

"Leonardo is what I am called at my place of employ here on Far London, good sir."

"You mean the place where you work?"

"Yes," I said, remembering to nod my head in affirmation. "At my place of work. I am currently associated with the Claiborne Galleries."

"You are, huh?" he said dubiously.

"Yes, good sir." I bent over and hunched my shoulders together, a near-perfect posture of nonaggression. "May I pass now, please?"

He shook his head. "I don't have anything on my master list about an alien named Leonardo."

I could have pointed out that Men were as alien to Far London as the Bjornn were, but it would have been inconsistent with the Dialect of Supplication, and I had already offended him once. Therefore I bent even lower.

"My papers are in order," I said, staring at the gray titanium. "I beg of you, good sir: If I am not allowed to perform my function, the House of Crsthionn will be dishonored."

"First we've got to determine what your function *is,*" he said. "There's about 200 million credits' worth of artwork on display inside. My job is to make sure your function isn't to steal it."

"Or maybe eat it," added his companion with a smile.

"Please, good sirs," I persisted. "If you will but summon Hector Rayburn or Tai Chong, they will attest to my identity and my right to be here."

"We got a Rayburn or a Chong inside?" asked the attendant of his companion.

"Beats me," replied the other one. "I can check on it."

"Okay. You do that." The attendant turned back to me. "All right now, Leo."

"Are you addressing me, good sir?" I asked.

"Who else?"

"You have forgotten my name, good sir," I said gently. "It is Leonardo."

"A thousand pardons," he said, imitating my tone of voice and bowing low. "Leonardo." Suddenly he straightened up. "Suppose you go around to the east side of the building while we check this out. If either of them vouches for you, I'll send word to pass you through."

"I am very anxious to join my associates, good sir," I said. "Can I not wait right here?"

He shook his head. "You're causing a traffic problem."

I looked behind me. There was no one in sight.

"A *potential* traffic problem," he said when I turned back to him. I realized that I had somehow given offense to him again, and therefore ceased using the Dialect of Supplication.

"Will this take very long?" I asked.

"What happened to the 'good sir'?" he asked, ignoring my question.

"It was obviously the improper form of address," I answered. "I am trying to decide which dialect will not offend."

"How about silence?" he suggested.

"I know of no wordless dialect," I replied truthfully. "Won't you please answer my question?"

"What question?"

"How long will I be kept waiting?"

"How the hell should I know?" he replied irritably. "It all depends on how many Rayburns or Chongs there are inside." He paused. "Look," he added, "I'm just doing my job. Now go around to the east side like a nice boy or girl or whatever you are, and someone will let you know when you've been cleared."

I turned around and climbed back down the steps. I was still unused to wearing shoes, and the slidewalk was moving so rapidly that I feared it might upset my balance, so I remained on the street, walked around to the east side of the multifaceted titanium and glass building, and found that it was deserted. I slowed my pace momentarily to admire a ceramic mosaic that was set into the metal wall at human eye level. Finally I came to a plain, unmarked door which was set into the building a tenth of a degree off center. It was locked.

I stood by the door and waited, feeling naked and somehow incomplete, as I always do when I am alone. I tried not to think of the warmth and security of the Family, but when you are the only member of your race on a strange world this is not always an easy thing to do. Five minutes passed, then ten more, and I was certain that with each passing second I was bringing further dishonor upon my Pattern Mother and my House, which made my own disappointment at the possibility of not being able to finally see one of the sculptures by the fabulous Morita seem pale and colorless by comparison.

Two human females passed by and stared openly at me. As they continued walking up the street, one of them whispered something to the other, and both of them began laughing.

And then, finally, Tai Chong stepped through the doorway and hurried over to me. "Leonardo," she said when she had reached my side, "I'm so sorry about this mix-up!"

"It is all right now that you are here, Great Lady," I replied, using the Dialect of Affinity, as I always did in her presence.

"Have you been waiting long?" she asked.

"No more than twenty minutes," I said, hiding my hands behind me so that she could not see them until their color returned to normal.

"This is intolerable!" she said angrily. "I'll have the security guards' jobs for this!"

"It was my own fault, Great Lady," I said. "I offended them through my ignorance of the proper form of address."

"Nonsense! They've been sending aliens around to this door all night."

The thought came to me that the gallery should have employed less sensitive and more forgiving guards, but I said nothing, and at last Tai Chong reached for my hand to lead me inside.

"Your color has changed," she noted as I reluctantly extended my fingers.

"I find it warm outside, Great Lady," I lied, for since she had not learned to identify the Hue of Emotional Distress, I had no desire to cause her further consternation.

"I had no idea that extremes of temperature affected you so greatly," she said sympathetically. "Would you like me to take you back to your hotel?"

"Please allow me to stay!" I said urgently, trying to control the panic in my voice.

"Well, certainly, if that's what you want," she said, staring at me as my color became brighter still. "I was just concerned about you."

"I thank you for your concern, Great Lady, but it is imperative that I proceed with my education and reflect credit upon my House." I paused. "Also," I added with a feeling of guilt, since I was addressing a personal consideration, "I have waited years for the opportunity to see a Morita sculpture."

"Whatever you say," she replied with a shrug. "But I'm still going to complain about the guards."

"It was my fault, Great Lady."

"I very much doubt it. By the way," she added as we entered the building, "I thought you were going to start calling me by my given name."

"I will make a renewed effort to remember, Great Lady," I said.

"I notice you don't have any trouble with Mr. Rayburn's name."

"He is not a Great Lady," I explained.

She chuckled dryly. "Someday, Leonardo, I must pay a visit to your world, with all its Great Ladies and not-so-great gentlemen."

Then we were in the main gallery, a large circular room with off-white ceramic walls and a faceted dome composed of bronzed solar glass, and the last of my discomfort vanished as I felt the warmth and closeness of the crowd. There were perhaps four hundred beings there, all brightly and elegantly clad, all but a handful of them human. Among the other races I discerned a Lodinite, three Ramorians, two Mollutei, a trio of feathered beings from the Quinellus Cluster, and off in a corner, proud and aloof, his gray, leathery arms folded across his narrow chest, was a Canphorite, whose glowing crystal medals proclaimed that he was a survivor of two armed uprisings against the human Oligarchy.

Tai Chong, still holding my hand, began escorting me

through the room, introducing me to various friends and associates of hers (whom I addressed gravely in the Dialect of Courtly Diplomacy, the imposed vagueness of which seemed to amuse them). Then Hector Rayburn, looking very dapper in his sleek, shining evening clothes, walked over and greeted us.

"I see you found him, Madame Chong," he said.

"Those bastards out front have created an Aliens Only entrance," she said, her anger returning.

Rayburn nodded his head. "I've heard they've been giving aliens a hard time all evening."

"It was only a minor misunderstanding, Friend Hector," I said.

"It was a major breach of manners," said Tai Chong.

"Well, there doesn't seem to have been any permanent harm done," said Rayburn easily. He ignored Tai Chong's outraged glance. "Leonardo, can I borrow a few minutes of your time?"

"Certainly, Friend Hector." I turned to Tai Chong. "If it is acceptable to you, Great Lady?"

"The Albion Cluster artwork?" she asked Rayburn.

"Yes," he replied.

She smiled at me. "Well, that's what you're here for. I'll meet you again after you've finished."

Rayburn led me out of the main gallery and down a narrow tiled corridor.

"She's going to be hell to live with for the next couple of days," he remarked.

"I beg your pardon, Friend Hector?"

"Madame Chong," he explained. "Her and her damned causes. *You* know those guards were just a couple of dumb clods who didn't mean any harm, and *I* know it, but you'll never convince her of it." He paused. "I wish she'd defend her human employees with the same vigor." Suddenly he seemed uncomfortable. "Meaning no offense, of course."

"I know you meant no offense," I replied carefully.

"She thinks she can change human nature overnight, and it just can't be done," he continued. "One of these days she's going to jump in and defend the wrong damned alien or schizoid killer or whatever she's defending that week, and then she's going to find herself in big trouble."

Before I could think of a diplomatic answer, we came to a small rectangular gallery that was filled with perhaps fifty paintings and holograms. There were nudes, portraits, landscapes, seascapes, spacescapes, still lifes, even some nonrepresentational pieces that had been created by a computer equipped with a Durham/Liebermann perception module.

Rayburn waited until I had briefly examined the collection, then turned to me.

"I've got a client who's interested in investing in a couple of pieces from the Albion Cluster," he said. "And since that's your field of expertise, I thought you'd be willing to let me pick your mind."

"I will be happy to help you in any way I can, Friend Hector," I answered. "How much money is she prepared to spend?"

"She's a he," he said. "And he'll go up to a quarter of a million credits. I've marked a couple of the likelier pieces in my catalog, but I'd like your input." He paused uneasily. "Also, authentication was never my strong point. I'd especially like to know if you think the Primrose is authentic." Suddenly his self-assurance seemed to return to him. "I'll make the final decision, and I'll take full responsibility for it. But I'd like your input, just the same."

"If I am to be of any use to you, Friend Hector, I must respectfully request that I be permitted to examine the artwork more closely."

He seemed relieved. "Certainly. I'll be back in a few minutes." He walked to the doorway. "I want to sample some of that Denebian wine before it's all gone." He paused as he saw my color darken. "You don't mind, do you? I mean, there's nothing I could do here but stand around and watch you."

"No, Friend Hector," I lied. "I do not mind."

"Good. I *knew* all this stuff Madame Chong was spouting about Bjornns not wanting to be alone was just her imagination." He stepped out into the corridor, then stuck his head back in. "You won't forget to check the Primrose?"

"I will not forget, Friend Hector," I said.

"Fine. I'll see you in a little while."

Then he was gone, and I forced myself to concentrate on the artwork rather than my isolation, and gradually the feeling of nakedness retreated behind my total absorption with the work at hand.

Most of the two-dimensional paintings were between six and ten centuries old, though there was one (and not a very good one, at that) which seemed to date back almost three thousand years. The majority of the holograms, especially those composed in *static/stace*—electrostatic patterns frozen in stasis—were no more than a century old, though, again, there was one that seemed to date back almost five millennia, back to the days when the race of Man was first expanding into the galaxy.

All but two of the pieces were undeniably created by human hands, and I felt there was a chance that one of the other two was also. Only two of the artists were of truly major stature—Jablonski, who had lived a thousand years ago on Kabalka V, and Primrose, who had achieved a certain notoriety on Barios IV before his work fell into disrepute—but all of the pieces fell into clearly defined and easily identified schools of the Albion Cluster.

I examined the Primrose, a minor work by a no-longer-major artist, determined that the canvas was from Barios IV and that the signature was not a forgery, and went on to the rest of the collection.

One painting in particular captured my attention. It was a portrait of a woman, and while it lacked the technique of the Jablonski, it nonetheless held my interest. Her features were exquisitely chiseled, and there seemed to be an air of loneliness about her, a sense of a deep longing for the unattainable. There was nothing in the title to identify her—indeed, it was simply called "Portrait"—but she must have been a very important lady, for I had seen her likeness twice before, once in a hologram from Binder X, and again in a painting from Patagonia IV.

I walked over to the Jablonski and two of the more exotic *static/stace* holograms and tried to concentrate on them, but something kept pulling me back to the portrait, and finally I returned to it and began studying the brush strokes, the subtle nuances of light and shading, the slightly off-center positioning of the model.

The artist's name was Kilcullen, which meant nothing to me. A rapid analysis of the texture of the canvas, the chemical composition of the paint, and the style of the near-calligraphic signature in the upper left-hand corner led me to place the painting's age at 542 years, and its point of origin as one of the human colonies in the Bortai system.

Suddenly I sensed a feeling of warmth and relief, and instantly knew that I was no longer alone in the room.

"Welcome back, Friend Hector," I said, turning to him.

"Well," he said, sipping from an elegant crystal wine goblet, "is the Primrose authentic?"

"Yes, Friend Hector," I replied. "But it is not one of his better paintings. It may bring 250,000 credits because of his reputation, but it is my judgment that its value will not increase appreciably in the years to come."

"You're sure?"

"I am sure."

He sighed. "That's a pity. I have a feeling the Jablonski will cost too much."

"I concur, Friend Hector. It will bring half a million credits at least, and quite possibly 600,000."

"Well, then," said Rayburn, "have you any suggestions?"

"I very much like *this* painting," I said, indicating the portrait.

He walked over and studied it for a moment. "I don't know," he said at last. "It's quite striking from across the room, but the closer you get, the more you realize that this Kilcullen was no Jablonski." He stared at it for another moment, then turned to me. "What do you think it will bring?"

"Perhaps fifty thousand credits," I responded. "Sixty thousand if Kilcullen has a reputation in the Bortai area."

He stared at it once more and frowned. "I'm not sure," he mused. "We'd be going out on a limb, buying a painting by a virtual unknown. I don't really know if that qualifies as an *investment*. It may be worth fifty thousand on quality, but that doesn't mean it'll appreciate any faster than the inflation rate." He paused. "I'll have to think about it." He stared at the painting again. "It's striking, I'll give it that."

Just then Tai Chong entered the room.

"I thought I'd find you here," she said. "The auction is due to begin in another five minutes."

"We're on our way, Madame Chong," said Rayburn, and I fell into step behind him.

"Did you find anything of interest in there?" Tai Chong asked me.

"Perhaps one piece, Great Lady," I answered.

"The portrait of the woman in black?" she asked.

"Yes, Great Lady."

She nodded her head. "It caught my eye, too." She paused and smiled at me. "Are you ready to take a look at the Morita sculptures?"

"Oh, yes, Great Lady!" I said enthusiastically. "All my life I have dreamed of seeing a Morita sculpture in person!"

"Then come with me," she said, taking me by the hand. "You'll probably never see three of them on one planet again." She turned to Rayburn. "We'll be back in a few minutes, Hector."

"I'll hold the fort," he said easily. "We don't have a professional interest in anything that's coming up in the next half hour."

She led me through the circular gallery to a small room that was off to one side. I tried unsuccessfully to control my color, which was fluctuating wildly with excitement, and experienced a moment of almost physically painful embarrassment over such a display of passion concerning a personal and individual interest.

"May I see your credentials, please?" said a burly, purple-clad guard who was blocking our way.

"I was here not five minutes ago," answered Tai Chong.

"I know, Madame Chong, but those are my orders."

She sighed and withdrew her identification card.

"Okay. You can go through."

"Thank you," she said. "Come on, Leonardo."

"Not him," said the guard. "Or is it a her?"

"He's with me," she said.

"Sorry," said the guard firmly.

"Leonardo, show him your invitation."

The guard shook his head. "Save your time," he said to me. "Only gallery directors are permitted through."

"I am a ranking member of the House of Crsthionn," I said.

"That's an alien gallery?" he asked.

"Yes," I answered. It was easier than explaining the concept of a Bjornn House to him.

"I'm sorry. This is for the directors of human galleries only."

I was stunned. I did not know what answer to make, and so I said nothing, though my color registered total humiliation. I hadn't realized until that moment how much I had looked forward to seeing the Morita sculptures; it was as if the Mother of All Things was punishing me for having the audacity to place my personal interests above those of the House, even for a moment. And as I realized that the punishment was a just one, all possibility of anger was drained from me, to be replaced by silent acceptance of the justice of the situation.

But while *I* may have been silent, Tai Chong wasn't.

"What's going on here?" she demanded. "Leonardo has come to Far London on an exchange program, and is associated with the Claiborne Galleries. His papers are in order, and I will personally vouch for him."

"Madame Chong, we're at war with more than fifty alien races across the galaxy."

"*Not* with the Bjornn!" she snapped.

"Look, I'm just obeying my orders. If you've got a complaint, see the director."

"I most certainly will!" she snapped. "This treatment of an honored visitor is inexcusable!"

"Please, Great Lady," I said, tugging gently at her glittering sleeve and trying to hide my humiliation. "I do not wish to be the cause of such disharmony. I will see the Morita sculptures another time."

"By midnight they'll be in three different spaceships, all bound for God knows where," she replied. "There won't *be* another time."

"I will see them when they are auctioned."

"They're too heavy and bulky to move out to the auction room," she said. "That's why they're on display here." She turned to the guard. "I'm asking you one last time: Will you let my colleague into the exhibit?"

He shook his head. "I've got my orders."

I sensed that she was barely in control of her temper, and ignoring my own bitter disappointment, I gently touched her hand.

"Please, Great Lady," I said softly. "There are many other sculptures and paintings for me to look at."

"Damn it, Leonardo, doesn't this bother you at all?" she asked in obvious exasperation.

"I have been instructed that when I visit human worlds, I must obey human laws," I answered carefully.

"This isn't a law!" she snapped, glaring at the guard. "It's a policy, and I intend to protest it!"

"That's certainly your right," he said with the total unconcern of one who knows that he is not ultimately responsible for his own behavior.

She glared at the guard, her anger almost tangible, then abruptly walked back to the main gallery, leading me by the hand as if I were a small human child. I myself felt strangely tranquil: An even more vitriolic scene had been avoided, and the experience had reinforced the truth that one's personal desires and goals are ultimately unimportant.

I was new to human society, and this was the first time I had pursued my private wants, in however trivial a manner. It would not be the last.

2.

THE AUCTION WAS JUST BE-
ginning when we rejoined Rayburn, who was engaged in
animated conversation with an elderly woman who had
dyed her hair green to match the color of her emeralds. I
was quite calm, but I could tell that Tai Chong was still
seething with anger at the guard.

"Honored guests," said the auctioneer, "welcome to the
Odysseus Gallery's third semiannual auction. Tonight we
will be presenting 143 pieces for your consideration, the
majority of them from the worlds of the Albion and
Quinellus clusters—and, of course, the pièce de résistance
of this evening's offerings, a trio of works by the immortal
Felix Morita, which have been donated by the government
of Argentine III. I should add that all revenues received
for the Moritas will be used to combat the mutated virus
that has wrought such havoc in the Argentine system, and
that the Odysseus Gallery will be donating one-third of *all*
our commissions earned this evening to the Argentine III
Relief Fund."

"He'll still make ten times more than he would without
the Moritas," whispered Rayburn with a knowing smile.
"That was probably part of the bargain."

The auctioneer paused until the polite applause subsided. "Now let's get the evening off to a great beginning with a piece from Earth itself."

An ancient chrome sculpture was brought out. It had been crafted in Uganda in 2908 A.D. (or −2 G.E.), had somehow turned up on Spica II a century later, and was later added to the collection of Andrea Baros, a famed actress of the Late Republic Era. But while its history was fascinating, its lack of quality was apparent, and the auctioneer was soon trying unsuccessfully to get the interested parties to proceed with more than thousand-credit jumps.

Tai Chong tensely observed the bidding for a moment, and then turned to me.

"You stay with Hector," she said, and I could see that her rage had not dissipated. "I'll be back shortly."

"I hope you are not going to lodge a protest on my behalf, Great Lady," I said.

"That is precisely what I'm going to do."

"I would much rather that you didn't."

"But why? The museum's policy is indefensible!"

"Great Lady," I said, "it is difficult enough to be an alien in this society without calling additional attention to oneself by complaining about your treatment of visiting races."

"But you're not one of the ones we're at war with," she argued. "You're one of the—" She suddenly stopped speaking.

"One of the docile ones?" I suggested.

"One of the species with whom we have always had a peaceful and harmonious relationship," she answered awkwardly.

"There are more than two thousand sentient races in the galaxy, Great Lady," I pointed out. "No guard can be expected to recognize more than the minutest fraction of them, and since the Oligarchy is at war—"

"The Oligarchy is *always* at war with somebody," she interrupted.

"Given those conditions, the policy is sensible."

"To say nothing of being personally humiliating to you."

"The individual doesn't matter," I answered.

"The individual is *all* that matters!" she said decisively, and once again I realized just how truly *alien* she was.

We began attracting curious stares, and Tai Chong lowered her voice when she saw how uneasy I had become as a focal point of such attention.

"I'm sorry, Leonardo, but I have to lodge a protest," she said. "When they offend one of Claiborne's associates, they offend Claiborne. I have to stand up for my people, even if they won't stand up for themselves."

I could see that further argument would be fruitless, and I stood there silently as she walked off to find the director of the Odysseus Gallery. I forced myself to concentrate on the bidding, and tried not to think of the consequences of her action.

The Jablonski came up for auction in another moment, and when the opening bid was 200,000 credits, I knew I had been right about its eventual price. A private collector from the Antares sector entered the bidding at 450,000, and finally bought it away from a local museum for 575,000.

"Right on the button," said Rayburn. "You really know your stuff, Leonardo."

"Thank you, Friend Hector," I replied, glowing brightly with pride despite my uneasiness about Tai Chong's protest.

He stared thoughtfully at me.

"Do you really think we can get that portrait for fifty thousand?"

My pattern darkened ambiguously. "Unless he has acquired a reputation on Bortai or its neighboring worlds. If he has, then it may cost sixty thousand credits."

The Primrose was next, and although it was a typical representation of his Hex Period, it brought a disappointing 190,000 credits, which confirmed the decline in his stature.

Tai Chong, looking quite satisfied with herself, returned, and we watched without much interest as the next three pieces brought average prices.

Then it was announced that the first of the Moritas was about to be auctioned.

"The physical restrictions of the platform preclude our exhibiting it here," said the auctioneer, "but I trust you've all had a chance to see it. This particular Morita is number seven in your catalogs, a stunning mosaic of firestones and sun crystals entitled 'Dawn.' We will start the bidding at half a million credits."

The bidding reached three million in less than a minute. The Canphorite entered the bidding at four million, but it was finally sold to a large museum from Deluros VIII for 6,500,000 credits, which Tai Chong assured me was not a record for a Morita, although the auctioneer announced that it was indeed a record for Far London, a record he expected to last no more than forty minutes, which was when the next Morita was scheduled to be sold.

Tai Chong bid on a small hologram and lost out to the Canphorite, then purchased an exquisite still life from Terrazane.

A few minutes later Rayburn tapped me on the shoulder.

"Your portrait's up next," he said. "I think I may take a shot at it." He paused. "Fifty thousand tops, right?"

"That is my evaluation, Friend Hector," I replied.

"The next item," announced the auctioneer as the painting was brought onto the platform, "is an untitled portrait by Christopher Kilcullen, who first achieved fame as a naval hero whose vastly outnumbered forces destroyed the enemy during the Jhaghon Uprising of 4306 G.E." He paused, studying his notes. "After his retirement Commander Kilcullen turned to painting, and although he was not prolific, his work now hangs in museums on Spica II and Lodin XI, as well as on his native Bortai. This piece was donated by the Estate of the late Heinrich Vollmeir, governor of Mirzam X, and has a reserve of twenty thousand credits placed upon it."

"That is not a term with which I am acquainted, Friend Hector," I whispered.

"A reserve?" he said. "It means that the owner, or in this case his estate, has placed a minimum bid of twenty thousand credits on the painting, and has agreed to buy it back for that amount if there are no higher bids."

"From which the gallery takes its commission?" I asked.

"That's right—and I'll wager that Argentine III doesn't see a credit of any buy-backs that don't reach their reserves."

For almost a minute there was silence, and then Rayburn nodded to one of the auctioneer's spotters.

"I have a bid of twenty thousand from the Claiborne Galleries," announced the auctioneer. "Will anyone make it twenty-five?" He looked around the room. "Twenty-five thousand?" He waited another half minute. "Last call for bids," he announced. "Will anyone say twenty-five thousand?"

Suddenly he smiled at someone on the other side of the room.

"I have twenty-five thousand from Malcolm Abercrombie," he announced. "Will anyone say thirty?"

Rayburn nodded.

"I have thirty. Do I hear thirty-five?"

I looked across the room and saw a white-haired gentleman with thick, bushy eyebrows and deep age lines in his face hold up four thin fingers and then make a fist. The liver spots on his hand stood out even more than the plain platinum ring he wore.

"Who is he, Great Lady?" I asked Tai Chong.

"That's Malcolm Abercrombie," she replied.

"With which gallery is he associated?" I asked. "His name is unfamiliar to me."

"He's a collector," she replied. "I don't know much about him, except that he lives here on Far London and is said to be a bit of a recluse."

"Mr. Abercrombie bids forty thousand." The auctioneer turned back to Rayburn. "Do I hear fifty?"

Rayburn paused for a long moment, then nodded almost imperceptibly.

"I have fifty thousand. Do I hear another bid?"

Abercrombie held up five fingers, then made a fist and stuck out his index finger.

The auctioneer stared at him for a moment, puzzled. "I beg your pardon, Mr. Abercrombie," he said at last, "but is that fifty-one or sixty?"

"Take your choice," said Abercrombie in a loud, rasping voice, and a number of the people in the crowd laughed.

"I really cannot do that, sir," said the auctioneer uneasily. "Will you please state your bid?"

"Sixty," replied Abercrombie to a round of spontaneous applause.

"I have sixty thousand credits," said the auctioneer, looking straight at Rayburn. "Do I hear more?"

"That's the limit?" he asked me in a low voice.

"As an investment property, Friend Hector," I answered.

He paused again, then looked back at the auctioneer and shook his head.

"Do I hear sixty-five thousand?" asked the auctioneer, scanning the crowd without much hope for signs of interest. "Last call for bids."

"Seventy-five," said a voice at the back of the room, and everyone turned to see who the new bidder might be.

"I have a bid of seventy-five thousand credits from Reuben Venzia," said the auctioneer, and a small, olive-skinned man possessed of a large black mustache and a nervous manner nodded his head to confirm the bid.

"Who the hell is *he*?" asked Rayburn.

Tai Chong whispered something to the woman standing next to her, who in turn whispered back.

"He's a very successful businessman from Declan IV."

"Another collector?" asked Rayburn.

Tai Chong consulted with the woman again. "He recently bought an art gallery in the Daedalus system," she said to Rayburn.

"He's not going to last very long if he overbids by twenty percent," said Rayburn. "Who the hell does he think is going to buy it for what he'll have to ask?"

"I have 100,000 from Malcolm Abercrombie," announced the auctioneer.

"Maybe he plans to sell it to Mr. Abercrombie," said Tai Chong wryly.

Venzia made a swift gesture.

"The bid is 125,000 credits, from Mr. Venzia."

Rayburn turned to me.

"What's going on here?" he demanded. "I thought you told me that it would bring between fifty and sixty."

"That's what it *should* have brought, Friend Hector," I replied, my color reflecting the Hue of Bewilderment. "I am at a loss to explain what is happening."

I still had no explanation two minutes later, when the bidding reached 300,000 credits.

"It's just not that good a painting!" muttered Rayburn, obviously confused.

"Leonardo," said Tai Chong, "what can you tell me about this Kilcullen?"

"I have never heard of him before tonight, Great Lady," I answered.

"And if he lived in the Albion Cluster and his work was worth 300,000 credits, you would have?"

"Without question," I replied.

"Curiouser and curiouser," she murmured as Abercrombie bid 375,000 credits.

"Do I hear 400,000?" asked the auctioneer.

Venzia nodded, and an instant later a well-dressed young woman came over to the auctioneer and whispered something to him.

"The auction is suspended for sixty seconds," announced the auctioneer. His gaze sought out the olive-skinned little man. "Mr. Venzia, would you approach the podium, please?"

"Now, what can this be about?" mused Rayburn.

Venzia walked over to the podium and was soon engaged in an animated conversation with the auctioneer and two assistant directors of the Odysseus Gallery. Within seconds it was obvious that he had lost his temper, and a moment later he stalked out of the main gallery, his face livid with rage. "Mr. Venzia's bid of 400,000 credits has been disallowed," announced the auctioneer. "Are there any further bids?" He looked around the room. "Very well. The painting is sold to Mr. Malcolm Abercrombie, for 375,000 credits."

There was a rustle of appreciative applause, and Abercrombie walked forward to sign for his purchase.

"It doesn't make any sense!" muttered Rayburn. Suddenly he turned to Tai Chong. "I want to take another look at it."

"Be my guest."

"Can I take Leonardo with me?"

"I think you'd better," she replied. "After all, he's the one who made our appraisal."

"Come on, Leonardo," said Rayburn, stalking off to the small side gallery that had temporarily been turned into a receiving room, and I quickly fell into step behind him.

When we arrived we found that Venzia had gotten there ahead of us, and was arguing with Abercrombie, who was obviously uninterested in the little man.

"But you got it on a fluke!" Venzia was protesting.

"It's hardly *my* fault that you didn't have enough money on deposit here," said Abercrombie gruffly, tightening his grip on the painting as if he half expected Venzia to reach out and try to grab it.

"Three hundred fifty thousand credits should have covered that painting and half a dozen other Kilcullens as well!"

"It didn't," said Abercrombie.

"I want to know *why* it didn't!" persisted Venzia. "You and I both know that the damned thing isn't worth sixty thousand credits."

"If you know that, why did you try to bid 400,000 credits?"

"I have my reasons," said Venzia.

"They don't concern me," replied Abercrombie calmly.

"Look," said Venzia, "I'll pay you half a million credits for it right here and now."

"You don't have half a million credits."

"I don't have half a million credits *on deposit*!" snapped Venzia. "My bank will vouch for it."

"Your offer doesn't interest me," answered Abercrombie with some show of irritation. "Now go away before I have the security staff escort you out. I have work to do."

Venzia glared at him for a moment, then turned on his heel and stalked off toward the main entrance.

Suddenly Abercrombie noticed Rayburn and looked directly at him.

"Are *you* going to start accusing me of cheating, too?" he demanded.

"Not at all, Mr. Abercrombie," said Rayburn, stepping forward. "I just stopped by to congratulate you on your purchase."

"It went too damned high," said Abercrombie gruffly, ignoring Rayburn's extended hand.

"It went about seven hundred percent higher than *we* anticipated," agreed Rayburn. "Why did you buy it?"

"Because I wanted it," said Abercrombie. "If you've got any other questions, make them quick. I've got to arrange to have the painting shipped to my home."

"Do you mind if my colleague takes another look at it?"

"Your colleague?" repeated Abercrombie. He jerked a thumb in my direction. "You mean *that*?"

"This is Leonardo," said Rayburn. "He's our Albion Cluster expert."

I made a formal obeisance toward him and began approaching the painting.

"That's close enough," said Abercrombie ominously when I got to within about ten feet of him.

"Is something wrong, Friend Malcolm?" I asked.

His cold blue eyes stared directly into mine. "I don't have much use for aliens. Never did, never will."

"Then I shall content myself with examining the painting from here, Friend Malcolm," I said.

"I'm not your friend," said Abercrombie.

I studied it for a moment, and then Rayburn said: "Have you changed your mind, Leonardo?"

"No, Friend Hector," I replied. "I have not changed my mind."

"And now, if you're through," said Abercrombie, "I'm in a hurry."

"We're through," said Rayburn, turning to me as Abercrombie supervised the wrapping of the painting. "You're sure you've never seen anything by Kilcullen before?"

"No, Friend Hector."

"Does his work resemble that of any Albion Cluster artist who might reasonably bring that kind of price?"

"No, Friend Hector."

"Now listen to me, Leonardo," said Rayburn. "Two different men valued this painting at over 350,000 credits, and I'd like to know why your estimate is at such variance with theirs before I bid on any more pieces from the Albion Cluster. Mr. Abercrombie could be a collector who's simply infatuated with this single painting, but Venzia owns a gallery, so I'm going to put the question to you again: Is there *any* similarity between this piece and any other work from the Albion Cluster that might have brought a six-digit price?"

"None, Friend Hector," I said. "I do not wish to offend Friend Malcolm, but this painting is simply not worth that much money. In fact, the only resemblance it bears to any more noteworthy artwork is the striking similarity of the subject to that in a Binder X hologram which was sold for 150,000 credits almost two years ago."

Abercrombie turned to me.

"When you say subject, do you mean the model?" he asked sharply.

"Yes, Friend Malcolm."

"And you've seen that model before?" he persisted.

"I do not know, Friend Malcolm," I answered. "I have seen a remarkable likeness of the model in a Binder X hologram. But I have also seen an equally similar resemblance in a Patagonian painting, and Patagonia IV was abandoned 308 years before Kilcullen was even born."

"I suppose all humans look alike to you," suggested Abercrombie, and I had the feeling that he was intently observing my reaction.

"No, Friend Malcolm," I replied. "I find each of you quite distinctive. Otherwise I could not have made the human artwork of the Albion Cluster my specialty."

He stared at me for a long moment. I could sense his innate dislike of me, though I could ascertain no logical reason for it. Finally he turned to Rayburn.

"I want a word with you," he said. "In private."

"Why not?" replied Rayburn. He turned to me. "Why don't you rejoin Madame Chong, Leonardo? I'll be along in a minute."

"Yes, Friend Hector," I said, and, glad to finally be free of Abercrombie's unsettling presence, I returned to the main gallery.

"Where's Hector?" asked Tai Chong when she saw that I was alone.

"He is speaking with Mr. Abercrombie, who seems to have taken an intense dislike to me," I said. "I truly did nothing to offend him, Great Lady."

"I'm sure you didn't, Leonardo," she said soothingly. "I just hope you don't judge all Men by this evening."

"I don't judge them at all, Great Lady," I replied.

"Then perhaps you should."

She fell silent then, watching distractedly as a small three-dimensional spacescape from Thamaaliki II brought a moderate price, and an early Kamathi sold for somewhat higher than I would have anticipated, given its crudeness of line. Then Rayburn joined us, a curious expression on his face.

"Well?" demanded Tai Chong.

"He just made us the damnedest offer I've ever heard!"

"What was it?" she asked.

"In a minute," he replied. He turned to me. "Leonardo, I want the truth now: What do you think of Malcolm Abercrombie?"

"I think that he must be under considerable tension because of the auction, Friend Hector."

"Come on," scoffed Rayburn. "I said the *truth.*"

"I think he is a narrow-minded xenophobe with a totally inadequate knowledge of current art market values," I said, and I could feel my color registering the Hue of Absolute Honesty.

"That's more like it," said Rayburn with a chuckle. "He thinks even less of you."

"Get to the point, Hector," said Tai Chong irritably.

"The point, Madame Chong," said Rayburn, "is that Malcolm Abercrombie just offered the Claiborne Galleries our choice: an early Sabai ink sketch or fifty thousand credits."

"In exchange for what?" she demanded.

Rayburn grinned in amusement.

"A week of Leonardo's time."

3.

I SAT, ALONE AND UNEASY, IN
Malcolm Abercrombie's study.

I had arrived almost ten minutes early for my appointment with him and remained in the busy, bustling street for almost nine minutes, studying the bold structure of his enormous home, the mathematical precision of his formal gardens, the grace and beauty of the two large stone fountains that fronted the east and west wings of the house.

Finally, when I was certain that I could cause no possible disturbance by appearing before the appointed time, I stepped onto the automatic walkway, prepared to be instantly transported to the front door—and nothing happened.

I began to feel a sense of impending panic. The house was set back almost five hundred feet from the street, and given my physical structure and the somewhat heavy gravity of Far London, I could not possibly traverse the distance in the one minute remaining to me. I had been given three days' notice in which to prepare for our meeting, and I would nonetheless be late.

I had no choice but to begin walking—and the moment

I did so, a mechanical voice asked me whether I desired to approach the front door, the servants' door, the service entrance, or the door to the guest wing.

"The front door, if you please," I said with an enormous feeling of relief.

"I am sorry," said the voice passionlessly, "but my programming will not permit me to transport members of any non-human race to the front door. Will you please make another selection?"

"I have an appointment with Mr. Abercrombie," I said. "I do not yet know if I am to be a guest or a servant."

"My programming will not permit me to transport members of any non-human race to the guest-wing door. Do you wish to go to the servants' door?"

"Yes," I said. "And please hurry. I must be there in thirty seconds."

"I am programmed to move at only one speed. Please prepare yourself; I shall begin in ten seconds."

I sighed and braced my feet, and shortly the walkway began moving slowly and smoothly toward the house.

"You may not exit here," it announced as we passed the front door, and it repeated the order a moment later as we circled the east wing of the house. Finally it came to a stop in front of a less ornate door, and instructed me to get off and enter the house.

I did so, and a sleek, shining robot rolled up to me. It was only the third robot I had seen on Far London.

"Are you Leonardo?" it asked.

"Yes," I replied.

"You are expected. Please follow me."

It spun around and wheeled off down a paneled corridor, then paused and waited for me to catch up with it.

"If you will enter this study," it said, opening a door for me, "Mr. Abercrombie will join you shortly."

I walked into the study, so relieved that my tardiness would go relatively unnoticed that I was hardly aware of the instinctive uneasiness that overtook me once the door closed and I was alone and isolated again. I began examining my surroundings and prepared to be joined momentarily by Malcolm Abercrombie.

That had been forty-five minutes ago, and I was now feeling *very* naked and alone.

The study itself mirrored my impression of the man: cold, monied, aloof. It was a large room, too large really, with a number of doors, and its walls were remarkably empty of paintings and holograms. There was a polished hardwood desk facing the doorway through which I had entered, but other than an ashtray and an unused set of writing instruments, there was nothing on it: no papers, no computer terminal, nothing. The chair behind the desk was tall and narrow, and as I walked over I noticed that there was a small cushion on it to support Abercrombie's lower back. There were three high-backed leather chairs, expensive but uncomfortable, lined up along one of the walls, and between two of them was an onyx pedestal which held a small crystal bowl of Altairian design. A row of windows behind the desk overlooked an acre of shrubbery which had been meticulously trimmed into an intricate maze.

To keep my mind from dwelling on my isolation, I once again considered the best means of addressing my host when he finally arrived. He had already indicated some displeasure with the Dialect of Affinity, and since I had not requested the meeting, I rejected the Dialect of Supplication. The problem was that I didn't know if I was a guest, which would require the Dialect of Honored Guests, or a paid consultant, which would lend itself to the Dialect of Peers. And, of course, there was always the likelihood that I was merely to be an employee for a week, which would support either the Dialect of Craftsmen or (if there were to be no social intercourse between us at all) the Dialect of Business.

I was still pondering the problem when a door opened and Malcolm Abercrombie, dressed in browns and ambers as if to complement the decor of the room, entered the study and walked directly to his desk. A sweet-smelling Spican cigarette protruded from a solid gold holder in his mouth.

He sat down, took a final puff of his cigarette, then removed it from its holder and snuffed it out in the ashtray. He leaned back on his chair, fingers interlaced across his stomach, and stared at me. I stood perfectly still and tried to effect an air of serenity.

"Leonardo, right?" he said at last.

"Right you are, Malcolm," I responded.

He frowned. "Call me Mr. Abercrombie."

So much for the Dialect of Peers. I quickly changed to the Dialect of Craftsmen. "Whatever you wish, Mr. Abercrombie. I assure you that I meant no offense."

"I'll let you know when I'm offended," he replied. He stared at me again. "You look uncomfortable standing there. Grab a seat."

"I beg your pardon?"

"A chair," he said with a look of distaste on his face. "Unless your race is happier standing up. It makes no difference to me."

I turned to the three straight-backed leather chairs that were positioned against a wall.

"Shall I pull it up to your desk so that we may converse more easily?" I suggested as I walked over to one of them.

"Leave it where it is," he said gruffly. "We'll raise our voices if we have to."

"As you wish," I said, carefully seating myself on the chair.

"I suppose I should offer you a drink or something," said Abercrombie. He paused. "*Do* you people drink?"

"I have already had my daily ration of water," I answered. "And my metabolism cannot accommodate human stimulants or intoxicants."

"Just as well," he said. He stared at me again. "You know, you're the first alien I've ever allowed inside this house."

"I feel highly honored, Mr. Abercrombie," I said. I decided that the Dialect of Craftsmen was indeed the appropriate one since the Dialect of Peers did not permit social lies.

"Except for a couple of servants who didn't work out,"

he added. "Finally had to kick them out on their asses."

"I am sorry to hear it."

He shrugged. "It was my own fault for hiring aliens in the first place."

"You have hired *me*," I pointed out.

"Temporarily."

We sat in silence for a moment. Then he inserted another cigarette in his holder, lit it, and looked across the room at me.

"What the hell are you doing with a name like Leonardo?" he demanded suddenly.

"When I was younger, I aspired to be an artist," I replied. "I was not talented enough, but I have always kept my portfolio with me, adding to it from time to time. Shortly after I came to the Claiborne Galleries on an exchange program, I showed my work to Hector Rayburn. It included a Twainist interpretation of da Vinci's 'Mona Lisa' that appealed to him, and since my name is unpronounceable to humans, Friend Hector decided to call me Leonardo."

"It's a stupid name," said Abercrombie.

The Dialect of Craftsmen did not allow me to contradict my employer when he made so forceful a statement so I said nothing at all.

"It belongs on a bearded, paint-spattered Man," he continued, "not a candy-striped nightmare with orange eyes and a nose on the side of its face."

"That is an essential part of my Pattern," I explained. "My breathing orifice is between my eyes. Possibly you cannot see it from this distance."

"Let's keep the distance just the way it is," he said. "Seeing your nose isn't one of my priorities."

"I will remain here," I assured him. "You needn't be afraid of me."

"Afraid?" he said contemptuously. "Hell, I've lost count of the aliens I've killed! I was at the Battle of Canphor VI, and I spent three years in the Rabolian War. Maybe I've got to put up with some of you uppity bastards who wear clothes and learn Terran and pretend you're

Men, but I don't have to like it, or to rub shoulders with you. You stay where you are and we'll get along just fine."

Since he had such an obvious distaste for my presence, I became even more curious about why he had requested it, and addressed the question as delicately and inoffensively as the Dialect of Craftsmen would permit. It took three tries before I finally made myself clear.

"I have reason to believe that you might prove useful to me," he replied.

"In what capacity?" I asked.

"Who's conducting this interview, you or me?" he said irritably.

"You are, Mr. Abercrombie."

He took another puff of his cigarette, leaned forward until he could rest his elbows on his desk, and stared at me intently.

"How much do you think I'm worth?"

"I have no idea," I said, surprised by his question.

"Close to 600 million credits," he said, watching me carefully for a reaction. "If you do your job, you'll find that I'm not ungenerous, even to an alien." He glared unblinkingly at me. "But I want you to know that if you ever try to take advantage of me, I'm the least forgiving sonofabitch you'll ever meet. You swipe a single ashtray and I'll spend every one of those 600 million credits hunting you down. Understand?"

It was fortunate for both of us that I was not using the Dialect of Peers, for my answer would have gravely offended him and his reaction to it would probably have caused me acute physical discomfort. I merely said: "The Bjornn do not steal, Mr. Abercrombie. It is contrary to civil and moral law."

"So is war, but everybody keeps doing it," he said. "I've spent forty years putting together my art collection, and before I give you free access to it, I want to know a little more about you."

"If you have concern for the safety of your collection, there is no need for me to see it at all," I said.

"Yes there is," he responded.

"Surely you are protected by a security system," I said, my color deepening with the anticipation of seeing a fabulous private collection.

"It wouldn't be the first time an alien beat a system that was designed to stop a Man." He paused and frowned. "Why do you keep changing colors?"

"Only the intensity of my colors changes," I explained. "Not the colors themselves."

"Answer the question."

"It is the involuntary expression of a Bjornn's emotional state."

"And what does this particular expression mean?" he continued.

"That I am elated at the prospect of seeing your collection," I replied. "I hope the intensification of my color has not disturbed you."

"Anything I don't understand disturbs me," he answered. "What about the stripes? Do they change too?"

"No," I replied. "They, like the mark on my face that you referred to earlier, are essential elements of the Pattern of the House of Crsthionn."

"You mean they're some kind of tattoo?"

"Yes," I lied. After all, how does one explain the hereditary Pattern to a man who finds all colors and patterns inferior to his own?

"How old were you when you got your Pattern?" he asked with a show of curiosity.

"Very young," I answered truthfully.

"They gave it to you after you joined the House of Crsthionn?"

"No, Mr. Abercrombie," I said, trying to keep my answer simple and relatively truthful. "I became a member of the House of Crsthionn after I had my Pattern."

"Kind of like an initiation ceremony?" he asked.

"Not really," I said.

He decided to attack a parallel subject. "What about your wife? Does she have a Pattern, too?"

"Yes."

"What does *her* Pattern look like?"

"Very much like mine, I suppose," I responded. "I have never seen her."

He blinked. "You've never seen your own wife?"

"No, Mr. Abercrombie."

"Will you ever see her?"

"Of course," I said. "How else would we propagate?"

"Beats the hell out of me," he said. "Who knows how you aliens propagate?"

"I could explain it to you," I offered.

"Spare me the details," he said, distorting his facial features into a grimace.

"If you wish," I replied. "I meant no offense. To a Bjornn, the act of propagation is a natural function, just like ingestion and excretion."

"That's enough!" he snapped. "I didn't bring you here to tell me about your toilet habits."

"Yes, Mr. Abercrombie."

"It's disgusting and perverted."

"I am sorry that you should think so," I said. "Doubtless I have chosen the wrong mode of expression."

He stared at me for a long moment.

"You haven't got a hell of a lot of spunk, have you?"

"I do not understand you, Mr. Abercrombie."

"I wouldn't let anyone talk to *me* the way I've been talking to you. I'd spit in his eye and leave."

"You have offered to pay the Claiborne Galleries for my services," I explained. "I would bring shame to my House if I did not honor my commitment."

"But you'd *like* to take a poke at me, wouldn't you?" he continued.

"No, Mr. Abercrombie. I do not believe I would enjoy it at all."

"Jesus!" he muttered contemptuously. "At least the Canphorites went down fighting. What's the matter with you Bjornns?"

"Perhaps the answer is that, unlike Man and the inhabitants of Canphor VI and VII, the Bjornn do not descend from carnivores, and therefore lack your aggressive traits."

He stared at me for a moment, then shrugged.

"All right," he said. "Let's get down to business."

"Then my answers have satisfied you?"

"Not especially. But they've convinced me that you haven't got the guts to rob me." He got to his feet. "Follow me."

"At what distance?" I asked, recalling his stricture about not approaching him.

"Just shut up and do it," he growled, walking to a door. He opened it just as I reached him, and I followed him into a large, well-lit gallery, perhaps seventy feet long and twenty wide. Some fifty paintings and holograms hung on the dark wood walls, each by an acknowledged master.

"Exquisite!" I exclaimed, examining a Ramotti landscape from her Late Purple Period. "Such elegant brushwork!"

"Are you familiar with all the paintings?" he asked.

"No," I admitted. "A number of them are unfamiliar to me."

"But you know the artists?"

I looked again. "Yes."

"Three of them are phony. Tell me which ones."

"How much time have I?" I asked.

"As long as you want." He paused. "You're glowing again."

"I enjoy a challenge," I said—and the intensity of my color vanished an instant later as I realized what a self-centered statement I had uttered.

I walked up and down the gallery, pausing before each painting and hologram, analyzing them as quickly as I could. Finally I returned to Abercrombie, being careful to stop some ten feet short of him.

"You tried to trick me, Mr. Abercrombie," I said with a smile. "There are *four* fraudulent pieces."

"The hell there are!" he snapped.

"The Skarlos portrait, the Ngoni still life, the Perkins hologram, and the Menke nude are all duplicates."

"I spent 800,000 credits for the Ngoni!"

"Then you were deceived," I said gently. "Ngoni lived

on New Kenya five centuries ago, yet the paint is less than three centuries old."

"How can you tell?" he demanded.

I tried to explain how a Bjornn can analyze the chemical composition of paints and the diverse textures of canvas, wood, and particle boards, but since human eyes cannot see as far into the infrared and ultraviolet spectrum, it was beyond his comprehension, nor were there any dialects that could incorporate the proper terms into their Terran equivalents, which did not in fact exist.

"All right," he said. "I'll take your word for it." He paused, lost in thought, then looked up. "I'll send it to Odysseus for an authentication certificate, and if it doesn't pass muster, my agent on New Kenya is going to wish he'd never been born."

"Was I correct about the other three?"

He nodded his head.

"May I assume, then, that I am here to authenticate various purchases you have made or are considering making?"

"No," he said. "But I wanted to see if you knew your stuff." He paused, then added grudgingly: "You do."

"Thank you, Mr. Abercrombie."

"Come into the next room," he said, opening a door at the end of the gallery. I followed him into a small room—small for *this* house, at least—and found myself in a windowless enclosure, the walls of which were covered by seventeen paintings and five holograms, as well as a pair of exquisitely crafted cameos and a small statue —and each of them featured a likeness of the woman in the Kilcullen painting.

"Well?" he said, after allowing me to briefly examine them.

"I am most impressed," I said, the intensity of my color deepening once again. "I believe that four of the paintings were rendered prior to the Galactic Era."

"They were," he replied. "And the statue predates the birth of Christ."

"What religion does she represent?" I asked.

"None."

I felt confused. "But for the same woman to appear in artwork separated by so many thousands of years and trillions of miles would certainly imply that she is a formidable myth-figure in the history of your culture."

"She has nothing to do with the history of my culture," said Abercrombie adamantly.

"Then can there be some other explanation for why her likeness has appeared in so many diverse works of art?" I asked.

"I haven't got any idea," he replied.

"It is most curious," I said, standing back and comparing three of the nearer paintings. "It is obviously the same woman. She is always clad in black, and she possesses the same hauntingly sad expression in each rendering."

"I hope you're not suggesting that she posed for each of the artists," said Abercrombie irritably. "There's a seven-millennia span from the earliest to the latest. Men may be tough, but sooner or later we all die. Usually sooner."

"I am merely suggesting that possibly there is a single source, an ancient painting or carving, and that all these are simply interpretations of it."

"Maybe," he said dubiously. "But I sure as hell haven't been able to find it."

I walked slowly around the room once more, examining each piece in turn.

"They have another interesting feature in common," I said.

"What?"

"Not a single one was rendered by an artist of stature," I pointed out.

"You've never run across *any* of these artists before?" he asked, surprised.

"No," I replied.

"What about Kilcullen?"

"His name was unknown to me prior to the auction."

"Then how could you put a value of fifty thousand credits on the painting?" he asked sharply.

"By analyzing the painting's age, point of origin, general school, and quality, and then taking into account the artist's relative obscurity," I replied.

He seemed to consider my answer for a moment, then nodded his head.

"Do they have anything else in common that you can see?" he asked.

"You are the only other link that binds them together," I answered. I paused, aware of the possibility that he might take offense at my next question, but determined to ask it. "May I inquire about your interest in them, Mr. Abercrombie? The model's appearance in so many portraits is certainly an intriguing mystery, but I must point out that a number of them are relatively crude and amateurish."

"I'm a collector," he said with just a trace of pugnacity.

"Then she *does* have some meaning for you," I said.

"I like her face," he replied.

"It is a lovely face," I agreed, "but surely you must have some further reason."

"What makes you think so?"

"Two nights ago I saw you bid 375,000 credits for a painting that is demonstrably worth fifty thousand."

"So what?"

"I simply infer that you must have some reason to bid so much money, above and beyond your admiration for her beauty."

He stared at me for a moment, then spoke:

"I'm eighty-two years old, my health is deteriorating, my wife is dead, my two sons were killed in the Sett War, I haven't seen or spoken to my daughter in close to thirty years, I have one grandchild and I dislike her intensely, and I'm worth 600 million credits. What do *you* think I should do with my money—leave it to a woman I wouldn't recognize and another one that I can't stand the sight of?"

I moved a few feet farther away from him, stunned that he could so casually reject the concept and obligations of House and Family.

"Fifty thousand credits, 375,000 credits," he continued, "what the hell's the difference? I'd have spent five million credits on the Kilcullen if I had to. I can afford to buy any damned thing I want, and none of my money will do me any good once I'm in the grave." He paused. "That's where *you* come in."

"Please explain, Mr. Abercrombie."

"You said the other night that you had seen this model"—he gestured to one of the paintings—"twice before."

"That is correct."

"A painting and a hologram, you said."

"Yes. The painting was from Patagonia IV, although it was purchased by a resident of New Rhodesia, and the hologram was from Binder X."

"I want them—and any others you can hunt up."

"I am not aware of any others, Mr. Abercrombie."

"They're out there, all right," he said with conviction. "I've been tracking them down for twenty-five years, and I wasn't aware of the two you saw."

"I would not begin to know where to look for them," I said.

"You know where to begin looking for two of them," he replied. "You know where they were sold, and you can find out who bought them."

"I suppose I can," I admitted. "But that does not mean that their new owners will care to part with them."

"They'll sell, all right," promised Abercrombie. "You just find them for me, and I'll take it from there." He set his jaw firmly. "Then we'll start hunting for the others."

"I very much doubt that I will be able to find even the two works that I saw in a week's time, Mr. Abercrombie," I said.

"Then you'll take a month," he said. "So what?"

"You are only employing me for a period of one week," I pointed out.

"I'm employing you for as long as I need you," he responded sharply.

"But I have obligations to the Claiborne Galleries," I protested.

"You leave the Claiborne Galleries to me."

"I mean no disrespect, Mr. Abercrombie, but I have come to Far London on an exchange program, and I must—"

"Look," he interrupted me, "if I have to buy Claiborne lock, stock, and barrel to get what I want, I will! Is that clear?"

I could think of no reply, and so I made none.

"You'll be well paid," he continued less harshly. "Salary, expenses, you name it."

"But I am here to gain knowledge of Claiborne's procedures so that I may impart them to other members of my House, just as one of Claiborne's human employees is currently learning from the House of Crsthionn."

"Your House is in business to make money, isn't it?" he said.

"Yes, of course."

"Then I'll pay your House ten thousand credits a month for as long as you work for me. That's over and above your personal salary. Does that solve your problem?"

"I do not know," I said, perplexed, my color fluctuating wildly. "I will have to consider your offer very carefully."

"Let me make it easy for you. If you turn it down, I'll fire you right here and now. You'll lose your job, and your House won't get its money. How does that sit with your precious concept of dishonor?"

"Surely you do not mean this, Mr. Abercrombie!"

He stared coldly at me. "Try me," he said in level tones. "I don't make empty threats, and I always get what I want."

"Then I have no choice," I said unhappily. "I must accept your offer."

"Good. That's settled. I'll get in touch with Rayburn this afternoon and tell him our new arrangement."

"Hector Rayburn is my peer. The manager of the Claiborne Galleries is Tai Chong."

"Madame Chong," he repeated grimly. "I know all about her."

"She is very knowledgeable."

"She's also a bleeding-heart alien-lover who sometimes forgets which race she belongs to."

"You must not speak of my Great Lady like that!" I said as firmly as I could.

"Ah!" he said with a smile. "So you've got some spunk after all! Let me give you a little advice, Leonardo—save it for yourself and don't waste it on her. She's what I call a weekend bleeding heart, and that's the worst kind of all."

"I do not understand you."

"Madame Chong's the type who'll run out to one of your worlds on a weekend and march up and down the streets with you demanding whatever the hell it is you people demand—but comes Monday morning, when the Navy moves in and starts breaking open heads, she's back on Far London feeling like a fulfilled person and wondering who she can help liberate next weekend."

"I will listen no further to such things!" I protested, my color fluctuating wildly. "My Great Lady has been kind and considerate to me in every way."

"You can't put kindness in your bank account, or send it off to your House. I'm giving you coin of the realm —and nobody tells me what to say in my own home."

I could think of no reply, and so I remained silent.

"All right," he said with an air of finality. "That's settled."

"When am I to begin?" I asked at last.

"You've already started."

"But I must get Madame Chong's permission."

"I'll take care of it," he said.

"But—"

"Are you questioning my word?" he demanded ominously.

"No, Mr. Abercrombie," I said with a sigh of resignation. "Where shall I work?"

"Wherever you have to. If you need the library, use it. If you have to fly to the Albion Cluster, go there. If you need to buy something, buy it. Have everything billed to me. I'll call my bank and clear your name and ID with them."

"And if I want to study your collection?"

"I'll instruct the robots to let you in any time of the night or day—but only to see the collection. The rest of the house is off limits to you. Is that clearly understood?"

"Yes, Mr. Abercrombie."

"And one other thing."

"Yes?"

"There was a man called Venzia who went up to 350,000 credits for the Kilcullen painting the other night, and would have gone a lot higher if he hadn't messed up his credit deposit. See if you can find out why."

"Possibly he, too, is enamored of the model's face," I suggested.

"I doubt it."

"Might I ask why?"

"Because I haven't made any attempt to keep my purchases a secret, and he's never yet made me an offer for any of my artwork."

"I will look into the matter, Mr. Abercrombie," I said.

"See that you do," he said, dismissing me.

And this was how I left the employ of Tai Chong, who felt compassion for all races, and joined the service of Malcolm Abercrombie, who disliked all races equally —including, I suspected, his own.

4.

My Dear Pattern Mother:

Much has happened in the six weeks that I have been in the employ of Mr. Malcolm Abercrombie, and now that I am once again on Far London, I shall relate the details to you.

But first I think I should tell you about Mr. Abercrombie himself, since you expressed some dismay about my entering his employ, based on my first description of him.

He is, in truth, a most unusual man. I originally felt that he was a bigot; I was wrong. It would be fairer to say that he dislikes all races equally, including Man. And yet I am no longer uncomfortable in his company, possibly because he treats me with the same lack of cordiality that he treats everyone, even his own grand-daughter.

And, as if in contradiction to my assessment, he is also capable of acts of the utmost generosity and loyalty, although he does not like to be thanked for them, and indeed is at his most surly on those occasions when I have tried.

For example, I had to journey to Binder X on a mission

for him. Only one passenger ship per week flies there
from Far London, since it has little commerce with the
Inner Frontier, and when I applied for passage, I was
told that all the second-class seats had been taken and
that aliens (which is Man's somewhat curious term for
non-Men, since Man himself is an alien on more than a
million worlds) were not permitted to purchase first-
class compartments, even though I was demonstrably
able to pay for one and more than half of them had not
been sold. I reported my predicament to Mr.
Abercrombie, who made a single call—and suddenly I
was given not merely a compartment but a two-room
suite! It was such an act of generosity that I could not
bring myself to tell him that the moment the ship took off
I immediately left my quarters and spent most of the
journey in the second-class lounge, mingling with the
other non-human passengers. If he cannot understand
the concept of the House, how could I ever explain to
him the warmth and security of the Herd?

When I thanked him for sparing me this imagined
humiliation, he replied that I was his employee, and that
the insult was to him. It was not the treatment of aliens
as inferiors that bothered him; in fact, it is a concept
with which he is in wholehearted agreement. But the
treatment of Malcolm Abercrombie's servants as inferiors is evidently not to be tolerated, even when that
servant is myself.

He is truly a man of contradictions. One of the
wealthiest men on Far London, able to purchase anything that he desires, he nonetheless seems not to
enjoy his money. His knowledge of art is, at best,
limited, and yet he has spent a considerable portion of
his fortune on it. Most Men refuse to use robotic or
non-human assistants or employees, fearing the en-
croachment of the former and feeling contemptuous of
the latter, but Mr. Abercrombie's house is run by three
robots, and I am the only other sentient entity with
access to the premises. He has made an enormous
contribution to a local hospital in the name of one of his

deceased sons, and yet he distrusts doctors so much that he suffers with a very painful tumor at the base of his spine rather than allow them to remove it. He refuses to speak about either of his dead sons, though I feel certain that he loved them; he speaks constantly of his daughter and his grandchild, both of whom —unbelievably—he loathes. He spends thousands of credits on his gardens, and never walks through them or even looks at them from his window. He speaks to me in the most insulting manner, and yet I believe he would never permit any other Man to do the same, at least while I am in his employ. He pays me barely enough for my own subsistence, and yet I know he has made generous arrangements with both the Claiborne Galleries and the House of Crsthionn. He has a huge stock of wine, whiskey, and other human stimulants, but I have never known him to partake of any of them, nor does he keep them for visitors, of which he has absolutely none.

His library, both of books and tapes, is virtually nonexistent, nor has he an entertainment center in his house, and yet he rarely leaves, preferring to monitor his investments and issue his orders via his computer. He claims to have no interest in alien races, and yet whenever I mention the Bjornn, he always has questions about them. He is especially interested in the organization of the House, but seems totally incapable of understanding that it is the Pattern that determines the House rather than the reverse. And he is alternately mystified and outraged by the concept of blood mothers and Pattern Mothers, and although he disdains his own daughter's company, he cannot comprehend why I have no interest whatsoever in my blood mother. He is furious that his daughter married a man of whom he disapproved, which is perfectly understandable; while at the same time, he is mystified by the fact that I have no objection to the House having selected my Pattern Mate for me while I was still a child.

Perhaps the most fascinating thing about this singularly fascinating man is his obsession with a woman

who may never have existed, and who, if indeed she did
exist, has been dead for at least seven millennia.

In fact, it is this obsession that led to my current
employment, for in his quest for artwork featuring this
woman, Mr. Abercrombie has retained me in the dual
capacities of purchasing agent and researcher.

My first assignment was to fly to Binder X to obtain a
hologram featuring this particular woman. The voyage
took five uneventful days, during which time I made the
acquaintance of a number of Declanites and Darbee-
nans, who were making connections at Binder to their
own distant planets.

Once on Binder X it took me two days to trace the
hologram, and finally I presented myself to its owner, a
woman named Hannah Comstock. She was not the
person who had purchased it when I attended the
auction at which it had been sold a few years ago, but
had evidently bought it privately in the intervening years.

The attitude toward non-humans is considerably
more liberal on the worlds of the Inner Frontier, and I
had no difficulty securing an invitation to visit her at her
home, which was about five miles from the center of
Fort Rodriguez, the smallest of Binder X's five cities.

Upon arriving, I explained the purpose of my mission
—that I had been authorized to purchase the hologram
for Malcolm Abercrombie—and after her initial protes-
tations that she admired it too much to ever part with it,
she named a price that I considered to be at least half
again what it was worth. I relayed this information to Mr.
Abercrombie, who contacted her himself and concluded
the purchase while I was sleeping at my hotel.

When I arrived at Mrs. Comstock's house the next
morning to take possession of the hologram, I asked
her if she knew anything about its history. She did not,
but had purchased it because of the artist, a man
named Peter Klipstein. His name was unfamiliar to me,
and she explained that he was the man who had opened
up the Corvus system to human colonization, and that
they regard him as a great hero. She had therefore

concluded that Klipstein's name probably made the hologram quite valuable, at least to the Corvus colonists, and had purchased it primarily as an investment.

I inquired if she knew of any other Klipstein holograms, and she replied that she was unaware of the existence of any, and had indeed been surprised to find that he had created this one, although she had the signature authenticated before purchasing it.

Since my ship did not leave for New Rhodesia, my next port of call, for another day, I stopped by a local library and had the main computer bring up Peter Klipstein's biographical data for me. This was a mistake, since he has been the subject of no less than twenty-seven full-length biographies. Finally I had the computer sift through the biographies and supply me with a ten-thousand-word history of the man, which I shall now condense even further for you.

Peter Klipstein was a member of the Pioneer Corps, that branch of the government charged with charting and exploring new worlds for human colonization in the early days of the Republic, some twenty-five centuries ago. (Evidently the Pioneer Corps had been created at the onset of the Galactic Era, survived through both the Republic and the Democracy, and was disbanded only after the advent of the Oligarchy some four hundred years ago.)

After charting some six other systems, Klipstein came to the Corvus system, where he found one habitable world, Corvus II, and supervised the terraforming of another, Corvus III.

When he retired from the Pioneer Corps at age forty-seven, he settled on Corvus III, purchasing a huge estate that was unsuitable for farming, and lived in unthinkable isolation, far from family and friends. The Democracy was unable to closely monitor all the Frontier worlds it had accumulated, and when Corvus III was invaded by the Klokanni, their Navy was in no position to come to the aid of the embattled colonists. The planet was conquered in less than three days, and it was then that Klipstein began a one-man campaign of sabotage and terrorism that resulted in the abandonment of Corvus III by the Klokanni. When it was over, he was offered the governorship of Corvus III, which was now renamed Klipstein. He refused, and returned to live out his remaining years alone on his estate. There was no data in any of the biographies about his work as an artist, and I suspect that his output was minimal, for although it is obviously computer-enhanced, it is nonetheless a striking piece, and had he guided his computer in producing many more such works he would surely have received some measure of recognition within the field.

My other duty, in addition to purchasing renderings of the woman with whom Mr. Abercrombie has become so fascinated, is to try to find other works of art in which she is featured. Since her appearance in paintings created thousands of years and trillions of miles apart remains a mystery, I hoped I might clarify it by finding out what, if anything, the various artists had in common. To that end, I instructed the library's master computer to attempt to determine what background or experiences Klipstein might have shared with Christopher Kilcullen, an artist whose painting of the woman had recently been auctioned on Far London.

The answer was discouraging. Klipstein died almost two millennia before Kilcullen was born. They lived fifty-five thousand light-years apart. Klipstein was an explorer and mapmaker; Kilcullen, a career officer in the Navy. Neither had ever studied art, and while it seemed apparent that the hologram was Klipstein's only serious venture into the field, Kilcullen was well on his way to establishing a reputation at the time of his death. Klipstein was an atheist; Kilcullen, a devout member of a minor Christian cult. Klipstein had never married, and the biographies imply that he may have lived a totally celibate life; Kilcullen was married four times, divorcing his first wife and outliving his next three. Indeed, so diverse were their lives that the only thing I could find in common is that each, at one point, fought against overwhelming enemy strength with commendable courage, even heroism.

This led me to believe that the subject may not have been a real woman, but rather the representation of some ancient war goddess. The computer, however, was able to find no dark-haired goddess of war in human mythology. I then had it determine whether any dark-haired woman existed as a founding member or even a patron saint of the Navy, and was given a negative response, not very surprising considering that Klipstein's battle hardly qualified as an official action of the Navy.

I spent my final hours on Binder X in the library, trying to find some link between their lives other than the military, while the computer continued to insist that none existed.

Finally I had to leave for New Rhodesia, and I boarded a small passenger ship, my questions still unanswered. Fortunately this ship, too, had a complement of non-human passengers, and I was able to spend most of the voyage in their midst. I had to transfer ships at the little colony world of Morioth II. The remainder of my journey was almost unbearable, as there were only six other passengers, five Men and a Canphorite, and they kept entirely to their compartments. By the time we landed I had concluded that Klipstein was totally mad, for no sane being would willingly shut himself off from the warmth and safety of other members of his own species.

(In fact, my revered Pattern Mother, the thought has occurred to me that the galaxy is dominated by a completely insane race, for who but Man so cherishes the frightening concept of privacy? Certainly a case can be made for it.)

New Rhodesia is a lovely green and blue world. Its northern continent is composed almost entirely of heavily forested mountains, but its two southern continents, flat and crisscrossed by hundreds of rivers, are ideal for farming. It has a unique trade arrangement with its sister world, New Zimbabwe, which is some seven light-years distant, and supplies it with all of its metals and fissionable materials in exchange for grains and meats. Furthermore, the two worlds have pooled their resources to form an economic cooperative when trading with all other worlds of the Oligarchy.

The Lodinite ambassador met me at the spaceport (only Lodin XI, Canphor VI and VII, and Galaheen IX, of all the non-human worlds, have embassies on New Rhodesia). With his help it took less than an hour to locate the owner of the painting I sought, as New Rhodesia, being primarily an agricultural world, is far less populated than New Zimbabwe, where almost eighty percent of the people from this unique economic cooperative reside. The ambassador warned me that the New Rhodesians were more xenophobic than was common for a Frontier world, and even with his intervention on my behalf, I spent a full day working my way through an inordinate number of restrictions and petty statutes before I was allowed to leave the spaceport and proceed to my destination.

The man I sought was Orestes Minneola, a retired dietary chemist who lived in a luxurious apartment in Salisbury, a bustling city about two hundred miles west of the spaceport. He invited me into his main room and treated me with civility, but I could tell that my presence made him uncomfortable. When he learned the purpose of my visit, he allowed me to examine the painting, which he had hanging in another room, but he stated that it was not for sale as it possessed a certain sentimental value to him. I explained that Mr. Abercrombie would pay him considerably more than he himself had paid for it, but he remained adamant.

Finally, when he had convinced me that he was not merely assuming an aggressive bargaining position but indeed had no intention of parting with the painting, I asked him what particular attachment he had to the painting. He replied that Rafael Jamal, the artist, was one of his heroes, and had supposedly spent the last few years of his life working on the painting.

This seemed to confirm my conviction that the subject was indeed derived from an ancient war myth, and I inquired whether Jamal had fought for the Navy or for some independent force. Mr. Minneola seemed confused, and finally admitted that he had no knowledge whatsoever of Jamal's military record.

It was my turn to be confused, for I had never heard of a Man referred to as a hero unless he had excelled in military action. My host explained that I was mistaken, departed the room for a moment, and returned with a scrapbook of circus posters from all over the galaxy, explaining that he was an enthusiastic patron of circuses and a student of their history. He thumbed through the book until he came to a colorful if poorly rendered poster of a very young, athletic-looking man in skintight, sequin-covered garments, swinging on a device called a trapeze. This was Jamal, and according to Mr. Minneola he was a famed circus entertainer whose specialty was a quintuple somersault from one trapeze to another without benefit of a net. His career had ended with a tragic accident that left him paralyzed from the waist down, and he had died some four years later.

I thanked Mr. Minneola for his time and courtesy, began the search for a hotel (a number of them had vacancies, but non-humans were not permitted inside them), finally found a dilapidated hostelry on the outskirts of what the colonists termed the Native Quarter (although there were no sentient natives on New Rhodesia, and indeed it was simply a euphemism for ghetto), and reported to Mr. Abercrombie that I had located the painting but that the owner refused to part with it for any price. Far from seeming discouraged, the news seemed to excite him; like most Men, he seemed to cherish only those things for which he had to fight.

On the return flight, I was supposed to transfer ships at the orbiting hangar at Pellinath IV, but at the last moment we had to divert to Pico II, as the Bellum, Pellinath's only sentient race, were resisting incorporation into the Oligarchy's economic system, and the Navy had moved in to forcibly convince them to reconsider. No citizens or associate members of the Oligarchy were allowed in the area, and I had to wait on Pico for three days, until the Bellum had been beaten into acquiescence.

Though I found its bleak landscape and extinct volcanoes fascinating, I was told that Pico II was considered a minor and unimportant world by the Oligarchy, its sole claim to fame being the fact that the notorious criminal Santiago had once been imprisoned there more than two thousand years ago. It was a relatively underpopulated world then, and so it remains today.

I visited the local library and asked its computer for biographical data on Rafael Jamal, with special attention to his military record. It searched its memory for almost three minutes before replying that the only reference it had to Jamal was a single newstape article concerning his accident. I suggested that it tie in to a larger computer on Pellinath or some other nearby world, discovered that the fee for expending so much energy on this energy-poor planet was exorbitant, and decided to start running the names of the artists in Abercrombie's collection through it instead. The first seven names had indeed served in the military—but the eighth had not, and by the time the computer had processed the nineteen names it could find, it turned out that five of them had no record of military service. I refused to abandon my theory that the woman was some ancient military myth-figure until I had determined whether the five had seen some sort of unofficial guerrilla action, but I realized that I would have to wait until I could access the Far London computer.

When it became apparent that our stay on Pico II was to last more than a few hours, I decided to spend the rest of the afternoon in the Rarities and Collectibles Room. There were a number of books there—actual books, with paper and binding—and since I had never seen one before, I selected a number of hefty ancient volumes dealing with human art, went off to a cubicle in the Alien Section, and began thumbing through the pages of a book of modernist spacescapes. An hour later I had worked my way through about half the books when suddenly I came upon yet another portrait of Mr. Abercrombie's unknown woman.

As always, she was dressed in black, and, as always, the exquisite regularity of her features was highlighted by an expression of infinite sorrow. I quickly checked the pertinent data and found that the portrait was completed on Earth in 1908 A.D., in a country called Uganda. The artist was a naturalist named Brian McGinnis, who was known primarily for the discovery of two rare species of orchid that grew on the slopes of a volcanic mountain; his only prior artwork had been a series of pastels of various orchids.

The biographical sketch of McGinnis went on to say that he had been born in a country called Scotland, had received his education in botany and biology, had spent four years in the military, and had gone to Uganda, a wild and primitive land, at the age of twenty-eight. He published seventeen monographs, thirteen on orchids, three on local fauna, and one on volcanic formations, and died of an unknown disease at the age of thirty-six, in the year 1910 A.D.

I have analyzed such data as I had been able to accumulate on the four artists, and I am still convinced that my theory is correct. If Jamal had indeed served in the military, it was the only thing they had in common, other than the fact that all four were human males who had each committed the same woman to canvas or hologram—and I am confident that when I access a Far London computer, it will confirm Jamal's military service.

I then asked the library computer to determine the current whereabouts of the McGinnis painting, but again, it was unable to help me, nor could it give me any information concerning Reuben Venzia, a man about whom Mr. Abercrombie wants some information. In truth, I cannot understand why the people of Pico II have never bothered to upgrade their library computer.

I finally went back to my room, prepared to contact Mr. Abercrombie and relate this new find to him, but the hotel's subspace tightbeam did not have the power to reach Far London, and the cost of patching the message through Zartaska and Gamma Leporis IX, the least complicated route, was so great that I decided to wait until I returned to Far London to inform him of my discovery.

I spent the remainder of my time on Pico II in the library, examining every volume of artwork there in the hope of finding yet another rendering of Mr. Abercrombie's mysterious woman, but with no success; and when the announcement came through that the Navy had subdued the Bellum, I reported to the ship and continued my voyage back to Far London.

When I arrived I went directly to Mr. Abercrombie's house, and found, to my amazement, that the Jamal painting was already hanging in his gallery. I expressed my surprise that he had purchased it so quickly, when Mr. Minneola had seemed so determined not to part with it, and he replied triumphantly that when he went after something he always got what he wanted. In this case, to use Mr. Abercrombie's own words (and I apologize for his vulgarity): "I damned near had to buy him a circus of his own." His own purchasing agent, it would seem, had somehow circumvented the Navy's blockade to bring him the painting, which is how it arrived ahead of me.

He seemed elated when I told him of the McGinnis painting, and ordered me to spare no expense in tracking it down. When I explained that I didn't know how to begin, and suggested that the painting, which was far from famous and had been rendered six thousand years earlier, might very well no longer exist, he became loud and even abusive at the suggestion, insisted that I was trying to sabotage his attempts to complete his collection, and demanded that I leave his presence and get back to work.

To the hunger for privacy which I mentioned earlier, I must now add another trait Mr. Abercrombie possesses that is unique to the race of Man and might well be an additional symptom of mental instability: obsession.

This woman doubtless never existed. She can have no possible meaning for Mr. Abercrombie. She has never been rendered by an artist of note. And yet my employer has spent a considerable portion of his fortune purchasing her portraits, and I am convinced that had Mr. Minneola not been willing to sell his painting, Mr. Abercrombie would not have hesitated to steal it. All this because of a human woman with a hauntingly sad face.

I might add that the model herself remains a fascinating mystery. How is it that men separated by thousands of years and hundreds of thousands of light-years have come to render the very same subject? Why has she never been painted by one of the masters? In fact, why has she never been painted by any race but Man? Why is she never smiling, or wearing any color other than black? Other than the fact that all the men who painted her may have engaged in some form of armed conflict, what else do they have in common that I have somehow overlooked? Who is she, and what does she represent to them? Why has her name never been used in any of the portraits' titles?

I consider these fascinating questions constantly, and I am very grateful that I am a Bjornn and not a Man, or I, too, could fall prey to obsession.

As always, I wish you prosperity for the House and security for the Family.

Your devoted Pattern Son,

5.

I ENTERED THE LOCAL BRANCH of the library, presented myself to the head librarian, waited while he confirmed that Mr. Abercrombie would indeed pay for the computer time, and then was escorted to a small cubicle in what was labeled the "Off-World Section," but was in fact an area consisting entirely of non-humans.

The section was relatively crowded, and the feeling of uneasiness that had manifested itself as I walked from my hotel through the relatively empty Far London streets to the library had totally vanished by the time I activated the computer.

"Good morning," said a not-very-mechanical voice. "How may I serve you?"

"I require a brief biographical sketch about a circus performer named Rafael Jamal," I said in the Dialect of Command. "I especially want the details of his military record."

"Would you prefer a verbal answer or a hard copy?" asked the computer.

"May I have both?" I asked.

"Certainly—but it will cost more."

"That is acceptable."

"I require some preliminary data," said the computer. "To what race does Rafael Jamal belong?"

"The race of Man," I answered.

"Is he alive, and if not, when did he live?"

"He lived approximately 350 years ago, in the first century of the Oligarchy."

"What was his planet of residence?"

"I do not know," I admitted. "But I suspect that it was Patagonia IV, for he was an invalid at the time he produced a painting there, and he died shortly thereafter."

"Thank you," said the computer. "I am searching my library files."

There was a moment of silence.

"I am now accessing the Patagonia IV Public Information computer," it announced.

It went dark for perhaps twenty seconds, then came to life again.

"Patagonia IV is no longer a human colony. I am now accessing the Historical Census Files on Deluros VIII."

I waited patiently, and at last I had my answer.

"Jamal, Rafael," said the computer. "True name: Pedro Santini. Born 4503 G.E., died 4538 G.E. Unmarried, died leaving no heirs, estate finally sold at public auction. Resided until age sixteen on Delvania III, then joined the Balaban Brothers Five-Star Circus, where he worked as a trapeze artist under the name of Rafael Jamal until he lost the use of his legs during a fall on Patagonia IV in 4533 G.E. Left leg amputated in 4536 G.E."

"What about his military service?" I asked.

"He did not serve in the military."

"Then he must have seen some military action in an unofficial capacity," I insisted.

"That is incorrect," said the computer. "He went directly from school to the Balaban Brothers Five-Star Circus, and remained there until his accident."

"I cannot understand this," I said.

"If I have been unclear, I can translate my answer into 1,273 languages and dialects other than Terran," offered the computer.

"That will not be necessary," I said, lost in thought. Finally an idea occurred to me. "Would you please see if Delvania III underwent any military attack or civil disorder during the time that Rafael Jamal lived there?"

"Checking . . . No, it did not."

"Did the Balaban Brothers Five-Star Circus ever perform on a world that was in the midst of a military disturbance?"

"Checking . . . No, it did not."

"But it *must* have!" I said.

"The answer is negative," replied the computer. "May I be of any further service?"

"Yes," I said. "There are four men: Rafael Jamal, Brian McGinnis, Peter Klipstein, and Christopher Kilcullen. I want you to access their histories from the Historical Census Files on Deluros VIII, and then analyze the data and tell me everything that they had in common."

I went through the process of answering the computer's basic questions again, and then waited while it accessed the necessary data.

"Analyzing," it announced at last.

There was a full minute of silence, an extraordinary length of time given that it already had all the data it required.

"Rafael Jamal, Brian McGinnis, Peter Klipstein, and Christopher Kilcullen all belonged to the race of Man," said the computer. "All four were males. I can find no other similarities between them."

"Are you quite certain?" I asked.

"I am incapable of error," replied the computer. "It should be noted that the data on Brian McGinnis is minimal and was accessed from Earth rather than Deluros VIII, but since Rafael Jamal, Peter Klipstein, and Christopher Kilcullen have nothing in common other than their race, and gender, more information about Brian McGinnis would not change my answer."

"Thank you," I said with a sigh of disappointment. Just to be on the safe side, I had it analyze the artists whose paintings were hanging in Abercrombie's house, but it could find no connection between them, neither of military service nor anything else.

Finally another idea occurred to me.

"I want you to analyze a painting," I said. "Is that possible?"

"Yes," replied the computer. "Where can I access it?"

"There is a print of it in a book entitled *Britain in Africa: A Century of Paintings,* which was published on Earth in 1922 A.D. There are probably many copies still in existence, but the only one of which I am aware is in the library on Pico II. The painting is untitled, but it is the only one in the book by Brian McGinnis."

"I have located a copy of the book in the main library of Selica II, where access will be much more rapid and less expensive than Pico II," announced the computer. "Please stand by while I have its contents transmitted to me."

"I will wait," I said.

The computer darkened, then lit up a moment later.

"The painting by Brian McGinnis is now in my memory banks," it told me. "What facets of it would you like me to analyze?"

"The woman," I replied.

"I can find no data concerning the model's name or identity."

"It is entirely possible that she never existed," I said. "She has appeared in paintings, holograms, and sculptures from all across the galaxy over a span of more than seven millennia, and she seems to have been rendered only by members of the race of Man." I paused. "I have access to the paintings and holograms in the collection of Malcolm Abercrombie. Can you now go through your library to see if her likeness occurs in any artwork that is not a part of that collection?"

"Yes."

"And," I continued, "if you should find her likeness elsewhere, can you supply me with a hard copy of it?"

"Yes . . . checking."

The machine went dark again, and remained dark for so long that I finally became aware of my isolation from the other patrons and began walking around the library, drawing warmth and comfort from the proximity of the other beings there. When five minutes had passed I reentered my cubicle, and waited another ninety seconds until the computer came back to life.

"I have found seven sources which may be representations of the same woman," it announced. "They will appear on the holographic screen just to your left whenever you are ready."

"Excellent," I said, suddenly very excited. "Please begin."

A female face with high cheekbones and narrow eyes suddenly appeared on the screen.

"This is a statue of Proserpine, the Roman Queen of the Underworld," said the computer. "It was created in 86 A.D. by Lucius Piranus."

I studied the image. There were similarities in bone structure, and her hair may well have been black (though it was impossible to tell from the sculpture), but the eyes were too small, and she was smiling, whereas the woman I sought seemed consumed by a secret sadness.

"No," I said, disappointed. "This is not the same woman. Please continue."

Another face appeared on the screen, and this time it *was* the woman I sought, beyond any question.

"This is a silkscreen print of Kama-Mara, a dual spirit of erotic desire and death who is said to have tempted Buddha during his meditations. The artist is unknown; the date of the print is estimated at 707 A.D."

"It is her," I said. "But if she is an Indian spirit, why are her features not Indian?"

"I have insufficient data to answer your question," said the computer. "Shall I continue?"

"Please."

Another image appeared, so real that I could almost touch the sadness that emanated from it. It was *her* again.

"This is a painting of Mictecaciuatl, the Lady of the

Place of the Dead in Mexican mythology. Artist unknown, painting rendered in 1744 A.D."

"Please continue," I said, my enthusiasm returning.

Her face appeared again, this time in a hologram.

"This is an untitled hologram, created by Wilson Devers, a big-game hunter on Greenveldt, in 718 G.E."

There followed three more paintings from Earth, Spica II, and Northpoint, each of them an exact replication of Abercrombie's mysterious woman.

"There are no other portraits of her in your library banks?" I asked when the last of them vanished from the screen.

"There are no other accurate portraits of her," replied the computer. "If she was rendered so poorly as to be unrecognizable, or was the subject of a nonrepresentational painting, I would be unable to identify her."

"I see," I said. "Can you now give me a brief biographical sketch of the artists?"

"Including Lucius Piranus?"

"No," I replied. "Let us temporarily remove his statue from consideration."

"Two of the artists are unknown," began the computer. "Wilson Devers, born in 678 G.E. on Charlemagne, relocated to Greenveldt in 701 G.E., received his hunting license in 702 G.E., remained a professional hunter until his death in 723 G.E."

"Did he ever serve in the military?" I asked.

"No."

"How did he die?"

"He was killed by an errant sonic blast from a client's weapon. Shall I continue?"

"Please."

"Barien Smythe, born in 3328 G.E. on Sirius V, relocated to Spica II in 3334 G.E. . . . ." The computer paused briefly. "His profession is listed as spaceship designer, but there is enough data for me to conclude that he was actually employed by a rival cartel and engaged in industrial espionage. He died in 3355 G.E. as a result of an explosion that demolished an entire factory complex."

"And the other two?" I asked.

"Milton Mugabe, born on Earth in 1804 G.E. He became an aquaculturalist specializing in the breeding and harvesting of sharks, large carnivorous fish of Earth's oceans, and was killed by a shark attack in 1861 G.E. The other man is Enrico Robinson, born in 4201 G.E. He became a prizefighter in 4220 G.E., changed his name to Crusher Comanche in 4221 G.E., relocated to Northpoint in 4224 G.E., and died of internal injuries received during a prizefight in 4235 G.E."

"Do these artists share any single trait or experience in common with each other, or with the four that I mentioned earlier?"

"No."

"It didn't take you very long to determine that," I noted.

"I anticipated your question."

"Can computers do that?" I asked, mildly surprised.

"I am so programmed," it replied. "Although had you not asked it, I would not have volunteered the answer."

"I see. May I have hard copies of the illustrations?"

"Including the Piranus sculpture of Proserpine?"

"Yes," I said. "And while you're doing so, can you also give me a biographical sketch of Lucius Piranus?"

"He was a minor Roman artist, born in 43 A.D., relocated to Crete in 88 A.D., died of natural causes in 111 A.D."

"Thank you," I said.

"Is there any other way in which I may serve you?" asked the computer.

I sighed. "Not at the moment, I am afraid."

"I will, of course, keep your request for illustrations of the model and biographies of the artists on file, and whenever I access other library computers and share their memories, I will pursue your quest for further data."

"Thank you very much," I said.

"It is my function," replied the computer.

"Wait," I said, remembering Abercrombie's other directive. "There is one more thing I would like you to do for me."

"Yes?"

"I need an expanded biographical sketch of Reuben Venzia."

"May I please have your Security Access Code?"

"I do not know what that is."

"I can't release information on a living person, other than those who have been officially designated as Public Figures, to anyone without the proper Security Access Code."

"Can you at least tell me where to find him?"

"Certainly. He is sitting 263 feet north-northeast of you."

"You mean he's here now?" I exclaimed.

"Yes."

"Why?"

"I cannot attempt to answer you unless you have a Security Access Code," responded the computer.

"Thank you," I said. "That will be all."

The computer darkened again, while I tried to fathom why Venzia should be in this place at this time. Finally I left my cubicle, and as I began walking through the Off-World Section toward the exit, I saw Venzia rise from a table in the main section and begin walking on a course that was designed to intercept me just as I reached the doorway.

"Leonardo, isn't it?" he said, extending his hand as he approached me.

I stared at his outstretched hand rather stupidly for a moment, since no human except Tai Chong had ever willingly made physical contact with me. Finally I recalled that it was a sign of greeting, and I took it.

"That is correct," I said, utilizing the Dialect of Peers. "And you are Mr. Venzia. I recognize you from the art auction."

"Call me Reuben," he said easily. "Can I buy you a cup of coffee?"

"I am incapable of metabolizing coffee," I replied.

"Choose whatever you want," said Venzia. "I'd like to talk to you."

"That is most generous of you, Mr. Venzia."

"Reuben," he corrected me.

"Reuben," I repeated. "I must inform you, however, that I obtain my nourishment at restaurants which cater to non-humans."

"Fine," he said, heading toward the exit. "Let's go."

"I have never seen a Man in one of them," I continued.

"I'd like to see them try to keep me out," he said.

"Very well, then."

"I haven't seen you for almost two months," he remarked as we walked out into the open air. "Have you been off-world?"

"Yes," I said, choosing the sidewalk to the slidewalk as I always do. "Although I cannot imagine why you would expect to see me, even had I remained on Far London. After all, we met only once."

"Oh, people in the same line of business tend to run into one another, especially on a planet as underpopulated as Far London." He paused. "How did you like New Rhodesia?"

I came to a sudden stop and turned to him. "How did you know I went to New Rhodesia?" I asked.

"An educated guess," he said. He gestured down the sidewalk. "Shall we continue?"

I proceeded in silence, pondering his last remark, and uncomfortably aware of the curious stares that we were attracting. A non-human on a human world is always an object of curiosity and occasionally even derision, but for a Man to walk in company with one of us is so unusual that the onlookers didn't even try to hide their distaste and disapproval. I became uneasy and suggested to Venzia that he might prefer to lead or follow me in order to attract less attention.

"Let 'em look," he said with a shrug. "It makes no difference to me."

"It doesn't bother you?" I asked.

"Why should it?" he replied. "If they've got nothing better to do with their time, it's hardly *my* concern."

I considered his answer, which was typically human in

its careless lack of concern for the opinions or welfare of the Herd, as we continued walking. After we had gone two blocks we came to one of the restaurants I regularly frequented, and I led him inside.

"It's a bit of a dump, isn't it?" he commented, staring at the bare tables and wrinkling his nose at the myriad odors that assailed us. "Wouldn't you rather go to a nicer place? It's my treat."

"It is true that there are nicer places to eat," I acknowledged, aware from the reaction of the diners and waiters that even here we were objects of intense interest, "but I am not allowed to enter them. Besides, this restaurant is usually crowded; I find that comforting."

"You like crowds?"

"Yes."

He shrugged. "Have it your way." He waved to a waiter. "Let's have a table."

The waiter, a pale blue tripodal Bemarkani, approached us.

"Are you quite certain you wish to dine here, sir?" it asked Venzia.

"As a matter of fact, I'm quite certain that I don't," responded Venzia with an expression of distaste. "But my friend and I want a table. Now hop to it."

The Bemarkani's nostrils began flaring—its equivalent of a hostile glare—as if I were destroying the character of his establishment by bringing a Man into it, then led us to a table at the very back of the restaurant, where we could not be seen from the doorway.

"This won't do," said Venzia.

"May I ask why not, sir?" responded the Bemarkani.

"Take a look," said Venzia. "These chairs weren't built for Men. I'd have to be four feet tall and have a tail to fit into one of them. It's totally unacceptable."

The Bemarkani silently led us to another table, also toward the back of the room, and Venzia, after wiping the table off with a handkerchief, nodded and sat down.

"It's not really much better," he remarked, "but what the hell—nothing in here looks all that comfortable." He paused. "Where do you usually sit, Leonardo?"

"Wherever they place me," I replied.

"It must get pretty damned uncomfortable from time to time."

"It does," I admitted.

"Then why do you put up with it?"

"There are compensations."

"The crowd? If you'd make a stink about where they seat you, you could enjoy it in comfort." He paused. "Well, let's get our cheerful, smiling waiter back and tell him what we want."

I ordered a drink composed of pulped vegetable matter from Sigma Draconis II, a world very similar to my own, while Venzia asked for coffee, was informed that there was none available, and settled for a glass of water.

"It smells pretty awful in here," said Venzia after the waiter had left.

"The kitchen supplies the needs of some thirty to forty different races," I replied. "In time one gets used to the odors."

"Let's hope we're not here that long," he said devoutly. "May I ask why we are here at all?"

"We're here because I want to know the full extent of your interest in the paintings you've been tracking down," he replied.

"I see no reason why I shouldn't tell you," I said. "I have been retained by Malcolm Abercrombie to help him acquire certain works of art to add to his personal collection."

"Why you?"

"I beg your pardon?"

"I said, why did he choose you?" said Venzia. "I know a little bit about Abercrombie, and he'd sooner cut off his right arm than give the time of day to an alien."

"I had previously seen two pieces that he wanted, and he commissioned me to seek out the owners and purchase them."

"*Recent* pieces?" demanded Venzia intently.

"Recent is a relative term," I replied.

"Within the past ten years?"

"No. The most recent was from the very early days of the Oligarchy."

He lit up a small cigar, ignoring the hostile glances he received from two Teronis at the next table. "Did you have any luck?" he asked in a more relaxed tone of voice.

"Yes," I replied. "Mr. Abercrombie was able to obtain both pieces."

"And now you're trying to hunt down others featuring the same subject." It was more a statement than a question.

"That is correct."

"Well, you've gone about as far as you can with the library computer."

"How do you know what I asked the computer?"

He smiled again. "I told it to notify me if anyone began asking questions about Mictecaciuatl and Kama-Mara."

"You spied on me!"

"I wouldn't call it spying," he said. "I have no idea what questions you asked, though I can make a pretty good guess. How many paintings did the computer identify for you?"

I felt that he had no right to ask, but again, I could see no reason for not answering him. "Six."

"You discarded the Piranus sculpture?"

"Yes."

"Good decision." He exhaled deeply. "Well, six is all you're ever going to get out of this computer. And, to save you some wear and tear on your expense account, none of them are available."

"Have you purchased them yourself?" I asked.

He chuckled. "Hell, no. I don't want them."

"I am afraid that I do not understand," I said. "The first time I saw you you were trying to buy the Kilcullen painting for 400,000 credits."

"No, I wasn't."

"But—"

"I knew Abercrombie wouldn't let anyone outbid him," he interrupted, looking inordinately pleased with himself.

"I just wanted to see if there were any other interested parties."

"Why would you do that, if you have no interest in the paintings?" I asked.

"I have my reasons."

"Might I know them?"

He shook his head. "I don't think so, Leonardo."

"May I know why not?"

"Because I have a feeling that you can't tell me anything I don't already know—*yet*," he added meaningfully. "When you can, we'll get together again. I might have a job for you."

"I am already employed by the Claiborne Galleries."

"I thought you said you were working for Abercrombie," he said sharply.

"So I am. But Claiborne is my official employer during my tenure here. Abercrombie is paying them for my services."

"I'll pay even better."

"Leaving Claiborne against their wishes would bring dishonor to my House," I explained. "I could never do that."

"You won't have to leave them," said Venzia.

"I do not understand."

"Claiborne is one of the biggest art houses in the galaxy," he began. "They've got branches on seventy-three planets—"

"Seventy-five," I corrected him.

"Seventy-five, then," he said. "You hold forty or fifty auctions a year, and arrange God knows how many private sales."

"That is true," I acknowledged. "But I fail to see how—"

"Let me finish," said Venzia. "You have access to a lot of information about these auctions and sales."

"It is my understanding that you have recently purchased an art gallery," I said. "Surely you have access to the same information."

"I need *advance* access," he said, emphasizing the word.

"In point of fact, I need *you*."

"I could not even consider helping you," I said firmly. "It would be unfair to the other potential bidders."

"I'm not a potential bidder."

"But you own an art gallery."

"There's not a single piece of art on the premises," he replied. "It's just a mailing address on Declan IV."

"Then why . . ." I began, trying to formulate my question.

"Because I need the kind of information that an art gallery is privy to—but I'm finding out that large chains like Claiborne get it a lot faster than one-man companies."

"But if you don't want the artwork, what *do* you want?" I asked.

"The names and addresses of the artists."

"Claiborne handles almost a million transactions a year," I noted. "What could you possibly do with all those names?"

"I don't want all of them," he said. "Just the ones who painted the woman you and Abercrombie are so interested in."

"Why?"

He smiled and shook his head. "Not until you have something to tell me that's of equal interest."

"I have nothing to tell you."

"But you will."

"It would be unethical."

"How?" he persisted. "I'm not trying to cut Claiborne out of its commission, or preempt any potential bidders. I just need information."

"I cannot—"

"Don't say no yet," he interrupted. "Think about it for a day or two, and you'll see that what I want can't possibly harm Claiborne or the artists."

"Even if that were so, it would be disloyal to Malcolm Abercrombie for me to turn such information over to you, when he is employing me to find such information exclusively for him."

"It's not disloyal," he said irritably. "I told you: I don't *want* the damned paintings!" He paused and forced a tight smile to his lips. "We'll discuss it again in a few days. In the meantime, let me give you something as a gesture of my good faith."

"I cannot accept your money," I said. "Since I will not leave Claiborne to work for you, accepting payment would be unethical."

"Who's talking about payment? I have some information that will make your current job a little easier."

"My job?"

He nodded his head. "Have you got a pocket computer with you?"

"Yes," I said, withdrawing it from my pouch.

"Activate it."

I did as he asked.

"Contact the Deluros VIII Cultural Heritage Museum," he said, speaking very slowly and enunciating each word clearly so that the machine could not misinterpret him, "and use Access Code 2141098 to call up material on Melaina, a goddess who was also known as the Black Mare of Death; Eresh-Kigal, the Goddess of the Underworld; and Macha, the Irish Queen of Phantoms." He then placed his thumb over the sensor. "From Kenya's Mac-Millan Library on Earth, use this thumbprint for access to call up material on K'tani Ngai, Empress of the Dark Domain. And from the library computer on Peloran VII, call up material on Shareen d'Amato, who supposedly haunts the spacemen's cemetery there. No access code is required."

He stopped speaking and handed the computer back to me.

"And portraits exist of all these myth-figures?" I asked.

He nodded affirmatively. "The myths may differ, but the woman is the same."

"You are quite sure?"

"I could hardly expect you to consider my offer if I lied to you, could I?"

"No, you could not," I admitted. "I thank you for your help."

"My pleasure." He withdrew a small card and inserted it briefly into the computer. "That's my address on Far London and my vidphone access number. Contact me whenever you're ready to talk a little business." He got to his feet. "Since our conversation is finished, I trust you'll forgive me for leaving you here, but the truth of the matter is that the smell is making me sick."

"One last question!" I said so emphatically that I drew additional stares from the nearby tables and a surly look from the waiter.

"Just one, Leonardo," he replied. "There's a difference between good faith and philanthropy."

"Why has her portrait always been rendered by unknowns?"

"I wouldn't call them unknowns," answered Venzia. "Some of them were quite famous. I gather this Kilcullen was quite a military hero, and our boy on Patagonia IV was supposedly the greatest trapeze artist of his time."

"But they were unknown as artists," I persisted.

"True enough," he conceded. Once again he looked amused. "Good question, Leonardo."

"What is the answer?"

"I don't think I'm going to tell you."

"But you agreed to."

"I agreed to let you ask one more question," replied Venzia. "I never agreed to answer it."

"May I ask why not?"

He smiled and shook his head. "That's another question."

Then he was gone, and I was left alone at my table to wonder why a man who professed no interest whatsoever in possessing any of the various renderings of this mysterious woman should be so vitally interested in the artists, or why he had more facts at his fingertips than Malcolm Abercrombie had been able to amass in a quarter of a century.

6.

THE NEXT TWO WEEKS WERE uneventful. I was unable to find any other paintings of Abercrombie's model, and I spent most of my time investigating the list of names that Venzia had read into my pocket computer.

The results were puzzling. The renderings of Melaina, Eresh-Kigal, Macha, and K'tani Ngai to which he had referred me were all of our mystery woman—but when I delved further into the lore surrounding Melaina, the Black Mare of Death, I found five other renderings, all different. Curious, I next researched K'tani Ngai, and discovered that in every other portrait and carving, except the one in the MacMillan Library, she was a black woman, usually portrayed with the hands and feet of a leopard. The same held true for Macha and Eresh-Kigal.

The only other name on his list was Shareen d'Amato, and I had the Far London library computer access the computer on Peloran III. Its answer to my query was brief but intriguing:

D'AMATO, SHAREEN. DATE OF BIRTH, UNKNOWN. DATE OF DEATH, UNKNOWN. CLAIMED CITIZENSHIP ON BANTHOR III, BUT BANTHOR III POSSESSES NO RECORD OF HER.

"Wait!" I said excitedly. "Do you mean to say that Shareen d'Amato actually existed?"

YES.

"When and where?"

AS EXPLAINED, A COMPLETE BIOGRAPHY OF SHAREEN D'AMATO IS UNAVAILABLE.

"Give me such facts as you possess."

SHE WAS THE CONSORT OF JEBEDIAH PERKINS FROM 3222 G.E. TO 3224 G.E.

"That's all you know about her?"

YES.

"When was her portrait painted?"

IN 3223 G.E.

"By Perkins?"

YES.

"Give me Perkins' biographical data."

JEBEDIAH PERKINS, BORN 3193 G.E., SPACESHIP PILOT WITH KARANGA INDUSTRIES FROM 3215 TO 3219 G.E., PILOT WITH BONWIT CARTEL FROM 3219 TO 3222 G.E., PILOT WITH FALCON CORPORATION FROM 3222 TO 3224 G.E., DIED IN 3224 G.E. WHILE PILOTING A SHIPFUL OF SCIENTIFIC OBSERVERS TO THE VICINITY OF THE QUINIBAR SUPERNOVA.

"Did he get too close?" I asked.

UNKNOWN.

"Was Shareen d'Amato aboard the ship?"

UNKNOWN. IT IS GENERALLY SUPPOSED SO, BUT THERE IS NO VERIFIABLE DATA.

"Was there ever a photograph or hologram taken of Shareen d'Amato?"

UNKNOWN.

"Why is she believed to haunt the spacemen's cemetery on Peloran VII?"

UNKNOWN.

"Has anyone ever claimed to see her there?"

UNKNOWN.

"Thank you," I said, breaking the connection.

It was frustrating that the computer could supply so little information, but the one piece of positive data it had supplied was fascinating: Unlike all the other goddesses and myth-figures, Shareen d'Amato had actually lived, and had presumably posed for the portrait that now resided in one of the art museums on Peloran VII.

I found a vidphone booth in the library and called Abercrombie to tell him of my discovery.

"Interesting," he said after activating the vidphone and listening to my information. "What museum owns the painting?"

"I can find out by this afternoon," I said. "But the intriguing thing is that she actually lived!"

He shook his head. "I doubt it."

"But the computer said—"

"The computer is wrong," he interrupted me. "If she was born in the Third Millennium of the Galactic Era, how the hell did her image turn up on all those earlier paintings and holograms and statues?"

I hadn't considered that, and I had no answer for him.

"Start using your brain, Leonardo," he continued. "If this d'Amato woman actually existed, then the painting's an aberration, a fluke."

"I can research her more thoroughly," I suggested.

"How?" he asked contemptuously. "Your best bet was Peloran VII, and the computer there has already told you everything it knows." He paused. "Look—I'm not writing a scholarly thesis on this woman. I hired you to find her portraits, not to tell me that she shacked up with some spaceship pilot more than fifteen hundred years ago. Now track down the painting and find out how much they want for it."

"Yes, Mr. Abercrombie," I said.

He stared sharply at me. "By the way, I've never heard of Jebediah Perkins. How did you find out he had painted her?"

"Reuben Venzia told me."

"Venzia!" he repeated, leaning forward with interest. "Have you finished researching him?"

"I haven't yet begun," I replied. "He sought me out two weeks ago and volunteered some information concerning the woman in the paintings." I paused. "Thus far, everything he told me has been verified."

His eyes narrowed suspiciously. "And what did you give

him in exchange for this information?"

"Absolutely nothing, Mr. Abercrombie," I said truthfully.

"Nobody gives anything away for nothing!" he snapped. "Exactly what did you promise to give him? Paintings of *my* model?"

"Nothing," I repeated, shocked. "He asked for certain specific information concerning upcoming art auctions, but I refused to divulge it or help him in any manner."

"What kind of information?" he persisted.

"Information concerning portraits of the subject that you collect."

"And he gave you all this stuff on the paintings after you refused to help him?" said Abercrombie with obvious disbelief.

"That is correct," I said. "He is interested only in the subject herself. He has no interest in the portraits."

"No interest?" Abercrombie yelled. "He went to 350,000 credits for the Kilcullen painting, you lying, tiger-striped bastard!"

"But he never had any intention of purchasing it," I explained.

"Just how gullible do I look to you?" demanded Abercrombie coldly.

"He says that he was merely trying to . . ."

I suddenly realized that the screen was blank and I was talking into a deactivated vidphone. I checked to make sure that we hadn't been inadvertently disconnected, and then, experiencing a surprising sense of elation, I returned to the computer. I was unhappy that I had upset Abercrombie, of course, but I was also relieved that I would be able to continue my researches rather than have to go out to his house to explain in detail what I had learned. (Not that I couldn't have told him just as easily by vidphone or even computer, but he preferred to have his employees meet him in person, which made no sense to me at all, since once I appeared on his premises he usually ignored me for hours and then insisted that I cover everything we had to discuss in a brief sentence or two.)

I spent the next three hours having the library computer check various sources for more information about Shareen d'Amato, but it was unable to add anything substantive, though it supplied me with a number of romantic legends concerning her ghost, which supposedly haunted the cemetery, greeting the shades of departed spacemen and offering them drink and sexual comfort on their way to the next life.

Then, as I was about to leave the library to obtain nourishment, the computer came to life again.

"In my continuing search for data, I have found a book containing material on Brian McGinnis," it announced.

"Where is it?" I asked.

"In a small local library on Aguella VII."

"Aguella VII is not a human colony," I said. "I wonder how a book about an African botanist came to be there?"

"The book is not about McGinnis, but rather about the early days of Great Britain's colonization of Uganda," replied the computer. "It was donated, along with 308 other volumes about Uganda, by Jora Nagata, a structural engineer of Ugandan ancestry who emigrated to Aguella VII in 2167 G.E. and worked on several projects as a consultant to the Aguellan government."

"Can I access the book?" I asked.

"I have committed the pertinent sections to memory, and will reproduce them on the screen," answered the computer.

There followed some fifteen hundred words on McGinnis, whose primary claim to fame seemed to be that he occasionally displayed more bravery than intelligence in his dealings with the local fauna. Once, by the simple expedient of yelling and fluttering a white handkerchief in the wind, he diverted a stampeding herd of buffalo from a native village that he was visiting, and on numerous other occasions he went alone and unarmed into the jungle to observe the various carnivores. His discovery of the two new orchid species, one of which bore his name, was not even mentioned.

"Is that all?" I asked when I had finished reading.

"That is all the written text."

"You say that as if there's something else."

"There is a photograph of Brian McGinnis."

"Please let me see it."

Suddenly the screen was covered by a sepia-toned print of a young man, clad in short pants and short-sleeved shirt, his rifle cradled in his arms, a look of enormous pride on his bronzed face, standing with his foot on the neck of a large spotted cat which the caption said was believed to be a man-eater. There were four figures standing behind him: three were dark-skinned, obviously his assistants or colleagues. The fourth was pale-skinned, a woman, and I knew who it was before I ordered the computer to enlarge her image, since she alone was clad in black despite what I had read of the intense heat and sunlight that one encounters in Earth's equatorial zone.

It was *her*. She had the same sad eyes, the same prominent cheekbones, even the same hair style.

"Who is the woman?" I demanded.

"I cannot answer that," responded the computer. "There is no mention of her in the book, and she is not identified in the photograph."

"Do you recognize her?"

"She is the subject of the portraits that you have been seeking."

"Why did you not tell me about this photograph?"

"You specified that you were only interested in works of art, and while some photographs do indeed qualify as art, it is my best judgment that this photograph is primarily one of documentation."

"I am now interested in all photographs of this woman as well as all other artwork," I said. "Do you understand?"

"Yes."

"Do your memory banks contain any others?" I persisted.

There was a fifteen-second pause.

"No."

"I want you to reaccess all the library computers you have contacted on my behalf and determine if any of them contain photographs of the woman, and then continue your search for her among those computers that you have not yet accessed." I paused. "Start with the library on Peloran VII and see if it possesses a photograph or hologram of Shareen d'Amato."

"Have you any further instructions?"

"No. You can contact me at my hotel or Malcolm Abercrombie's residence as soon as you have further data."

I left the cubicle, walked to the vidphone booth, and placed a call to Abercrombie to tell him what I had learned—and also to get his input, since I now had proof that his mystery woman had lived at the turn of the twentieth century A.D., some two thousand years *after* her image began appearing in various human artwork. I knew that the science of cloning had not existed prior to the time of the photograph, but I was unable to formulate any other logical explanation that would encompass all the facts I had thus far amassed.

There was no answer, and, assuming him to be asleep or busy at his computer, I decided that I might as well begin the journey to his house, since he would doubtless demand my presence the moment I contacted him. I left the library with great reluctance, for I was certain that a photograph or hologram of Shareen d'Amato must exist somewhere within the Oligarchy and I was unbearably anxious to see it, but I realized that it would take the computer a considerable amount of time to arrange for its networking, and I decided that the sooner I left, the sooner I would be able to return.

It took me almost forty minutes to reach Abercrombie's estate, for the streets were crowded with lunch-hour traffic, and I lingered amid the crush of bodies, enjoying the sensation of warmth and security they inadvertently provided. Eventually I reached the outskirts of the city, and a few moments later I stepped onto the automatic walkway that led to Abercrombie's mansion.

"Please identify yourself," said the mechanical voice of the security system.

"I am Leonardo."

"Do you have an appointment?"

"I do not need an appointment," I replied, surprised by the question. "I work for Mr. Abercrombie."

"I have no record of a current employee named Leonardo."

"This is ridiculous. I was here two days ago."

"Two days ago you were employed by Mr. Abercrombie," replied the voice. "This afternoon you are not."

"There must be some mistake," I said uneasily. "Please check your records again."

"Checking . . . You are not in Mr. Abercrombie's employ."

"Please let me speak to him," I said.

"His standing order is that he will not speak to strangers."

"But I am *not* a stranger!" I protested.

"I am prohibited by my programming from contacting him on your behalf."

"Then I will approach the house and speak to him in person," I said, taking a step forward.

"I cannot permit entrance by unauthorized personnel," said the voice. "Please step back. In five seconds the walkway will possess a lethal electrical charge. Four. Three. Two."

I quickly moved backward.

"The walkway is now impassable," announced the voice. "Please do not approach the house via the lawn as precautions have been taken to prevent your access."

"Get the idea, you turncoat alien bastard?" boomed Abercrombie's amplified voice.

"Mr. Abercrombie, what is the meaning of this?" I asked, confused and frightened.

"It means that when I hire someone, even someone like you, I expect his loyalty!"

"I have given you my complete loyalty," I responded.

"I paid you to get me some background on that sonofabitch, not to consort with him!" he roared.

"I have not consorted with him," I explained. "He sought me out, and I rejected his proposition."

"Then why did you hide it?"

"I hid nothing."

"Bullshit! You met with him two weeks ago, and I still wouldn't know about it if you hadn't blundered and let it slip out!"

"I thought it too trivial to mention," I said. "He asked for my help and I refused it."

"You should have gone with him when you had the chance," said Abercrombie. "Now it's too late."

"I do not understand what you are saying, Mr. Abercrombie."

"Nobody double-crosses Malcolm Abercrombie! I paid you ten times what you're worth to help me get the only thing in the universe that I want, and the second you're out of my sight you start cozying up to that little wart Venzia. It serves me right for trusting an alien. That's one goddamned mistake I'll never make again."

"You are totally misinterpreting what I have said to you, Mr. Abercrombie."

"I'm properly interpreting what you haven't got the guts to say to me!"

"If I could just speak to you in person . . ." I pleaded.

"I've seen more of you than I care to see," he replied. "Now get the hell off my property."

"But this is just a misunderstanding!" I continued. "I implore you to give me the opportunity to explain!"

"It's over," he said. "I've already served notice to the Claiborne Galleries and the House of Crsthionn that I've terminated your employment because of your disloyalty. Now, unless you want me to report you to the police for trespassing, I think you'd better crawl off to whatever hole you came out of."

"You've told the *House*?" I repeated, as the full impact of what he said struck me.

"You heard me."

"The *House*?" I said again, my limbs so numb I could barely keep my balance.

There was no answer.

"But why?" I asked, still stunned. "I have served you faithfully. I have obtained your portraits. I have not betrayed you. You have everything you could possibly want. Why would you do such a thing?"

"Because I didn't get what I paid for."

"You did! I went to New Rhodesia and to—"

"I paid for your loyalty!"

"You received it. You have been too long alone, and you see enemies everywhere, but you have none."

"I'll be the judge of that. And after I finish with that little bastard Venzia," he promised, "you're going to wish *you* didn't have any enemies!"

"But—"

"If you're still on my property in thirty seconds, I'm calling the police."

And so, humiliated and miserable, I returned to my barren room, more isolated than I had ever been in my life.

Perhaps twenty times I began to write to my Pattern Mother, to explain the situation and Abercrombie's paranoid interpretation of it, but each time I got no more than two or three lines into the letter before I stopped. There was simply no way I could explain or excuse the fact of my termination. Personal dishonor would have been reprehensible enough, but I had dishonored the House, perhaps the entire race of Bjornn.

Suicide seemed the only possible course of action, yet suicide at this moment might bring even greater dishonor upon the House of Crsthionn, since I was still officially on an exchange program with the Claiborne Galleries and I had commitments to keep. In truth, I needed the ethical guidance of my Pattern Mother, but since it was she whom I had dishonored, I could not bring myself to ask for it.

I finally decided that I would tender my resignation when Tai Chong reopened the gallery the next morning, and the moment she accepted it I would return to my room and find the oblivion I now longed for.

PART 2

The Man Who Stole It All

7

I WENT TO THE CLAIBORNE
Galleries the next morning and asked for an audience with
Tai Chong. While I was waiting to see her, I paced
restlessly through the public display area, staring at the
various pieces without really seeing them. After a few
minutes had passed and she still had not called me into
her office, I walked to the back of the gallery and sat down
at my desk, glancing at the data that had accumulated in
my computer file without reading it. A moment later
Hector Rayburn approached me with an amused grin on
his face.

"I hear Abercrombie finally sacked you," he said.

"That is true, Friend Hector," I replied.

"Well, you stuck it out longer than any of us thought
you would," he continued. "Welcome back."

"I am only here to see Tai Chong."

"Oh? Are you going back to Bjornn?"

"My world is Benitarus II," I replied. "My *people* are
the Bjornn."

"Same difference," he said with a shrug. "Is that where
you're going?"

"No, Friend Hector," I said truthfully, since the dishonored are not permitted burial within the Benitarus system.

He seemed to lose interest in my future. "What's Abercrombie like?" he asked eagerly. "Is he as rich and crazy as they say?"

"He is quite wealthy, Friend Hector," I said, sneaking a brief look at Tai Chong's closed office door. "I am not competent to analyze his mental state."

"Did you find any paintings of that woman for him?"

"A few," I said.

He stared at me. "What's the matter with you today, Leonardo? Usually you're so full of talk and questions that I can't keep up with you. Today you're acting like you've lost your best friend."

"I have been disgraced."

"How?"

"Malcolm Abercrombie fired me for disloyalty," I said, my color reflecting my humiliation.

"So what?" said Rayburn. "I've been fired three times, and I'll probably be fired five more. It's an occupational hazard, that's all. When it happens, you have a drink, you get laid, and you forget about it." He paused. "Hell, you don't even have to hunt up another job. You've still got one with Claiborne."

"It is not that simple, Friend Hector."

"It's precisely that simple, Leonardo," he responded. "You Bjornns just don't have the right perspective."

"But it is *our* perspective," I replied, "and it is the one with which I must live."

My computer interrupted to say that Tai Chong was now ready to see me.

"Look," said Rayburn, "after you get through with her, stop by my desk and we'll go out and hang one on. I know a little place about three blocks from here that'll serve *anyone*." He smiled suddenly. "It'll be my treat."

"I thank you for your offer and your friendship, Friend Hector," I said, rising to my feet, "but I must refuse it."

He shrugged. "Well, if you change your mind, let me know."

I promised that I would do so, and then walked over to

Tai Chong's door, stood in front of the sensor until it had identified me, and entered the office as the door slid into the wall.

"Leonardo," she said, standing up and walking over to take my hand. "I'm so sorry about this mix-up!"

"The fault is mine, Great Lady," I said. "I have dishonored the Claiborne Galleries and the House of Crsthionn."

"Nonsense," she said, brushing aside my confession. "That bigot managed to hunt down less than thirty paintings in a quarter of a century. You found him two in a month and he had the temerity to fire you!"

I stood motionless for a moment, trying to assimilate what she had said. At last I found my voice.

"Am I to understand that you are not angry with me, Great Lady?"

"Of course not."

"But I was fired."

"Without cause."

"It was for speaking with Reuben Venzia."

"Freedom of speech and freedom of association are a couple of universal rights that seem to have escaped Malcolm Abercrombie's attention," she said contemptuously. She gestured toward her vidphone. "I was in the process of reminding him of them when you arrived a few minutes ago."

"You must not antagonize him on my account, Great Lady," I said, my color reflecting my distress.

"I did it for Claiborne," she replied firmly. "*Nobody* goes around abusing *my* employees!"

"That is what I wish to speak to you about."

"My speaking with Abercrombie?"

"No. My position as one of your employees."

"Of course you're one of my employees," she said reassuringly.

"I am here to submit my resignation."

She looked surprised. "Your resignation? What are you talking about, Leonardo?"

"I have dishonored my House."

"You have *not*."

"We come from different cultures, and it would be meaningless to argue the point with you, Great Lady," I said.

"Then don't argue it."

"I will not. But I must insist that you accept my resignation."

"Have you applied for another job?" she asked sharply.

"No, Great Lady."

She relaxed slightly. "What will you do if I accept your resignation? Return to your House?"

"I will perform the ritual of suicide."

"You'll do *what*?" she demanded, her expression one of shock.

"I will take my own life to abrogate the dishonor I have brought upon the House of Crsthionn."

"Just because you were fired?" she asked disbelievingly.

"Yes."

"But that's insane!"

"To a human, perhaps," I replied calmly. "But to a Bjornn, it is both proper and expected."

She shook her head vigorously. "I can't permit you to kill yourself, Leonardo."

"It is not your decision, Great Lady."

"Let's discuss it calmly and rationally," she said, flustered.

"I mean no offense, Great Lady, but I would much prefer that you accept my resignation with all due haste, as I must write my Pattern Mother and put certain of my affairs in order before performing the ritual."

She stared at me silently for a moment. Then an expression of dawning comprehension briefly crossed her face, and she cleared her throat and spoke.

"You could have taken your life last night," she said, listening carefully to her own words as if each sentence might lead her to the next. "You could have done it this morning. And yet you came to my office first, and you insist that I accept your resignation." She paused and looked intently into my eyes. "What if I refuse to accept your resignation, Leonardo?"

"It had never occurred to me that you might not honor my request, Great Lady."

She continued staring at me. "Your House signed an exchange contract with Claiborne," she said at last. "Your *House*," she repeated slowly, accentuating the word, "not you. What if I insist that you honor that commitment?"

I sighed. "If you refuse my resignation, then I shall have to fulfill my House's obligation to you."

"And you won't kill yourself?"

"I will not perform the ritual until my obligation to you is over."

"Then your resignation is refused," she said decisively.

"You are a very intelligent woman," I said ruefully.

"And you are a very live employee of the Claiborne Galleries," she replied with a relieved smile. "At least for the next ten months."

"Nine months and twenty-three days," I corrected her.

"We'll discuss it further when we're both in better spirits," she said. She exhaled deeply, as if dismissing the subject for the present. "In the meantime, you're going back to work for Malcolm Abercrombie."

"He will never take me back."

She grinned triumphantly. "He already has."

"But why?" I asked.

She held up a small hologram of a painting. "Does the subject look familiar?" she asked.

I stared at it. It was a portrait of Abercrombie's mysterious woman.

"I recognize the model," I replied. "But I have not seen this painting before."

"No one on Far London has." She paused. "When Abercrombie contacted me yesterday to inform me that he had fired you, I of course demanded the reason. Once I found out that Venzia had approached you, it occurred to me that he wouldn't have done so unless he thought you had something—or could get something—that he needed. So I spent a few hours going through all the electronic brochures we receive each week for upcoming auctions and private sales, and I came up with *this*." She indicated the hologram. "Is this what he wants?"

"Just the information, Great Lady," I said. "Not the painting itself. He collects information about the woman the way Abercrombie collects her portraits."

"I wonder why?"

"I do not know, Great Lady."

She paused, as if considering Venzia's interest, then shrugged. "At any rate, this portrait is being sold by Valentine Heath, a collector we've dealt with a number of times in the past. He prefers to sell directly to us, rather than go through the bother and uncertainty of an auction." She paused. "When you arrived, I was telling Abercrombie that we'd found another portrait of his lady, and that a condition of our obtaining it for him was his willingness to rehire you and offer written apologies to you, Claiborne, and the House of Crsthionn."

"He is a proud man," I said. "Surely he did not agree to your terms."

"He is also an *obsessed* man," she replied.

"He agreed?"

She smiled. "He agreed. You're back in his employ."

"But I don't want to go back!" I blurted out, surprising myself with my audacity.

"Surely it's preferable to suicide."

"Suicide is honorable," I said. "There is nothing honorable about working for a man who holds me in contempt and thinks me a liar."

"Prove to him that he's wrong."

"But—"

"Look, Leonardo," she interrupted. "Hector teases me because I'm always campaigning for our alien brothers, and in a way he's right: I make a lot of speeches and go on a lot of marches, but I never accomplish anything tangible. Well, this is my opportunity to actually *do* something, and teach a very distasteful man a very distasteful lesson at the same time." She paused and smiled at me. "And the fact that you're a Claiborne employee is going to make it all the sweeter."

"But couldn't someone else go to work for Mr. Abercrombie?" I asked. "Not only do we dislike one another, but my reason for being here is to learn your methodology and increase my exposure to different schools of artwork, neither of which I have done since I began working for him."

She shook her head. "You're the one he fired; you're the one he's got to take back. Besides, how can I give lip service to total equality and then not enforce it when I finally have the chance?" She clasped her hands in front of her. "Don't look so glum, Leonardo. I even got him to make substantial reparations to your House."

"You did?"

"Absolutely. Nobody abuses *my* aliens."

"I am most grateful to you, Great Lady," I said sincerely.

"You can prove it by not killing yourself," said Tai Chong.

"I promised that I would not perform the ritual while I am in your employ," I assured her.

"You still plan to do it when you leave?" she asked, surprised. "Even though he's agreed to take you back?"

"I do not know," I answered. "I will require ethical guidance from my Pattern Mother."

"But surely she'll tell you not to! Your House is getting more money now than they were originally!"

"It is the money of a guilty conscience," I replied.

"Nonsense!" she snapped. "It's the money of a stupid bigot who made a serious blunder and had to pay for it."

"I shall take your assessment under advisement," I said noncommittally.

"We'll talk about it again at a later date," she promised. There was an uneasy pause. "I have a feeling that our interview is over, Leonardo."

"Then am I to report to Mr. Abercrombie now?"

She shook her head. "No. As a matter of fact, I've already arranged for your passage to Charlemagne."

"To Charlemagne, Great Lady?"

"I am not unaware of your feelings toward Mr.

Abercrombie," she said. "And *someone* has to authenticate Valentine Heath's painting." She paused uncomfortably. "I was unable to purchase a first-class compartment for you, Leonardo. They simply will not allow you to occupy it."

"I take no offense, Great Lady."

"Well, *I* do," she said. "To make amends, I've reserved the Director's Suite for you at the finest hotel on Charlemagne."

"Charlemagne is very near the center of the Oligarchy," I said.

"Yes, it is," she replied, staring at me questioningly.

"My field of expertise is the work of the Albion Cluster, which is at the edge of the Inner Frontier. Surely you will require someone else to authenticate the painting."

"According to Valentine, it's only two years old," she replied. "Just have him introduce you to the artist and you'll have authenticated it as far as I'm concerned."

"But I do not know how to appraise or value it, Great Lady," I protested.

"It makes no difference. Whatever we pay Valentine, we'll make a profit when we resell it to Abercrombie."

"Then, since it is only two years old and you do not care about its value, why send anyone at all to authenticate it?" I asked, puzzled.

"Two reasons," she replied. "First of all, I intend to bill Abercrombie for every expense you incur on the trip —and I want you to take your time on Charlemagne. View it as a paid vacation."

"And the second reason?"

"I don't know much about the woman who appears in the paintings," she continued. "But it's obvious from the extent of Abercrombie's collection that she lived and died a very long time ago—which means that the artist who painted Heath's picture must have had some source material. See if you can find out what it was. If it's a work of art maybe it will be for sale, too, and we can purchase it for Abercrombie." She paused. "And one other thing, Leonardo."

"Yes, Great Lady?"

"If Reuben Venzia contacts you again, tell him you've considered his offer and you're willing to deal with him."

"But that would be unethical."

"We have, for all practical purposes, already purchased Valentine Heath's painting. There is no possible way Venzia can get his hands on it—but if he's got information that might prove useful to us, we don't want to shut off all communication with him."

"And what of Malcolm Abercrombie, who fired me yesterday for precisely what you are ordering me to do this morning?" I asked, suddenly aware of the irony of the situation.

"You leave Abercrombie to me," she said with grim determination. She got to her feet and escorted me to the door. "Everything will work out for the best." She placed a number of documents in my hand. "This," she said, gesturing to one of them, "is your Employment Pass, which will give you access to all public buildings on Charlemagne. They're pretty sophisticated out there," she added, "and I doubt that anyone will ask to see it. And this," she said, pointing to another, "is your Class B Passport, which will allow you to travel within five hundred light-years of Charlemagne for a period of thirty days, in case the artist is on some nearby world. And since we don't have an office in that system, this is the code number for a line of credit I've established with the Charlemagne branch of the Trustees' Bank. It's cued to your voiceprint, since your retinagram keeps confusing the security sensors. You can draw up to twenty thousand credits." She paused. "That's just in case Abercrombie has second thoughts about honoring his commitment to you. I assume you have his account and credit numbers?"

"Yes, Great Lady."

"This is a hologram of Valentine Heath, so you'll be able to recognize him at the spaceport."

"I should think it would be far easier for him to recognize a Bjornn disembarking from a human ship, Great Lady."

"Probably," she agreed. "But just in case he's late, or tied up elsewhere, you'll find his address coded on the back of it, and you can contact him at his home." She withdrew a small hologram. "And this," she said, handing it to me, "is a print of the painting you'll be authenticating."

I studied it briefly. "It is the same woman," I said.

"I know," she replied. "You don't forget that face once you've seen it."

I looked at the print again, and saw a strange script beneath it. It seemed almost legible, but the more I tried to make sense of it, the less I succeeded. Finally I handed it back to Tai Chong.

"I cannot read the writing below it, Great Lady."

"That's one of the newer script fonts they've been using in some catalogs," she explained. "It's called Antares Elegant, I believe. It looks lovely, but I can see why it might be difficult for you to read." She stared at it. "It says that the artist's name is Sergio Mallachi. Have you ever heard of him?"

"No," I replied. "Does it also give the title of the painting?"

"Yes," said Tai Chong. She shrugged. "It's rather odd, and just a bit intriguing."

"What is it?" I asked.

"The Dark Lady."

8.

THE SPACEPORT AT CHARLE-
magne made me realize just how minor a world Far
London actually was.

To begin with, we did not land on the planet itself, but
docked instead at a huge orbiting hangar, where a public
address system issued instructions to arriving passengers,
directing them to connecting flights, customs inspections,
orbital hotel accommodations, and shuttle flights to the
planet's surface.

Once I determined that Valentine Heath was not among
the crush of people waiting at the dock, I went directly to
the customs area, waited until my luggage had been
subjected to a sensor scan, had my passport validated, and
then took a very slow slidewalk to the shuttle departure
dock. The next planetary shuttle was not due to leave for
almost an hour, and since the food aboard the ship had
been created with the human palate in mind, I began
looking for a restaurant that catered to non-humans.

To my surprise, I couldn't find any. Humans and
non-humans alike mingled in a number of restaurants,
and nobody seemed to find this at all unusual. I entered
one of them, still half-expecting to be told that aliens, or at

least Bjornns, were not welcome, and was immediately escorted to a small table along one of the walls. Just behind me were two Men, discussing some sporting event while drinking coffee, and to my left was a table housing two Teroni and a Lodinite. The Teroni were eating the slick, greasy meat that was the staple of their diet, while the Lodinite was munching on a nondescript mass of vegetable matter.

The menu appeared—in Terran—on a small computer screen above the table, and although I could read it, I requested a Bjornn translation, just to see what would happen. After a moment I realized that this was a shocking breach of manners for a guest, but before I could cancel or countermand the order, the requested translation appeared, and, not wishing to cause further difficulty, I ordered a drink composed of the crushed pulps of fruits from Charlemagne's tropical zones. Immediately two columns appeared on the screen, the first a list of races who would find the drink physically harmful (three of them —the Domarians, the Sett, and the Emrans—were warned that this particular blend of fruits would be potentially fatal to them), the second a somewhat smaller list of races who would not undergo any ill effects but whose metabolism was such that the drink would act as an intoxicant.

Since the Bjornn appeared on neither list, I verified the order, was served almost immediately, and spent the next quarter hour sipping the drink and enjoying the feeling of warmth and security that emanated from the mass of nearby patrons. Finally I decided that it was time to leave, so I fed Abercrombie's credit number into the computer, waited until it was confirmed, and returned to the shuttle dock.

Once there, I was again struck by Charlemagne's complexity. Most of the human worlds I had visited had one or, at the most, two major cities, for Man had assimilated so many planets so quickly that he had barely begun to populate them. Successful colonies usually began as small cities which continued to spread as more and more Men emigrated to them; unsuccessful colonies began and ended as mere outposts. But while I had heard of Deluros VIII, with its seventeen billion Men, and other major worlds such as Earth, Spica VI, Terrazane, and Sirius V, I had never actually experienced any planet where Men covered more than the tiniest percentage of the surface.

Now, however, I was deluged with information about Charlemagne. There were perhaps twenty lines of various colors running across the polished flooring of the dock, and passengers were instructed to follow the color to the shuttle which would transport them to their destination: red to Centralia, purple to Blackwater, gold to New Johannesburg, orange to the Eastern Frontier District, and so on. My information was that Valentine Heath lived in the city of Oceana, and I followed the appropriate line to the proper shuttlecraft.

The craft itself was compartmentalized like any other spaceliner of the Oligarchy, with a first-class cabin containing perhaps three dozen comfortable seats created for the human figure, and, further back, the second- and third-class sections, divided into oxygen and chlorine environments, and filled with a miscellany of seats that could accommodate anything from a six-ton Castorian to a diminutive Tretagansii.

As I prepared to make my way back to the second-class section, however, I noticed that a Canphorite was sitting at the very front of the first-class cabin, and that a trio of blue-tinted beings who had entered ahead of me were in the process of seating themselves in the cabin as well.

I turned to a uniformed woman who was directing traffic within the craft.

"Excuse me, Great Lady," I said.

"Yes?" she replied.

I indicated an empty seat just ahead of me. "Is it permitted?"

"Is what permitted?"

"Am I allowed to sit here?"

"Of course," she said. "In fact, once we start the engines, you're not allowed to stand."

"I was referring to the first-class cabin, Great Lady."

"There are no classes on shuttle flights," she replied.

"But the structure of the cabin is such that—"

"The shuttle was built for use in the Spinot system," she explained. "We recently purchased it, and we haven't renovated it yet. Just take any seat you want."

"Thank you, Great Lady," I said.

I walked up the aisle and looked into the second-class section. It was quite crowded, and ordinarily I would have immediately entered it and sought out a seat, but although the first-class cabin was less than half full, I decided that this one time I would ride in it, just to experience what human passengers experienced. My decision made, I walked to a seat and strapped myself into it, making sure that the webbing was spread evenly across my body and wondering what Abercrombie and my Pattern Mother would say if they could see me now.

The brief trip to Charlemagne's surface was uneventful, and a few moments after landing I stood at the disembarkation gate, looking for Valentine Heath. I couldn't find him, and finally I approached a computer terminal to ask if he had left a message for me. He had not.

I decided that the best thing to do would be to register at my hotel and then try to make contact with Heath. To that end, I went to the baggage reclamation area, retrieved my luggage, and registered my voiceprint with a representative of the Oceana Police Department.

As I walked out the exit and stood in the bright Charlemagne sunlight, I found myself facing a seemingly endless line of vehicles. The nearest of them pulled directly in front of me, and its back door sprung open.

"Welcome to Oceana," said the driver, a stocky, balding human with an ingratiating smile. "Where are you headed?"

"I wish to be taken to the Excelsior Hotel, my good man," I said in the Dialect of Honored Guests.

"Have you got a reservation?" he asked.

"Most certainly," I responded, entering the vehicle and taking my luggage with me. "Why do you ask?"

He shrugged, and the vehicle began moving. "Just that they usually operate at capacity. I thought I'd save you a trip if you hadn't booked ahead."

"That is most considerate of you."

"It's my job," he said. "Is this your first visit to Charlemagne?"

"Yes, it is," I said.

"I hope you enjoy your stay."

"I have every confidence that I shall," I said, looking out the window at a vast expanse of brown dried grass. "May I ask you a question, my good fellow?"

"Go right ahead."

"Your fair city is called Oceana," I noted. "Where is the ocean?"

He laughed. "Wrong time of year."

"I do not understand."

"We're just a couple of hundred miles south of the equator, so instead of summer and winter we get dry and rainy seasons. Do you see that plain?" he asked, gesturing out the window.

"Yes."

"Well, when the rainy season comes, it becomes a lake almost two hundred miles wide and about eighteen inches deep. The first man to set up shop here came right after the rains and thought it was an ocean, so he named the place Oceana. By the time he found out what a blunder he'd made, the name had already been approved by the Pioneer Corps and registered by the Cartography Department back on Caliban, and it would have been just too damned much trouble to change it." He paused. "That's the reason the spaceport is so far from the city. If it were any closer, it'd be under water for half the year."

"How very interesting," I said.

"It's more embarrassing than interesting," replied the driver with another laugh. "We still get an occasional tourist here who books his vacation just based on the name."

We reached the outskirts of Oceana, a metropolis of shining steel buildings and angular glass towers, of broad thoroughfares cleaving through tastefully arranged commercial and residential areas. Finally the clusters of buildings pressed closer and closer together, seeming almost to touch the frail, wispy, low-hanging clouds, and the vehicle came to a stop.

"Here we are," announced the driver.

I completed the transaction, then emerged from the vehicle and approached one of the six liveried doormen, who in turn took my luggage and escorted me inside to a relatively small reception area which was surrounded by a plethora of very exclusive shops and boutiques. I became increasingly aware of the fact that there was only one other non-human within sight, a tripodal being wearing the hotel's gold and magenta colors and a maintenance insignia, but no one else seemed to take notice of it, and I was shortly ascending to the sixty-fourth floor via an express elevator.

Once there, I walked down a short, brightly lit corridor until I came to a door at the end of it. I spoke my name, waited until my voiceprint registered, and then walked into my suite as the door receded.

I found myself in an oversized sitting room that contained four chairs, a large couch covered by white Tumigan leather, a small, well-stocked bar made of Doradusian hardwoods, a stone fireplace, and a large window that overlooked the city.

Standing at the bar, a half-filled glass in his hand, was a tall, elegantly groomed, expensively tailored man with hair the color of the sun-scorched Oceana grasslands and oblique green eyes that had just a touch of gray in them. I instantly recognized him as Valentine Heath.

"Come in and make yourself comfortable," he said easily. "Sorry I couldn't get out to the spaceport, but I wouldn't have spotted you anyway. They told me you were a Bjornn."

"I am," I replied.

He looked surprised. "I've met a couple of Bjornns in the past," he said, "and they certainly didn't look like you."

"Doubtless they belonged to a different House," I said.

"They were green and black, and their skins seemed to be covered by endless patterns of concentric circles."

"That would be the House of Ilsthni," I said. "They are jewelers."

"Right," he said with a smile. "Anyway, I'm pleased to meet you, Leonardo. I'm Valentine Heath."

"May I ask you a question, Mr. Heath?" I said. I was about to address him as "Friend Valentine," but I decided against the Dialect of Affinity until I could determine how and why he had broken into my suite.

"Of course—and call me Valentine."

"Why are you here, Mr. Heath?"

"Valentine," he corrected me. "I thought you might have some difficulty locating my address. It's my understanding that you've never been to Charlemagne before, and Oceana's got a pretty complex street grid and an absolutely nonsensical numbering system."

"I seem not to be making myself clear, Mr. Heath," I said. "Why are you here in my room?"

"I hope you don't think it insensitive of me, Leonardo, but there are four entrances to the hotel. I was afraid I might choose the wrong one and miss you."

"But the security lock is coded to my voiceprint. How did you get in?"

"Never trust security locks, Leonardo," he said with a smile. "Any maid or bellman can gain entrance to it. If I were you, I'd leave my valuables in the hotel safe." He paused. "Can I fix you a drink?"

"No, thank you."

"Something to eat, perhaps? Room service offers quite a large selection and they deliver within ten minutes."

"No, thank you."

"Well, then, why don't you relax and we'll just have a pleasant visit."

"I am not tired," I said. "Perhaps I could see the painting now."

"Later," he said. "Let's get to know each other first."

Suddenly I began to feel very uneasy in the presence of a

man who had broken through my suite's security system and seemed totally uninterested in showing me the painting that I had come all this way to appraise.

"Let us get to know each other while walking around your city," I suggested. "I found it quite fascinating as I drove through it."

"It really doesn't come to life until after dark," he replied. "If you want to see Oceana, you must wait until the sun goes down."

I didn't want to alert him to my fears, but it seemed imperative that I leave the suite and surround myself with witnesses to whatever fate he had in store for me.

"While on the spaceliner from Far London, Friend Valentine," I said, emphasizing the form of address, "I read that Oceana has an outstanding art museum. If it is open, perhaps we can go there."

He shook his head. "I hate to disappoint you, Leonardo, but it's been closed for renovations."

"How can that be?" I said. "The article said that it was built only two years ago."

"It seems that someone robbed it last week, and they're installing a more sophisticated security system." He walked over to a chair and sat down. "So why don't we just spend the afternoon here?"

I stared at him for a moment, looking for telltale bulges in his clothing that would signify the presence of a weapon. I could not discern any, but I realized that it didn't matter anyway: He was far larger and stronger than I was.

Mustering my courage, I said: "Friend Valentine, my luggage has not yet arrived. I think I should go back down to the lobby to make sure that it has not been misplaced."

"The porter will be bringing it along any minute now," he assured me. "He's probably loaded it onto a cart with a bunch of other bags, and is dropping them off one room at a time."

"Nevertheless," I said, "I have some personal belongings that are quite dear to me."

He pointed to the hotel intercom console. "If you're

really worried about it, call up the reception desk and see if your luggage is on its way."

"I would feel much more secure if I were to go in person," I said truthfully, edging a step toward the door.

He shrugged. "If you're *that* worried, go ahead."

"You don't intend to stop me?" I blurted out.

He seemed amused at the idea. "Why should I want to stop you?"

"I thought . . . that is, it seemed . . ." Flustered and embarrassed, I was unable to form a cogent sentence.

"Are you all right?" he asked. "You just changed colors."

"It is the Hue of Humiliation," I explained. "I thought, for some reason, that you wanted to keep me here."

Heath chuckled. "You're free to go anywhere you want." He paused. "On the other hand, I'm afraid I'll have to take advantage of your hospitality until nightfall."

"I don't understand."

"It's quite simple, really," he said. "The police are looking for me."

"You are a fugitive?" I exclaimed, my fears returning.

"No, just a suspect."

"Then why do you hide from the police?" I asked. "Surely the best course of action is to make yourself available to them and answer their questions truthfully."

"That's only the best course of action if you're innocent," he replied with a smile. "I happen to have done exactly what they think I did." He paused. "I really hate to inconvenience you like this, Leonardo, but it's only for a few more hours. Once it's dark out, I'll have no difficulty eluding them."

"Did you kill someone?" I asked, backing away from him.

"Certainly not! I'm an opportunist, not a murderer."

Suddenly a thought occurred to me. "The painting—is it stolen?"

"I'd never steal anything so mundane," he replied. "The brush strokes are really quite trite, you know."

"But you *do* steal paintings?"

He took a sip of his drink, then looked up with an amused expression on his face. "You make me sound like an art thief, Leonardo."

"Are you?"

"No."

"For a moment," I said, relaxing somewhat but still ready to retreat again, "I thought you might be responsible for the closing of the art museum."

"I am," he replied calmly.

"But you just said you aren't an art thief!"

"'Art thief' is too limited a description. I also steal jewelry and a number of other beautiful things." He paused. "I prefer to think of myself as a master criminal. It sounds so much more professional."

"Why are you telling me this?" I asked.

"Because I'm imposing on your hospitality," he said. "And because an alien can't testify against a human being on Charlemagne."

"But I can tell the police what I know."

He shrugged. "They already know what I've done. Proving it is another matter altogether." He smiled at me. "Besides, we're going to be friends, and that would be a decidedly unfriendly thing to do."

"I cannot be friends with a thief," I said adamantly.

"Of course you can. I'm actually a very likable fellow. In point of fact, it's my stock in trade. Without it, I'd have a much harder time in my chosen profession."

"But why be a thief at all?"

"It's my parents' fault. I personally view myself as a victim rather than a thief."

"What have your parents to do with it?"

"They spent too much money." He finished his drink and leaned forward in his chair. "You see, the Heaths have been a monied family for more generations than you can imagine, and of course, no Heath would ever stoop to working for a living. My own education prepared me to do nothing but squander the family fortune—so you can imagine my disappointment when I found out that Father's taste in women and Mother's passion for gambling had left me precious little to squander." He paused. "I was totally unqualified for even the most menial position —but I do have a cultivated and exquisitely developed sense of taste, if I say so myself . . . and since I had been raised to expect certain of life's amenities, it was only natural that I should drift into the one profession for which I am temperamentally suited."

"What makes you temperamentally suited to be a criminal?" I asked.

"Like all spoiled children, I was raised to care about no one except myself, of course," he replied. "If I respected other people's rights, I would undergo enormous moral conflicts every time I plied my vocation. Fortunately, I suffer no such qualms, and of course, if it weren't for people like myself, the insurance industry would soon undergo a serious recession, so in my own way I'm actually benefiting the economy."

"I knew there were thieves in some alien societies," I said, "but I never thought to meet one who took such pride in his work."

"Why not be proud of what I do? It's an art form, and I'm certainly a better thief than Sergio Mallachi is a painter."

"I feel I must point out to you that I am carrying no currency with me," I said.

"I'd never steal currency," he said disdainfully. "It's much too easy to trace the serial numbers."

"It is even easier to trace a stolen portrait," I noted.

"Ah!" he said with a smile. "But people *spend* currency. They keep their art treasures under lock and key. The trick is to steal things that are so famous that their new owners would never display them publicly. That's why I deal with collectors, and why I never support public auctions." He paused thoughtfully. "Of course, I make it my business to supply collectors with *anything* they want, including honestly procured artwork, and I frequently act as a middleman for them. And," he concluded, "I occasionally act as a consultant for clients who have an abundance of wealth and an absence of taste. Usually I arrange for them to purchase paintings like *that*," he said, pointing to an exceptionally poor abstract that hung behind the couch.

"But if you came by the Mallachi portrait honestly, you could have auctioned *it*," I pointed out.

"Then people would want to know why I don't have everything auctioned," he replied. "Consistency may be the hobgoblin of little minds, but inconsistency does tend to bring one to the attention of the police computers."

"I don't know if I should even be talking to you," I said, uncomfortably aware of the fact that I had been captivated by his manner and that my fear and apprehension had all but vanished. "You represent immorality and disorder and dishonor."

"You overestimate my importance, Leonardo," he replied easily. "I'm merely an opportunist in quest of opportunities, nothing more. If anything, you should feel some sympathy for me; I'm working harder than any Heath in the past five hundred years, doing my best to restore the depleted family treasury." He paused and seemed to survey his surroundings for the first time. "God, what dreadful taste the decorator had! Bare walls would be better than this hideous metallic wallcovering!" He shook his head. "I'll wager they've hung sporting prints in the bedroom."

"What did you steal from the museum?" I asked.

"Just one piece," he said with a shrug. "You wouldn't think the police would become so incensed over a single piece of artwork, would you?"

"It all depends what it was," I said.

"A Morita sculpture," he answered.

"A Morita!" I exclaimed.

He nodded, looking quite pleased with himself. "One of his most innovative."

"But surely the police will find it when they examine your home!"

"It all depends which home they examine," said Heath with no show of concern. "I've got eleven of them, all under different names, and only three of them on Charlemagne. You don't mind if I pour myself another drink, do you?" He got to his feet and walked over to the bar. "You're sure I can't fix one for you?"

"No."

"As you wish." He smiled again. "But where are my manners? Can I order some native Bjornn drink for you? Room service has an adequate selection."

"I am not thirsty, thank you."

Just then the porter knocked at the door.

"Come in," said Heath in a loud voice, and the door opened a moment later. "Just put everything in the bedroom," he ordered, directing the porter through the room and tipping him on the way out.

"Thank you, Mr. Leonardo," said the porter. "Enjoy your visit to Oceana."

"I'm sure that I will," answered Heath, ordering the door to close.

"But *I* am Leonardo," I said.

"True," agreed Heath. "But *I* am more likely to need an alibi than you are."

"For what?"

"Who knows? The day is young yet."

"You are a thoroughly reprehensible person," I said.

He smiled. "But charming. Poppa Heath always held that if you couldn't cultivate a fortune, you should at least cultivate the illusion of one—and that, of course, requires charm."

"Malcolm Abercrombie has a fortune, and is perhaps the least charming human I know," I said.

"Abercrombie? He's the man who wants the portrait of the Dark Lady, isn't he?"

"Yes."

"Why? It's an ugly piece of art. I was almost ashamed to offer it to Tai Chong, but my creditors have expensive tastes and I really must generate some income this week."

"He collects representations of her."

"I didn't know she posed for any other artists."

"She did not pose for the portrait you have offered for sale," I said. "She has been dead for more than six thousand years."

"Nonsense," he scoffed. "She was Mallachi's mistress. For all I know, she still is."

"You must be mistaken," I said. "I have seen a photograph of her from the days when Man was still Earthbound."

He shook his head. "You may have seen someone who *looked* like her."

"I could not be mistaken. I have seen the evidence."

"I don't suppose Mallachi could be mistaken either," replied Heath. "After all, he painted her."

"I wonder if I could speak to this Mallachi," I said.

"I don't see why not," answered Heath. "Of course, I'll have to track him down. He doesn't live on Charlemagne."

"I would appreciate it."

"I'll see what I can do," said Heath. "By the way, how many other portraits of the Dark Lady does Abercrombie own?"

"Twenty-seven."

A predatory look passed across Heath's face. "Are any of them by well-known artists?"

"Why do you wish to know?" I asked.

He smiled disarmingly. "I'm just making conversation —unless you prefer sitting here in silence until nightfall."

"You are an admitted art thief," I replied. "I do not know if I can answer your question."

"You're hurting my feelings, Leonardo."

"If so, then I am sorry."

"I'm a very sensitive person."

"I have no doubt of it," I said.

"But you still won't tell me anything about Abercrombie's collection?"

"I require ethical guidance from the House of Crsthionn before I reply."

"Crsthionn," he repeated. "That's not the word you used before."

"Crsthionn is *my* House. Earlier I was speaking about the House of Ilsthni."

"So you were," he said. "They're the jewelers and

you're the art dealers." He paused. "Tell me something, Leonardo."

"If I can."

"Why do you look so different from the jewelers? After all, you're all members of the same race."

"We are physically as similar to each other as human beings are," I replied.

"Structurally, perhaps—but you're orange and violet, and you've got broad stripes all over you. The other Bjornns were covered with circles, and were green and black."

"Men come in different colors, and yet you are all Men. It is our Pattern and our color that determine which of the thirty-one Houses we will enter, and yet we are all Bjornns."

"You mean you're stuck with a profession based on the markings you have at birth?"

"Were you not, by your own admission, forced into your own immoral profession due to an accident of birth?" I asked.

"Touché." He grinned. He paused for a moment. "Still, had my parents not squandered away my birthright, I would have had numerous fields open to me. You, evidently, did not."

"You make it sound limiting, and I assure you it is not. Every profession has numerous different duties and disciplines connected with it."

"But you still have to enter that profession," he persisted.

"We become part of that House," I said. "There is a difference."

"I don't see it."

"Unlike you, we are descended from herd animals, and so we have an overriding instinct to *belong*, to be a part of the Family. The greatest tragedy that can befall a Bjornn is to be born with a Pattern other than those of the thirty-one Houses."

"Does it happen often?" asked Heath.

"Perhaps once in two thousand times," I replied. "The

child is ostracized, and dies almost immediately."

"It sounds rather barbaric to me."

"Far from it. The race strives for genetic purity, and to allow a non-Patterned into the society is to court disaster."

"How many generations are you inbred?" he asked.

"You still do not understand," I said. "Mating frequently takes place between members of different Houses, expressly to avoid the less desirable traits of intensive inbreeding. I myself am such a product. My mother was of the House of Krylken, and my father, whose Pattern I bear, was of the House of Crsthionn."

"So he raised you?"

"I was raised by my Pattern Mother."

"I'm getting all confused," said Heath. "I thought your mother didn't have the same Pattern."

"She did not. I was given to a matriarch of the House of Crsthionn—my Pattern Mother—and it was her obligation to see that I was cared for and instructed in the ethos of the House of Crsthionn."

"What about your father?"

"What about him?"

"Didn't he have something to say about it?"

"I have never met him. He left Benitarus II before I was born."

"Why? Had he broken some law, or were they just upset with his choice of wives?"

"Neither," I replied. "Bjornn society is a matriarchy. Males are infinitely replaceable; females are the source of strength and stability within the House. Therefore, all males leave the House, and usually the planet, upon reaching maturity, lest they prove disruptive to the orderly life of the House."

"From what you've said, it seems to me they'd miss the social life of their Houses."

"Desperately."

"Do they ever return?"

"Only for breeding, or to take further instruction in the ethos of their Houses." I stared directly at Heath. "One meets many deleterious influences while traveling abroad in the galaxy, and occasionally one must return home to reimmerse oneself in the moral imperatives of the Bjornn."

Heath looked amused. "I do believe I've just been insulted."

"If so, then I apologize."

"Graciously accepted," he said. "And now, shall we get back to discussing Abercrombie and his collection?"

"I am ethically compelled not to."

"Ethics can be *such* a bother," he said wryly. "Especially, it would seem, for a Bjornn."

"I come from a very harmonious and honorable society," I replied. "Doubtless I was inadequate in my description of it."

"I doubt it. I get the distinct impression that it stifles a certain type of individual initiative."

"The individual is nothing. The House is all."

"You don't really believe that nonsense, do you?" he asked.

"I most certainly do."

"Well, after a couple of weeks with me, you'll have a more practical outlook."

"We shall not be together that long."

"Certainly we will," he replied easily. "You've got to examine the painting, and then you wanted to meet Mallachi. That's four or five days right there."

"But you said two weeks," I pointed out.

"So I did."

"What will consume the extra time?" I asked.

"Oh, I'm sure we'll think of something," he answered confidently, and somehow I knew that I had not heard the last of his questions about Malcolm Abercrombie and his collection.

9.

As night fell, I still had not formed a judgment concerning Valentine Heath. He was interesting and amusing, and he treated me with civility and respect; but if he was to be believed (and I saw no reason to doubt him), he was a thoroughly amoral felon who was currently harboring stolen artwork and would doubtless be selling some of it to an unsuspecting Tai Chong before too much longer. Even before we descended to the ground floor of the Excelsior Hotel, I had decided to remain in his company only long enough to obtain the Mallachi painting, and then to return to Far London as quickly as possible.

"Shall we hire a vehicle, or is there some form of public transportation you would prefer?" I asked as we approached the front door.

"Public transportation?" he repeated with a mock grimace. "Rubbing shoulders with the proletariat while they exhale smoke and garlic in your face? Bite your tongue, Leonardo!"

"Then I will flag down a vehicle," I said, stepping outside.

"Allow me," he said, signaling to a large, luxurious silver vehicle that was halfway down the street. It immediately came to life and pulled up to the door.

"My pride and joy," he said, opening a door for me. "Even the cigar lighter is fusion-powered. What do you think of it?"

"It is quite large," I remarked as I climbed into the immense back seat.

"If you're thirsty, there's a built-in bar," he said, joining me and pressing a button that raised a small liquor cabinet between us.

"No, thank you."

"There's also a video with an octaphonic sound system," he continued.

"How interesting," I said.

He pressed another button, and I stifled a yelp as the entire seat began vibrating.

"For those days when you're bone-weary from dodging the police," he explained.

He knocked on the opaque glass that separated us from the front seat, and the driver, a Mollutei, slid the panel back.

"Yes, Mr. Heath?" he said through a translator pack, which came out in perfect Terran.

"The subterranean penthouse, James," he said.

"Yes, Mr. Heath," replied the Mollutei, sliding the glass panel shut again.

"What is a subterranean penthouse?" I asked.

He chuckled. "An underground apartment."

"I noticed that you called your driver James," I said. "I was not aware that the Mollutei possessed human names."

"They don't. But I can't pronounce his name, so I call him James." He paused. "The last one, if I recall correctly, was Oscar."

"I am delighted to discover that you are willing to employ non-humans."

"As I believe I mentioned, their testimony is not allowed in Charlemagne's courts," replied Heath. He paused. "Also, they work for less money than humans, and I'm continually trying to cut expenses—not that it ever does any good. I was brought up never to settle for second best, but no one thought to teach me how to *afford* the best. My professional life has been an endless round of trial and error."

"Obviously you haven't made too many errors," I noted, "since you are still at large."

"Oh, I've made my share," he answered easily. "But so have the police. You'd be surprised at how long it takes them to realize that someone in my position could be a thief. A stock-market swindler, a manipulator of government contracts, a buyer of political favors—these things are expected from a man of obvious wealth and breeding. But a thief in the night? It never seems to occur to them."

"Then why were you forced to hide in my suite?" I asked.

"*Almost* never," he amended. "And of course by the time they catch me, the Morita will have already been placed with a person who has even less reason than I to make its possession a matter of public record, and then I'll be given a clean legal bill of health and a series of profuse apologies, and the police will wait even longer before suspecting me of the next theft."

"It seems very convenient," I said disapprovingly.

"To say nothing of illogical," he added. "Consider the folly of arresting the typical disadvantaged underworld character for stealing a precious gem or a rare painting. I mean, he's barely able to pay for a clean shirt; how could he possibly be the man they're after? Whereas *I* require upward of half a million credits a month just to meet my basic expenses, and I have no visible means of support. If the police just looked at things logically, they'd round up every member of the idle rich and keep them all imprisoned without bail until the culprit confessed."

"It is a very interesting point of view," I admitted.

"And not without a basis in fact," he continued. "I never worry about being robbed when I go out among the unwashed masses, whereas I always go armed to the teeth when traveling among my peers." He turned to me. "Remember, Leonardo: The moment a man tells you that he has no need for money, grab your wallet and run."

"And what should I do if he tells me that he is a thief?"

"We're all thieves," he said with a smile. "I just happen to be an honest one."

"Is that not a contradiction in terms?" I asked.

"Of course. Whoever said that a man can't be contradictory?" He looked out the window. "Ah! Here we are."

I reached for the door handle, but he gently grabbed my hand.

"Not just yet," he said. Then he activated an intercom switch. "Twice around the block, James." He turned back to me. "If you don't mind, we'll take an extra minute or two to make sure we're not being followed and that the entrance to my building isn't under surveillance."

"And if it is?"

"Then I'll disguise myself as a neighbor and take the painting out right under their noses."

"What if the real neighbor should make an appearance?" I asked.

"You're looking at him," said Heath with a smile.

"I do not understand."

"I keep two apartments in the building. The one in the basement is rented in my own name, but the one on the sixth floor is leased by an elderly gentleman with a white beard and a very noticeable limp. He rarely emerges from his apartment, just often enough so that the neighbors can identify him."

"Am I to understand that you maintain two identities in Oceana?"

"Three, actually," he said. "It's a bother, but you never know when they'll come in handy." He spoke into the intercom again. "That will do, James. Park about a block away after you let us out, and keep a watchful eye out for us."

The vehicle came to a stop, and we emerged into the warm, dry night air.

"This way," he said, leading me to the front door of a large steel and glass apartment complex.

We entered a small foyer and waited for the security system to identify Heath.

"Good evening, Mr. Heath," said a metallic voice.

"Good evening," replied Heath.

"You have a companion," said the voice. "Please identify him."

"This is Leonardo, of the race of Bjornn, a business associate from Far London. He will be my guest for the next few hours."

"Registered," said the voice.

Suddenly a section of the wall slid back and Heath walked through, gesturing me to follow him. We followed a well-lighted corridor to a nearby elevator, and a moment later had descended to the basement level.

"Here we are," he said, walking to a door and standing before it while his voiceprint and retinagram were cleared. Then it slid silently into the wall, and we entered his darkened apartment.

"Lights," he commanded.

Instantly the various lamps and light fixtures came to life, and I found myself in an elegantly furnished room that was equipped with a plethora of entertainment devices ranging from a full-sized holographic video to a number of highly complex games of skill, all keyed to a single computer. A recording of a string quartet serenaded us in decaphonic sound, while hypnotic ripples of light formed intricate pastel patterns on the walls and ceilings. A display case along one wall held some twenty sculptures and artifacts from around the galaxy, most of them quite small and delicate, each of them stunningly executed. A chrome tabletop floated two feet above the ground in front of a fur-covered couch, and on it were three leather-bound books from Earth.

"Can I get you a drink?" asked Heath.

"No, thank you," I said.

"You are the driest creature I've ever met," he noted. "Are you getting hungry? I've got an exceptionally well-equipped kitchen, though I must confess that I've never cooked a meal in my life. You'll have to fix it yourself."

"Perhaps later," I said. "I would like to see the Mallachi painting now."

"If you wish," he said, walking into another room. He

returned a moment later with a large canvas, which he propped up on the couch. It matched the hologram Tai Chong had given me.

"Dreadful, isn't it?" he commented as we both looked at it.

"He is not very skilled," I admitted.

"I wouldn't have had the gall to offer it to Tai Chong," continued Heath, "except that the woman is so beautiful that she almost overcomes the inadequacies of the artist." He continued to stare at the painting for a moment. "She really is quite striking, isn't she?"

"Yes, she is," I agreed. "Do you know if Mallachi has painted any other portraits of her?"

"I doubt it," answered Heath. "In fact, to the best of my knowledge this is his first painting."

"Can you tell me anything about him?"

"Not very much," replied Heath. "He spends most of his time on the Inner Frontier, though he makes his home on Quantos IX. He never talks about his profession, but from bits and pieces I've managed to pick up, I believe him to be a bounty hunter, and a highly successful one at that."

"If he is a wealthy man, and he does not paint for a living, why did he give you the portrait to sell?" I asked.

"I gather that she left him a few months ago."

"And he is so heartbroken that he wants no reminders of her in his home?"

"Or so furious."

I studied the sad face in the painting. "Did he say why she left him, or where she might have gone?"

Heath shook his head. "I hardly know the man, Leonardo." He looked at the painting again. "Do you really think Abercrombie will want this thing?" he asked dubiously.

"He will want it."

"The man has no taste at all."

"He collects portraits of her," I said.

"He must be a completist."

"He would like to be."

"How hard can it be?" asked Heath. "After all, she can't

be thirty-five years old. How many people can have painted her?"

"More than you might suppose," I replied. "Men have been painting and sculpting her for eight thousand years."

"She must have a commonplace face."

"Have you ever seen it before?" I asked.

He stared at her portrait once more, then shook his head. "Never," he admitted.

"Did Mallachi ever speak of her?"

"You make it sound like we're old friends," complained Heath. "In point of fact, I've met the man twice. The only thing he told me was that he met her out on the Frontier somewhere."

"How long were they together?" I asked.

He shrugged. "Who knows?"

"I think I would like to speak to Mallachi," I said.

"Why?"

"To find out if she really exists."

"I already told you: She was his mistress."

"But you never saw her."

"That's right."

"Do you know anyone who did?" I asked.

"No."

"Then he might have been lying."

"What reason would he have had to lie?" asked Heath.

"It is my observation that Men frequently lie without a reason," I said.

"True," agreed Heath amiably. "But why do you care if she exists or not?"

"Her portrait has appeared throughout human history, frequently as a myth-figure. If she does *not* exist, if by his statement Mallachi meant that because of his profession he embraces the Goddess of War or Death, then he must have had some source or inspiration for her portrait—and if I can find it, I will attempt to purchase it for Malcolm Abercrombie."

"And he'll buy it sight unseen?" asked Heath.

"Yes."

"He's really that obsessed with her?"

"Yes."

A predatory look crossed Heath's face. "I have a feeling that there's a handsome profit to be made out of all this."

"You are making one," I pointed out.

He offered me another of his disarming smiles. "Yes, of course I am."

"Where is Sergio Mallachi now?" I asked.

"Hopefully he's on Quantos IX," said Heath. "Let me make a quick vidphone call to a mutual friend and I'll make sure."

He left the room, and I spent the next few minutes thumbing through the three leather-bound books on the floating table. Two of them were different editions of the Bible, and the third was a translation of the works of Tanblixt, the great Canphorian poet. I was perusing the latter when Heath reentered the room.

"We're out of luck," he announced. "Mallachi's on some Inner Frontier world named Acheron."

"I am not acquainted with it."

"Neither am I, but allow me to hazard the guess that it's one of the nastier planets out there."

"Why?"

"Because Acheron is another name for Hell."

"Can you find out its coordinates?"

"I'm not sure it's worth the effort," said Heath.

"Why do you say that?"

"Because Mallachi was due to return to Charlemagne two weeks ago." He paused. "Given his profession, that could mean he's dead."

"I see," I said.

"Your color is darkening," noted Heath.

"It reflects my disappointment."

"Don't give up yet," said Heath. "I'll contact my friend every day. There's always a chance he'll show up before you return to Far London." His gaze fell on the book I was holding. "Are you interested in poetry?" he asked.

"I am interested in books," I replied.

"Lovely things," he agreed. "Terribly anachronistic, though. I could probably keep the entire library of Oceana in a bubble module half the size of that book you've got in your hands."

"Doubtless," I agreed.

"Still, they're nice to have around—if one can afford them."

"I was surprised to find that you possess two copies of the Bible," I remarked.

"Oh? Why?"

"With no offense intended," I said, structuring my observation in the Dialect of Diplomacy, "you seem an unlikely student of your race's codified moral precepts."

He uttered an amused laugh. "I don't *read* them. I just collect them."

"That answers my question," I said.

"You're really quite good at this, Leonardo," he said admiringly.

"At what?"

"At slipping the verbal knife between my ribs in your quiet, self-effacing way."

"I assure you that—"

"Spare me your assurances," he interrupted. "I'll let you know when I'm offended."

I could think of no reply, and so chose to remain silent.

"Tell me more about the Dark Lady," he said at last. "Has she got a name?"

"I have no idea," I replied. "I would have thought *you* knew."

He shook his head. "Mallachi only referred to her the one time, and all he said was that she was his mistress." He paused thoughtfully. "I wonder how she got in all those paintings of Abercrombie's?"

"I do not know," I said. "My original premise was that she represented a mythic war figure, but that theory has been disproved."

Heath grimaced. "Here we are speaking of her as if she never existed, and yet I know for a fact that she was alive less than a year ago."

"That is untrue," I said. "You have never seen her. You know only that Mallachi claims she was his mistress."

"Why would he lie to me?" demanded Heath. "I had no interest in her."

"Why would she appear in more than thirty works of art dating back almost eight millennia if Mallachi were telling the truth?" I replied.

"How should I know?" he said irritably. "Coincidence?"

"Do you truly believe in such a coincidence?"

"No," he admitted. "But I do believe that there's a logical explanation, even though we haven't come up with it. Maybe—"

At that instant he was interrupted by a high-pitched beeping sound.

"What was that?" I asked, startled.

Heath was already on his feet. "That was James, signaling me that we're no longer alone."

"The police?" I asked.

He nodded. "I fear we're going to have to make a rather abrupt exit."

"But why?" I asked. "If, as you say, you came by the Mallachi painting legitimately, you have nothing to hide."

He looked amused. "In this room alone I can see three books and more than a dozen alien sculptures that are in need of hiding—and you haven't seen what I've got in the bedroom." He paused, staring unhappily at his art objects. "I don't suppose I've got time to pack them and take them along, more's the pity." Suddenly he walked decisively toward the door. "All right," he said. "Let's go."

"Why do you not simply disguise yourself as your other identity?" I asked.

"Because my makeup's in the sixth-floor apartment," he said. "Do hurry up, Leonardo."

"I have nothing to fear from the police," I replied.

"You want to meet Mallachi, don't you?"

"As you say, he may be dead by now."

"He may also be alive."

"Then I shall find him in my own good time," I said. "The police are my friends, not my enemies."

"Don't bet on it," said Heath. "You might find it

difficult to explain how an alien came to be alone in an apartment with all these stolen goods." He grinned. "They might even think you were the thief." He must have seen my horrified reaction, because he continued, even more persuasively: "At the very least, they'll think you're involved in all this, and unfortunately the building's security system will confirm that I described you as a business associate and that you didn't disagree."

"No Bjornn has ever been arrested! I will disgrace the House of Crsthionn!"

"Then stop wringing your hands and come with me," said Heath.

"But even if we escape, they will still know I was here."

"So what?" he said. "Tai Chong ordered you to inspect the painting. She'll explain everything to the police."

"The painting!" I exclaimed. "We cannot leave without it. That is my purpose for being on Charlemagne!"

"All right," he said calmly. "Pick it up. We've still got a minute or two before the police get through the security system and figure out which elevator to take."

I raced to the painting and carried it back to the door.

"Now follow me," he ordered.

He stepped out into the corridor and walked rapidly to a service lift. I had to adopt a shuffling run to keep up with him, but twenty seconds later we had ascended past the main floor.

"Where are we going?" I asked.

"My other apartment," he explained. "It would be just a bit awkward to try to take the painting out past the police, so we'll store it there for the time being."

"And then what will we do?"

"You worry too much, Leonardo."

We got off at the sixth floor, walked down a corridor, and stopped before a door. Heath stared intently at it for an instant, then walked right past it to the stairwell.

"What is the matter?" I whispered.

"The police are in the apartment."

"How do you know?"

"Whenever I leave the apartment, I always put a little

piece of dark tape, no more than an inch or so, where the door meets the wall. It pulls loose if anyone opens the door."

"Could it have been removed by a maintenance worker?" I asked.

"Do you want to take the chance?" he responded.

"No," I admitted.

"Neither do I."

"What now, Friend Valentine?" I said, falling into the Dialect of Affinity more from terror than any valid reason.

"Well," he said, "while I've always admired video heroes who bound catlike across the rooftops of a city, I very much doubt my ability to emulate them, so I suppose we'll have to depend on intelligence rather than agility." He paused, lost in thought. "There's a helioport on the roof, but that's much too obvious. And they've doubtless got men stationed at the rear entrance."

"Please hurry!" I said urgently.

"We're in no immediate danger," he replied. "They'll simply assume that I'm out on the town, and will keep a watchful eye on the building's entrance."

"The security system will tell them you are here!" I said.

"So it will," he said, surprised. "I had quite forgotten that." He turned to me, an amused expression on his face. "You know, you have the makings of a truly exceptional fugitive, Leonardo."

"Please!" I said.

"Well, we can't go up and we can't go down. I suppose the audacious approach is the best. Follow me."

We climbed down a flight of stairs and emerged on the fifth floor.

"What do we do next?" I asked nervously.

"We very calmly walk out through the front door," he answered.

"Surely you are not serious!"

"I most certainly am."

"But they know I am a Bjornn!" I protested. "They will be looking for me!"

He smiled. "But they don't know what a Bjornn looks

like. If they've ever seen one before, which I for one doubt, they probably think that you're green and black with a circular pattern. Believe me, to them you'll just be another alien."

A set of elevator doors opened. Heath walked over, looked into the empty compartment, but did not enter it.

"I *knew* you were jesting," I said as an enormous sense of relief swept over me.

"Not at all," he replied. "I'm simply waiting for a crowded elevator."

"Why?"

"Because then we'll be members of a group coming down from the upper levels of the building, and the police are looking for two individuals coming up from the basement."

"And you think *that* will fool them?" I demanded incredulously.

"Let's find out, shall we?" he said as a partially full elevator stopped at our floor, and I had no choice but to follow him into it.

My hue became several shades brighter as my terror increased, and between that and the Mallachi painting I felt hideously conspicuous when we finally emerged into the lobby. Heath had struck up a conversation with an elderly gentleman, and continued talking to him as we came to a trio of uniformed police at the front door of the building. He even nodded pleasantly to one of them, and to my absolute amazement the officer nodded back and paid no further attention to any of us.

As the group split up upon leaving the building, we followed a foursome that had turned to our left—the opposite direction from where the Mollutei was waiting with Heath's vehicle—and rode the slidewalk until we were out of sight of the police. Then Heath took a small communicator from his pocket and signaled to the Mollutei, and a moment later his vehicle pulled up next to us.

"Well done, James," he remarked as we clambered into it. "I think you'd best take us to the spaceport."

"Where are we going?" I asked, my heart still pounding rapidly in my chest.

"It will be a few hours before the police realize how easily we fooled them, but once they do, they're going to be very cross with us. When that unhappy moment occurs, I think it would behoove us to be a long distance away—so I guess we might as well try to find Sergio Mallachi after all." He leaned back on the seat and grinned. "Next stop—Hell."

10.

MY FIRST SENSATION WAS one of stiffness. Every joint in my body seemed frozen, and it took an enormous effort of will just to move my fingers.

Then, as feeling gradually returned to me, came the hunger: overwhelming, voracious, insatiable.

Finally there was the light, beating against my eyelids and forcing my eyes to water even before I could open them. I tried to wipe the tears from my face with my hand and found that I could not bend my arm sufficiently.

Suddenly a voice, distant and remote, impinged upon my consciousness.

"Welcome back," it said. "I trust you slept well."

I tried to ask where I was, but my lips would not respond to my mental commands and all that came out was an unintelligible noise.

"Don't try to speak or move yet," said the voice, and now I recognized it as Valentine Heath's. "You're just waking up. You'll be fine in another two or three minutes."

I forced an eye open and tried to look at him, but my pupil was completely dilated and I couldn't focus.

"Where am I?" I managed to mumble, as more feeling returned to me.

"Aboard my spaceship," answered Heath.

"Where is your ship?"

"About three weeks out of Charlemagne, or four hours from Acheron, depending on which direction you're facing."

Finally I was able to reach my face with my hand, and I wiped away the tears and gingerly touched my head.

"What happened to me?" I asked.

"You've had a little nap."

"For how long?"

"Almost three weeks."

"I do not understand."

"I put you in the Deepsleep chamber a couple of hours after we left Charlemagne," he replied. "You were becoming an emotional basket case. You kept ranting and raving about dishonor and disgrace. When you demanded that I divert the ship and take you to Benitarus II, I decided that the best thing to do was put you into Deepsleep until we reached Acheron."

Suddenly it all came back to me: the police, the narrow escape from Heath's building, the fact that I was now a fugitive from justice. I remained surprisingly calm in the wake of these memories, a condition that was doubtless attributable to my weakened physiological state. I tried to sit up, but pains shot through my head and back and I uttered a startled yelp.

"Don't try to move yet," said Heath soothingly. "It'll take your body another couple of minutes before it's back to normal. Also, if you're like me, you should be starving: The Deepsleep chamber slows your metabolism down to a crawl, but even so, you can work up quite a hunger after a few weeks. Can I have the ship's galley prepare some food for you?"

"Yes, please."

"All it carries are soya products, but it can make them up to taste like almost anything." He paused thoughtfully. "Since the Bjornns descend from prey rather than predators, I suppose steak is out of the question?"

"Vegetation will be sufficient," I answered.

"Would you care for some salad dressing?" he asked.

"No."

My vision had cleared enough for me to see him shrug. "Vegetables it is," he replied, reaching forward to tap out his instructions to the galley on a computer terminal.

Finally I was able to sit up, and I carefully swung my legs over the edge of a plastic cocoon. I felt a momentary dizziness, but it quickly passed.

"Handy things, these Deepsleep chambers," remarked Heath. "I can't imagine why the commercial spaceliner companies don't install them. They keep one from going mad with boredom during long voyages." He smiled. "I set mine to wake me up six hours ahead of you, just in case you were still feeling distraught."

It was a typically pragmatic human response, and I could not bring myself to take offense at it.

"Are we still fugitives?" I asked.

"I have no idea," replied Heath. "One does not, after all, contact the police to ask them if they're still looking for you." A light flashed on his terminal. "Ah! That would be your salad. Do you feel up to walking to the galley?"

"I will try," I said, getting gingerly to my feet. To my surprise, I felt quite good, even somewhat refreshed.

"I told you it would just take a couple of minutes," he said. "And you have the added advantage of having aged only a day or so during the past three weeks."

Since a Bjornn is concerned with the quality of his life rather than the length of it, I made no response, but merely followed him to the galley, where a container of vegetable matter awaited me. I was so hungry that I grabbed some of the larger pieces and stuffed them greedily into my mouth before I even sat down.

"Feeling better now?" asked Heath after I had finished the entire meal.

"Yes," I said.

"Good."

"I must speak with you."

"Be my guest," he said.

"I must return immediately to Benitarus II."

"You're not going to start that all over again, are you?"

"I have been tainted by my association with human beings," I said. "I have been shamed by my employer, and now I am being sought by the police, and in my ignorance I do not know how either situation came to pass. All I know is that every moment I remain away from Benitarus I risk bringing further disgrace upon myself and dishonor to my House."

"Leonardo, we're four hours away from Acheron. We're probably six weeks from Benitarus."

"Nevertheless, further contact with you is morally polluting. I must return to my home, and reimmerse myself in the rote and ritual of Bjornn life."

He shook his head. "It's out of the question. Not only is Benitarus half a galaxy away, but it's the very first place the police will think of looking for you."

"It is?" I asked, panic-stricken.

"It is."

"We cannot allow this to happen! My Pattern Mother must not be forced to speak to human police!" Suddenly a terrifying thought came to me. "They might be there already!"

"If they are, it's too late to worry about it."

"You don't understand!" I cried. "This would be the ultimate disgrace!"

"Look," he said. "Once we're done here I'll come with you to Far London. You can deliver the painting to Abercrombie, and I'll explain the situation to Tai Chong, who can fix things with the Charlemagne police. Then you can go anywhere you want to go."

"That may be too late!" I insisted.

He shrugged. "All right," he said soothingly. "I'll contact her now, while we're approaching Acheron. Will that make you happier?"

I nodded, momentarily unable to speak. Heath spent the next few minutes sending a subspace message to Tai Chong, summarizing what had happened and exonerating me of any wrongdoing, and asking her to relay his message to my Pattern Mother.

"Satisfied?" he asked when he had finished.

"Why are you doing this for me?" I asked.

"Because I'm an exceptionally decent and caring person."

"Very few Men perform acts of charity without the expectation of some profit," I said. "You have done nothing during our period of association to convince me that you are one of them."

Heath seemed amused. "What a cynic you've become, Leonardo." He paused. "In point of fact," he added, "I'm also very curious about the Dark Lady. You've made her history seem most intriguing."

"So intriguing that you would transport me here and then to Far London at your own expense, with no thought of recompense?" I asked dubiously.

"Let us say that my interest in her is not entirely philanthropic, and let it go at that," he replied.

The ship suddenly shuddered, and I almost fell down.

"We're braking to sublight speed," Heath announced. "We ought to be able to see something now."

He activated the viewing screen.

"There it is," he said. "It even *looks* hot. Let me get a readout on it."

He instructed the computer to provide him with the essential data on Acheron, a reddish world perhaps five thousand miles in diameter, with two small oceans and almost no cloud cover. The surface was pockmarked with impact craters, the poles were the same color as the equator, and it had a single moon, no more than twenty-five miles in diameter, which raced across the sky as if trying to escape from the uninviting world below it.

"Why would anyone choose to live here?" I asked, staring at the world in the ship's viewing screen.

"It used to be a mining world," replied Heath.

"Has it been mined out?"

He shook his head. "No. They simply found a number of richer worlds and abandoned it."

"Then who lives here?"

He glanced at the readout. "Hardly anyone. The population is less than three hundred. It's just an outpost world now, a drop point for traders and miners."

"Does it ever rain?" I asked.

"Not very often," he replied. He referred to the readout again. "Let's see. The average temperature at the equator is thirty-four degrees Celsius, average at the north pole is twenty-nine degrees Celsius. Average annual rainfall at the equator, six inches; at the poles, zero." He grimaced. "The gravity is a little lighter than we're used to—not so much that we'll be doing backflips when we walk, but enough so that we won't have to expend too much energy, which will help to make up for the heat. Sentient races: none. Local fauna: none. Local flora: sparse and primitive." He looked up at me. "I'm surprised they found three people to live here, let alone three hundred."

"What is the atmospheric content?"

He checked the readout. "Thin, but breathable. Given some of these trace elements, I have the awful premonition that it will smell like raw sewage."

We spent the next few hours recuperating from the effects of the Deepsleep chamber and watching as the red globe became larger and larger and finally filled the entire screen.

"We are getting quite close," I noted. "Should you not request permission to land?"

"They don't seem to have a spaceport," he replied. "The ship's sensors have located a small town with about two dozen ships parked just north of it. I suppose that's where we're expected to put down."

"I hope they do not view this as an act of aggression."

He laughed. "What have they got that anyone could possibly want?"

We entered the atmosphere a few minutes later, and shortly thereafter set down at the edge of a ramshackle town that possessed a single street, composed primarily of domed houses and stores that had been half-buried in the dirt and then covered with layers of dried mud to give them extra insulation from the sun's piercing rays. The entrances, like the buildings themselves, were well below ground level, and consisted of ramps rather than stairs. There had been two cross-streets once, but now they were deserted, lined only with the skeletal remnants of dilapidated buildings.

When we emerged from the ship, we found a small, dark-haired, dark-eyed man, dressed in an out-of-fashion, dust-covered suit, waiting for us.

"Welcome to Acheron," he said, ignoring me and extending his hand toward Heath. "My name is Justin Peres. I'm the mayor."

"Valentine Heath," said Heath, taking his hand. "And this is my associate, Leonardo." He looked at a cloud of dust blowing down the center of the empty street. "I'm surprised Acheron needs a mayor."

"We don't," admitted Peres. "But we *do* need food deliveries, and those idiot bureaucrats back on Deluros VIII won't pay for them unless we've got an official government." He smiled. "You're looking at it." Suddenly the smile vanished. "And as the official government, I'd like to know your purpose here." He stared first at Heath and then at me. "You sure as hell don't *look* like bounty hunters."

"We're not," replied Heath.

"Well, *that's* a pleasant change," he said. "What's your business here?"

"I'm looking for a friend," said Heath. "Possibly you know him."

"If he's on Acheron, I know him, all right," answered Peres. "What's his name?"

"Sergio Mallachi," I said.

He looked surprised. "Speak Terran, do you?" He stared at me. "Boy, you sure wouldn't guess it to look at you."

"About Mallachi . . ." said Heath.

"You're too late."

"Do you know where he is?" asked Heath.

"Yes."

"Would you be willing to share that information with us?"

"I don't think it'll do you much good," said Peres. "He's in the cemetery at the south end of town." He looked sharply at Heath. "You're *sure* you're not bounty hunters?"

"I am an artists' agent," replied Heath. "I sold a portrait that Mallachi painted, and I've come to deliver his money."

"And what's the alien?" asked Peres, jerking a thumb in my direction but not bothering to look at me.

"As I said, he's my business associate."

Peres shrugged. "Well, this *is* the Frontier," he said with a look of disapproval. "I can't tell you who to deal with." He paused for a moment. "You're here to pay him for a painting, you say?"

"That's right."

"Are you sure you've got the right Sergio Mallachi?" asked Peres dubiously.

"Absolutely."

"The bounty hunter?"

"Yes."

"Well, I guess you'll have to hunt up his family and turn the money over to them," said Peres. He paused for a moment. "He *really* painted pictures?"

"One picture," replied Heath.

Peres shook his head unbelievingly. "Well, you learn something new every day. I'll bet it was a picture of his ladyfriend."

"A dark-haired woman?" asked Heath, suddenly intent. "Pale skin, dark eyes?"

"That's the one, all right." Peres paused. "Sorry you had to come all this way for nothing."

"It's all part of the business," replied Heath. "But as long as we *have* come all this way, I for one would like a drink before we start the long return voyage. My associate and I would be happy if you'd join us as our guest."

"He drinks, too?" asked Peres. He seemed to consider the proposition. "Might as well," he said at last. "It's safer than standing around out here, that's for sure."

"Is standing here unsafe for some reason?" I asked nervously.

"It could be," said Peres, heading off toward the town, which was perhaps four hundred yards distant. Despite the lighter gravity, the heat quickly took its toll of me, and it was all I could do to keep up with the two humans. Suddenly I saw a slight movement on one of the rooftops. I blinked my eyes to make sure that it wasn't a heat mirage, then stared again—and found myself looking at a gray-clad man positioning himself in the shadow cast by the slightly taller next-door building.

We reached the street, and again I seemed to sense figures lurking in the darkened interiors of buildings. Hunching over so that I wouldn't stand out against the stark landscape, I hurried ahead, my instincts urging me to join the two humans in front of me.

"What's the matter, Leonardo?" asked Heath, suddenly noticing my posture. "Did you injure yourself?"

"No."

"Then what's wrong?"

"Nothing," I said, not wishing to discuss my observations in Peres' presence.

Heath stared at me, shrugged, and continued walking. We came to the tavern a moment later, and gratefully entered its cool interior. It was relatively empty, with two groups of men clustered around two large tables, drinking and engaging in desultory conversation. Around the periphery of the room sat three other men, hard-faced and unsmiling, dressed in nondescript browns and grays, seated at small individual tables. One of them toyed with a glass of whiskey, the second was playing solitaire, and the third, somewhat older than the other two, was simply sitting with his elbows propped up on his table, his hat drawn low over his head, his eyes closed. Something about them fascinated and terrified me, and I moved closer to Heath, glancing furtively at each in turn.

"Well, Mr. Peres," said Heath, walking to an empty table, "what does one drink on Acheron?"

"I'll take a brandy," replied Peres as he and I joined Heath and sat down at the table. "But visitors usually prefer beer, at least until they adjust to the climate." He stared directly at me. "I don't know what the hell *you* drink."

"I think Leonardo could use a glucose solution," remarked Heath, turning to me. "I've never seen you so pale. You must be dehydrated."

My hue reflected my fear, of course, but I did not dare say so. "I will be fine as soon as I recover from the heat," I replied. "I would like a glass of water, please."

"Water it is," said Heath, looking down at the tabletop computer and frowning. "I see the buttons for brandy and beer, but I can't find water listed here."

"It doesn't work anyway," said Peres. "Not all that much on Acheron does. I'll take care of it."

He walked to the bar and returned a moment later, carrying our various drinks on a tray, which he set on the table in front of Heath, and slightly beyond my reach. Heath, seeming more amused than offended by his attitude toward non-humans, simply passed the water over to me.

"So tell me, Mr. Peres," said Heath, drinking half of his beer in a single swallow, "how did Sergio Mallachi die?"

"He was killed right here in this tavern."

"By some killer he was hunting down?"

"I suppose you could say so," replied Peres.

"That sounds like a very ambiguous answer," noted Heath.

"He was a killer, all right—but that's not why Mallachi came after him." Peres sipped his brandy. "It was over the woman. She had left Mallachi a few months ago and hooked up with this youngster, and Mallachi came here looking to kill him. Called him out right there in the middle of the floor, and the Kid killed him."

"Well," said Heath, "nobody ever said being a bounty hunter made him a good insurance risk."

"True enough," agreed Peres.

"And you say he was killed by a young man?"

"Right. Everyone just calls him the Kid." Peres smiled a knowing smile. "Not many men use their real names out here on the Frontier—especially if they're wanted by the law."

"And the woman?" asked Heath intently. "What happened to her?"

"She's right here," replied Peres calmly.

"Here?" repeated Heath, startled. "In this building?"

Peres shook his head. "No. Here on Acheron. She's down the street, locked away in the jail."

"What did she do?"

"Not a damned thing," said Peres.

"Then I don't understand . . ."

"The Kid's still on Acheron," explained Peres. "He's out in the desert somewhere."

"You're sure?"

Peres nodded. "As long as his ship's here, we know he hasn't left the planet."

Heath nodded toward the three men. "Then what are these bounty hunters doing here? They should be out looking for him."

"The Kid has used Acheron as his headquarters for close to five years, and he knows those mine tunnels better than anyone. A man would have to be crazy to go in there and try to dig him out, especially when we've got better ways to bring him back."

"You're using the woman as bait?"

"That's right."

"How do you know he won't leave without her?"

"There's two more bounty hunters out by his ship."

"If his hideout is well equipped, he could stay out there for years," said Heath.

Peres shook his head. "He'll show up either today or tomorrow," he said confidently.

"What makes you think so?"

"Because we transmitted a message over all our radio bands that she's being executed tomorrow night."

"Why should he believe you?" asked Heath.

"No reason," admitted Peres. "But *I* didn't send it. *She*

did." He paused. "In fact, the whole thing was her idea."

"She *wants* him to walk into a trap?"

"Evidently," said Peres. He couldn't hide a look of bewilderment. "Doesn't make much sense, does it?"

"Not unless she thinks he can live through it," agreed Heath.

"Not a chance," said Peres. "There must be a dozen bounty hunters stationed around the town. Word about Mallachi's killing went out, and they swarmed down on Acheron like locusts." He sighed. "There's still ore to be mined here. I've got a feeling it's going to be a little harder to interest investors in Acheron after a couple of killings —the one we've had, and the one we're going to have."

"Perhaps you should try selling it as a tourist attraction, with monuments on the spots where Mallachi and his killer died," suggested Heath. "In fact," he added thoughtfully, "it's not inconceivable that the Kid will take a couple of bounty hunters with him and give you a couple of more monuments."

"Would *you* come all the way out here to see where a bunch of killers died?" asked Peres skeptically.

"No," admitted Heath. "But . . ."

"But what?"

"But I abhor all forms of crime and violence. People without my scruples might very well be fascinated."

"Maybe," said Peres without much conviction.

There was a momentary silence, as each man finished his drink.

"What will happen to the woman after this young man is killed?" asked Heath at last.

"We'll let her go."

"I wonder if I might see her before we leave," said Heath.

"Why?" asked Peres suspiciously.

"She lived with him," replied Heath. "She might be able to tell me if he's got any heirs, and where I can find them. Also," he added confidentially, "I'm curious to meet a woman who is so intent on summoning her lover to his death."

"How do I know the Kid didn't send you to help her escape?"

"You can check my ship's flight log," said Heath. "We've been in space for three weeks, and you tell me Mallachi was killed two weeks ago."

"I just don't know . . ." said Peres meaningfully.

"I'd be *very* grateful," said Heath.

"*How* grateful?"

Heath pulled out a billfold and counted out three hundred credits.

"Is the alien coming too?" asked Peres.

"Yes," said Heath, adding two more fifty-credit notes to the pile of bills on the table.

Peres stared at the money for a moment, then took it and stuffed it into a pocket.

"Let's go," he said, getting to his feet.

I joined them as they walked to the door and up the ramp onto the hot, dusty street.

"This way," said Peres, turning to his left.

We walked about fifty feet and stopped.

"That's it," he said, indicating a low light-colored structure. "It used to be an office building, but we haven't had any businesses here in close to twenty years, and we needed a jail, so we appropriated the place and rigged the doors and windows with an electronic force field."

I looked where he was pointing, and suddenly I saw *her*. Her features were in such exquisite proportion that she appeared beautiful even to a member of a different race. She was clad totally in black, her dark eyes seemed sad and brooding, her hair looked exactly as it had been portrayed in all the paintings and holograms. She stood motionless before a window, staring beyond us to the far end of the street.

"I *knew* she existed!" exclaimed Heath.

"Whoever said she didn't?" asked Peres, puzzled.

"Oh, some art dealer who should have known better," replied Heath with a smile.

"By the way," said Peres, pausing to light a small cigar, "I ought to warn you that she's not much of a talker. Any conversation you might have with her is likely to be pretty one-sided."

"That's quite all right," said Heath, staring at her intently.

"Well," said Peres, stepping forward again. "We might as well get this over with."

Suddenly a door opened a few feet ahead of us, and a tall, burly, dark-skinned man emerged.

"You'd better get off the street," he said softly, his gaze fixed on a spot somewhere behind us.

"What's the matter?" asked Heath.

"Just do what the man says!" snapped Peres urgently, pulling Heath by an arm into an empty building while I scurried down the ramp after them.

"What happened?" demanded Heath. "What's going on?"

Peres led us to a window and pointed to the slim figure of a young blond man who stood, motionless, at the far end of the street.

"He's come for her," he said.

11.

THE KID STOOD STILL, SUR-
veying the situation. From time to time his gaze would
freeze on a rooftop or the interior of a building, and I
knew he had pinpointed yet another of the bounty hunters
who lay in wait for him.

He was dressed in a faded, nondescript brown outfit. A
laser pistol rested in a holster at his side, no longer
connected to its battery pack, ready for instant use. A
sonic pistol was tucked into his belt, a rifle was slung over
his shoulder, and the handle of yet another pistol could be
seen peeking out from the top of his left boot. He wore no
hat, and the hot wind whipped through his golden hair so
that it framed his face much as the halos in religious
paintings framed the faces of human saints.

Evidently the man who had told us to go inside was out
of range, for the Kid paid no attention to him, but
concentrated instead on studying the nearer buildings.
There were perspiration stains beneath his armpits, and
the back of his shirt clung moistly to him, but he seemed
in no hurry to move either into town or back out into the
desert.

"It's suicide!" said Heath, staring out the window at
him. "Doesn't he know it's a trap?"

"He knows," said Peres.

"Does he think he can take them all?"

Peres shrugged noncommittally.

I turned to look at the jail. The Dark Lady stood in the window, staring intently at the Kid, her face serene. I wondered what he had done to make her betray him in this manner.

"Here it comes!" whispered Peres excitedly, for the Kid had withdrawn his laser pistol and begun slowly walking down the street toward the jail.

There was a brief motion on the roof, the laser blinked, and an instant later a bounty hunter rolled down the gentle slope and fell heavily to the ground.

The man who had told us to get off the street drew a projectile weapon and fired it. Evidently he missed, for the Kid whirled and activated his own weapon as the man dove for cover. An instant later the man lay dead just outside our door, his face burnt black. I stared at him in horrified fascination, appalled that any race should consider such an end either heroic or romantic.

We heard another gunshot. The Kid spun around, his pistol flying some forty feet through the air, and I realized that he had been shot in the arm. He immediately grabbed the projectile weapon from his boot and fired back, then turned as he saw another figure in the store to his right. I do not know what kind of weapon was trained on him, but he fell to the ground and rolled over twice, blood pouring from the gaping hole where his left ear had been, fury masking the pain in his face. Then, kneeling, he fired into the store.

Two more laser pistols blinked, one from a rooftop and one from the tavern, and a number of bullets tore up the ground around him. The Kid fell backward as if hit in the chest by a heavy object. Then, as his body was rapidly covered by smoking scorchmarks of burning flesh and his vision was obscured by his own blood, he feebly removed his sonic pistol and aimed it at yet another bounty hunter.

I wanted to close my eyes, but I found that I could not do so. Instead I stared at him, transfixed, as he tried again and again to kill as many of his antagonists as he could before he died. It was so contrary to anything I had ever experienced that, even though the grim pageant was enacted right in front of me, I was totally unable to comprehend why he would keep fighting when he had already incurred perhaps ten mortal wounds, why he didn't just give up and accept the inevitable.

The air continued to be filled with the explosions of projectile pistols and the constant blinking of laser beams, while the Kid, his body jerking and spurting blood and ganglia as each bullet and beam found its mark, one eye hanging out of its socket by the thinnest shred of tissue, clawed feebly at his pocket with the only two fingers that remained on his hand, vainly reaching for one last weapon. Finally I could stand to watch the slaughter no longer and I turned my head away.

Perhaps by chance, perhaps by design, I found myself looking once more at the Dark Lady. Her hands were stretched out to the Kid, as if beckoning him to rise from where he had fallen and come to her, and her face, which had been so pale and emotionless, suddenly seemed flushed with excitement. She must truly have thought him capable of fighting his way past all the bounty hunters and rescuing her, for a moment later the hauntingly sad expression had returned, and I knew instinctively that he had finally died.

And then, suddenly, she was staring directly at *me*, an unfathomable expression on her face. I found this so disconcerting that I immediately averted my eyes.

"Well, that's that," remarked Peres with a sigh of relief.

"What a waste," commented Heath. "How many did he take with him? Four?"

"Three, I think," said Peres. "We'll have to check 'em out and see who's still twitching."

"It was horrible!" I said.

Peres turned to me. "I would have thought you'd like the sight of human blood."

"Surely no one could enjoy the sight of such butchery! It is immoral to take another being's life, no matter what the justification!"

Peres looked amused. "If you think *that's* immoral, wait until you watch them fight over who fired the fatal shot. We're likely to have two or three more killings before it's settled."

"What happens to the woman now?" asked Heath.

Peres shrugged. "I suppose we'll let her go." Suddenly he grinned in amusement. "She's going to need a good travel agent. I plan to confiscate the Kid's ship as payment for the damage he did during the shootout."

"But to release her with no means of leaving the planet is unconscionable!" I exclaimed, surprising myself by my boldness.

Peres turned to look at me as if I were some insect that he would sooner swat than converse with.

"Well, I sure as hell don't plan to keep feeding her for free," he said at last.

"Where will she go?" I asked.

"How the hell should I know?" he replied. "She'll probably hook up with one of the bounty hunters."

"They are all killers," I persisted, realizing that it was a breach of manners, but unable to stop myself.

"What's it to you?" demanded Peres. "You think she'd rather go off with a striped little monster like yourself?"

"There's no need for acrimony," said Heath smoothly. "My associate has a point, Mr. Peres. Rather than forcing her to leave in the company of one or more cold-blooded killers, let us at least allow her the choice of coming with us."

Peres stared at him for a long moment. "What do you want her for?" he asked suspiciously.

"Me?" repeated Heath, surprised. "I don't want her at all. It's a simple act of humanity. She's stranded here, you insist that she leave by the end of the day, and the only other people who might consent to take her are ruthless killers. We have room in our ship if she chooses to join us, and I can drop her off at any planet between here and Charlemagne. I doubt any of the bounty hunters have any intention of leaving the Inner Frontier, so at least I can get her a little closer to where she's going."

"How do *you* know where she's going?" asked Peres. "Hell, she's out here, isn't she? Maybe she *likes* the Frontier."

"She can always reject my offer," replied Heath. "But at least I'll feel better for having made it."

Peres paused. "What's your real interest in her?"

"Just what I told you."

"But you wanted to see her even before the Kid showed up."

"I don't find her any the less interesting just because he's dead," said Heath. "And I still have to find out who gets Mallachi's money."

"You sure the two of you aren't just planning to take her on some sort of perverted joyride across the Frontier?" asked Peres suspiciously.

"I can't imagine why that would concern you if it were true," said Heath, "but the fact of the matter is that it's not. No man of breeding would take advantage of a woman in such a predicament. I am a gentleman; she is a lady in some distress. It's as simple as that."

"There ain't ever been anything as simple as that," responded Peres emphatically. "If you take her off and nobody ever sees her again, I'd have to carry that burden with me to the grave."

And suddenly even *I* knew where the conversation was leading.

"I realize that would be a terribly heavy burden," said Heath sympathetically.

"Damned right," agreed Peres.

"What do you suppose it would take to lighten it?"

Peres smiled. "Another thousand ought to do it."

"Seven hundred," said Heath quickly.

"Eight."

"Done," said Heath.

"All right," said Peres, suddenly businesslike. "How do you want to arrange it?"

"Some of the bounty hunters might take umbrage at the sight of Leonardo and me leading her off to my ship," replied Heath. "Perhaps it might be better if you were to bring her to us there."

"Do any of them have any reason to think she'd rather go with them?" asked Peres.

"Frankly, I have no idea," answered Heath. "But I see no reason to put temptation in their path, so to speak. You're the mayor; you'll have much less difficulty taking her to the ship than we would."

"And if she doesn't want to go?"

"You're kicking her off the planet, and she has no friends and no money," said Heath. "Why *wouldn't* she want to go?"

"She's a strange woman. You never know with her."

"Just tell her that she's got two choices: come with us or stay in jail."

"But I don't *want* her in my jail," protested Peres. "She's nothing but trouble—and damned near everyone she latches onto ends up dead."

"Then convince her to leave Acheron with us."

"All right," said Peres, though his expression implied that he didn't think she'd agree.

"Look," said Heath. "Would you rather *I* spoke to her?"

Peres shook his head. "She'll take one look at the alien, and then nothing could get her to go with you. I'll take care of it."

"Fine," said Heath. He glanced out the window and looked down the street toward the Kid's corpse, where four bounty hunters were arguing among themselves and gesticulating wildly. "As soon as they've settled their financial differences, we'll go directly to my ship."

"I'll meet you there in half an hour," said Peres, opening the door and walking up the ramp to the street.

"Well, Leonardo," said Heath, smiling and rubbing his hands together, "we've got her!"

"It was the only civilized thing to do," I agreed. "I could not countenance her being forced to leave in the company of killers."

Heath chuckled. "In case it's escaped your attention, she *came* here after being in the company of a bounty hunter, and she then took up with an outlaw."

"Nevertheless, these are terrible men," I said with a shudder. "How can they kill like that?"

"You'd be surprised at what a man can do when there's money involved," replied Heath. "And before you condemn them, don't forget that bounty hunters are the closest things that the Frontier worlds have to police."

"But it was brutal, premeditated murder!"

"The Kid knew they were here. He didn't have to come."

"Why did he?"

"I beg your pardon?"

"The Kid," I said. "Why did he come back if he knew there were bounty hunters waiting for him? I do not understand his actions."

"You heard Peres," said Heath. "He came back for the woman."

"But he must have known he would never live to rescue her," I persisted. "Why did he willingly throw his life away?"

"Maybe he thought he could make it," said Heath without much conviction.

"That is an unacceptable answer," I replied. "I know he saw at least four of the bounty hunters; he had to know there were still more he could not see."

Heath shrugged. "I really don't know, Leonardo. Men under pressure do strange things."

"But he was not under pressure," I pointed out. "He was safe out in the desert. He knew the mine tunnels so well that no one dared go after him."

"But he thought the woman would be killed tomorrow night."

"If he believed her plea for help, he must have known that he could not possibly save her. If he did not believe it, then he had no reason to come back."

"True," admitted Heath thoughtfully.

"Then what is the answer?"

"I don't know," he said, checking the window to see if the bounty hunters had dispersed yet. "Maybe we'll get it from the Dark Lady."

12.

"CAN I GET YOU ANYTHING to drink?" asked Heath.

He had just put the ship on automatic pilot after leaving Acheron's atmosphere, and the three of us were sitting at a table in the galley, the one place in the tiny vessel that could accommodate all of us.

"Something hot, please," said the Dark Lady.

Those were the first words she had uttered since Peres had delivered her, and I marveled at the musical quality of her voice. She seemed totally at ease, and her demeanor was still serene.

Heath brought her a cup of coffee.

"Thank you," she said, holding it in both hands but not making any attempt to drink it.

"Is there anything else I can do for you?" he inquired.

She shook her head.

Heath seemed to be considering how to engage her in conversation. It was not so much that she seemed aloof, but rather that in her absolute tranquility she seemed to barely be in contact with the reality that surrounded her.

"That was a terrible ordeal you were forced to undergo back on Acheron," he began awkwardly.

She continued warming her hands on the coffee cup and made no reply.

"We will do everything in our power to make you comfortable," he continued. "Is there anything we can get for you—anything at all?"

She stared at him for a long moment, and though her face retained its serenity, I had the distinct impression that she was amused by his discomfort.

"You have questions to ask," she said at last. "Ask them now."

"What is your name?"

"You may call me Nekhbet."

He grimaced. "It may take me some time to learn to pronounce it properly."

"I have other names that are easier to pronounce."

"Would one of them be Shareen d'Amato, Great Lady?" I asked.

I had thought my question would surprise her, but she merely turned and stared at me curiously.

"And Eresh-Kigal?" I continued.

"You are a very surprising alien," she said with a hint of amusement.

"And I'm a very confused human," said Heath. "Who are Shareen d'Amato and this Erash-whatever?"

"They are just names," she replied.

"Yours?" asked Heath.

She nodded.

"What's your real name?" he asked.

"Ask your friend," she replied. "*He* knows."

"Leonardo?" asked Heath, surprised. He turned to me. "All right—who is she?"

"She is the Dark Lady," I said.

She smiled her acknowledgment.

"May I ask you a question, Great Lady?" I continued.

"Yes."

"Have you ever heard of a man named Brian McGinnis?"

She closed her eyes for a moment, then opened them and gazed at a bulkhead as if she were staring through it into the dim and distant past.

"Who the hell is Brian McGinnis?" asked Heath.

"A man who died almost six thousand years ago," I replied.

"Brian McGinnis," she said at last. "It has been a long time since I heard that name."

"Did you know him?" I asked.

"How could she know him, if he died six thousand years ago?" demanded Heath, annoyed.

"Your friend is right, alien," she said with a smile. "How could I know a man who died so many years ago?"

"I mean no offense, Great Lady," I said, "but you have not answered my question."

"I have the impression you know the answer." Her dark eyes locked on mine. "Am I correct?"

"I believe so, Great Lady," I said, surprised that I felt so little fear of her. "May I ask if you also knew Christopher Kilcullen."

"You have done your homework well, alien," she said with no hint of hostility. "I commend you."

"But you do not answer me," I said.

"There is no need to."

"Still, I should like to hear it from your own lips, Great Lady," I persisted.

She smiled again. "No doubt you would." She paused. "You are not destined to have everything in this life that you seek, alien."

There was a momentary silence.

"You *did* tell us to ask questions," said Heath at last.

"*You* may ask them," she replied.

"Fine," said Heath. "While we're on the subject of men you might know, what about Malcolm Abercrombie?"

"Who is Malcolm Abercrombie?" she replied.

"He collects your portraits," said Heath. "In fact, he's spent a considerable fortune on them."

"What is that to me?" she asked serenely.

"Would you like to meet him?"

"I shall never meet him," replied the Dark Lady. It was said not with a show of defiance, but as a simple statement of fact.

"He would like to meet you."

"Then he shall be disappointed."

"In fact," continued Heath persuasively, "I would venture to say that he would pay a great deal of money to make your acquaintance."

"I have no need of his money, and no desire for his company," said the Dark Lady.

"Then possibly you would do so as a favor to me."

"I owe you no favors."

"I realize that it is less than gallant to mention it, but we *did* rescue you."

"You are quite correct," said the Dark Lady.

"Then I'm sure we can reach an understanding," said Heath with a smile.

"You are quite correct about being less than gallant," she replied. "And I understand you perfectly, Valentine Heath." She took a sip of her coffee, then got gracefully to her feet. "Now, if you do not mind, I would like to rest."

"May I ask you one last question, Great Lady?" I said.

She turned to me. "Only one."

"Are you human?"

"Of course she's human," interjected Heath. "Just look at her, Leonardo."

She stared directly at me, but made no reply.

"Please, Great Lady," I said. "I truly do not know the answer to my question."

"The answer is no," she said at last.

"You're an alien?" demanded Heath unbelievingly.

"No, I am not."

Heath looked annoyed. "You've got to be one or the other."

"If you say so," she replied tranquilly. "Now could you please direct me to my quarters?"

"Certainly," said Heath, getting to his feet and walking to a door. "You can have my cabin."

"Thank you," she said. "That is very generous of you."

He flashed a smile at her. "What are friends for?"

"You are not my friend, Valentine Heath," she replied placidly as she walked into his cabin and closed the door behind her.

"How did she know my name?" said Heath, returning to the table. "I didn't mention it to her."

"Perhaps Mayor Peres did," I said without conviction.

He nodded his head vigorously. "That must be it." He pulled a bottle of liquor out of a cabinet, mixed himself a drink, and sat down. "Well, Leonardo, what do you think of our guest?"

"She is the Dark Lady," I said.

"I know she's the Dark Lady. You told me she was the Dark Lady. *She* told me she was the Dark Lady." He looked annoyed again. "Maybe I'd be more appreciative if someone would tell me just what the Dark Lady is."

"I do not know," I said.

"What was all this about Brian what's-his-name?"

"He was a human who lived almost a millennium before your race achieved interstellar flight."

"What about him?"

"He painted her portrait," I said.

"Obviously he painted someone who looked like her."

"I have seen a photograph of the two of them together."

"You're sure?"

"I am sure."

"And Kilcullen? Was he another of the artists?"

"Yes."

"And he, too, has been dead a long time, I presume?"

"Yes, though not as long as McGinnis."

He frowned. "Interesting," he mused.

"I would say that it is frightening," I replied. "Except that I am not frightened by her."

"Why should you be?"

"Because she is not human and she is not alien."

"What she mostly is is not truthful," scoffed Heath, sipping his drink. "She's as human as I am."

"Then how did she come to know about Brian McGinnis?" I persisted.

"Probably the same way you did."

"I have seen representations of her that predate the McGinnis painting by over two thousand years."

"Do you think she's the only black-haired woman who

ever lived?" demanded Heath.

"No," I said. "I think she is the only black-haired woman who has lived this long."

"Do you know what the human life expectancy is?" he snapped.

"Yes," I replied. "But she is not human."

"She looks human, she lives with humans, she gets painted and sculpted by humans, she takes human names. Does that sound like an alien to you?"

"She said that she is not an alien."

He snorted contemptuously. "Once you've eliminated human and alien, what else is there?"

"Could she be a psychic or spiritual manifestation?" I asked.

He pointed to her half-empty cup. "Manifestations don't drink coffee."

"I was unaware of that," I said. "Doubtless you have encountered manifestations before."

"Damn it!" he snapped, finishing his drink. "I know this is especially difficult for a Bjornn to grasp, but not all women tell the truth." He put his drink on a table and walked to the ship's computer. "We'll solve this once and for all. Activate!"

"Activated," replied the computer. "Waiting . . ."

"How many sentient beings are aboard this ship at this moment?"

"Three," answered the computer.

"Who?"

"Yourself, a Bjornn named Leonardo, and a human woman whose name may or may not be Nekhbet, Shareen d'Amato, Eresh-Kigal, or the Dark Lady."

"Give me some physical data on the woman."

"Height, five feet six inches. Weight, 128 pounds. Hair, black. Eyes, black. Age, between twenty-eight and thirty-six years, based on skin texture and skeletal structure, with a possible error of . . ."

"Deactivate," commanded Heath. He turned to me. "Does that sound like an apparition?"

"No," I said.

"Then are you satisfied?"

"No."

"No?" he repeated. "Why not?"

"Your computer is a machine, and as such, it can only analyze the data it was programmed to analyze. It cannot take into account the facts I have accumulated about the Dark Lady's past."

He stared at me for a long moment.

"You know, you're becoming rather argumentative," he said. "I trust I'm not the cause of this newfound aggression."

"I apologize if I have offended you," I said.

"I'm not offended, just surprised." He sighed. "All right, Leonardo, what do *you* think she is?"

"I do not know."

"You've no explanation for why she claims to have known these long-dead artists?"

"No," I said. "And I should point out that most of the men who painted her were *not* artists."

"Oh?" he said, surprised. "What were they?"

"I have been unable to establish a common link among them," I admitted.

He seemed to consider the problem for a moment, then shrugged and mixed himself another drink.

"Well, there's no sense driving ourselves crazy worrying about it. Maybe Abercrombie will be able to figure it out."

"Why should Malcolm Abercrombie chance upon the solution?" I asked. "He knows even less about her than you do."

"We're going to deliver her to him," said Heath.

"I do not understand."

Heath smiled. "Perhaps 'deliver' is the wrong word. We're going to negotiate with him for the pleasure of her company."

"You cannot sell one sentient being to another!"

"Nobody's selling anything, Leonardo," he said easily. "We're just performing a social service for two people who might find out that they have a lot in common."

"She is not a piece of property to be rented by the

hour!" I said, horrified.

"Who said anything about prostitution?" asked Heath innocently. "From what you tell me, between his age and his tumor, Abercrombie's probably past the point of being able to do anything about it even if he wanted to." He leaned forward. "But he's spent tens of millions of credits buying paintings of her. The man's got an obsession that's taken up a third of his life. Surely the chance to actually see her in the flesh, to know that she exists, to talk to her and maybe commission an artist of his own choice . . . it's got to be worth *something* to him."

"She said that she will never meet Abercrombie."

"And I'm sure she believes it," replied Heath. "But believing something doesn't necessarily make it true. Hell, she also believes that she isn't human."

"This is kidnapping!" I protested.

"We would be guilty of kidnapping if we had taken her against her will," he said. "She came with us voluntarily."

"But she did not know what you planned to do."

"You seem to think that she's some kind of royalty, to be treated with deference and abject respect," complained Heath. "Let me remind you that she consorts with killers, she arranged for her lover to be brutally slaughtered by bounty hunters, she's been kicked off Acheron, and she hasn't got a credit to her name. She should be grateful that we consented to take her along at all." He paused. "Look," he said more reasonably, "if it will appease your conscience, I'll give her ten percent of whatever I can get from Abercrombie. It'll probably be more money than she's ever seen at one time."

"She will not accept it."

"Of course she will."

"She will not," I repeated. "She has already said as much."

"She will, when she realizes that the alternative is being delivered to Abercrombie and *not* getting ten percent."

"I cannot permit this!"

"Leonardo," said Heath, "let me be absolutely straightforward with you. I find myself in a somewhat awkward financial position." He paused and sighed. "In point of fact, I am currently a fugitive from justice. I can't go back to Charlemagne for the foreseeable future, and I'm sure the police have frozen all my assets there. They will doubtless have put a trace on all my credit accounts, so I don't dare use them either. I must have a prompt infusion of cash, and this seems to afford me the best opportunity of obtaining it."

"You will obtain money when Tai Chong pays you for the Mallachi painting."

He shook his head. "That will barely be enough to refuel the ship." He paused. "I wasn't raised to mingle with the common herd, Leonardo. It may be unpleasant, but there it is: I require money to maintain the quality of my life."

"And what about the quality of *her* life?" I demanded.

"She was in a prison cell when we found her," he said. "What kind of quality was that?"

"For whatever reason, she was there voluntarily," I pointed out. "You are doing this against her will."

"You're becoming tiresome, Leonardo," he said. "I liked you much better when you were completely subservient."

"I cannot stand by silently and let you do this to a *lady*."

He arched an eyebrow. "Would it be different if she were a man?"

"It would still be immoral."

"But you wouldn't be as upset?"

"It is a heinous crime no matter who the victim is," I said emphatically.

"But worse if it's a woman?"

"All females are sacred."

"That's a strange world you come from," he said.

"It is *my* world," I responded. "I believe in it, and I cherish it."

"Well, next time we're in this situation, I'll be certain to kidnap a man," said Heath. "In the meantime, the subject is closed."

"The subject is *not* closed," I said. "I must make you understand what a terrible crime you are contemplating."

"The subject *is* closed," he said firmly. "Or am I going to have to put you in the Deepsleep chamber again?"

I realized that I could be of no service to the Dark Lady were I to continue arguing, so I meekly agreed, and waited until he fell asleep a few hours later. Then I silently entered her compartment to inform her of Heath's intentions.

It was empty.

I examined the interior of the small ship and could find no trace of her, and finally I woke Heath.

"What are you talking about?" he demanded as he got up off his bunk. "People don't just vanish from a spaceship! Where is she?"

"She is gone," I said.

"Gone where?"

"I do not know."

"We'll see about this!" he muttered, walking rapidly to her compartment. He practically tore it apart, even looking beneath the bunk and in the undersized closet. This done, he proceeded to the control room, the storage area, the lavatory, and back to the galley.

"What the hell is going on here?" he demanded. "Computer—activate!"

"Activated," announced the computer. "Waiting . . ."

"How many sentient entities are currently aboard the ship?"

"Two."

"Have any of the hatches been opened since we left Acheron?"

"No," answered the computer.

"Is there any way we could have jettisoned the Dark Lady without our knowing it?"

"No."

"Has she made any effort to leave the ship?"

"No."

"Then what has become of her?" asked Heath.

"I do not know," said the computer.

PART 3

The Man Who Wanted It All

13.

Heath came in from the wooden deck that overlooked the snow-covered mountains, rubbed his hands together vigorously, and walked over to the bar.

"Beautiful day!" he enthused. "A bit nippy, but beautiful."

"If you find it cold, why do you go out?" I asked without much interest.

"Do you know what this place cost me?" he said with a laugh. "All the realtor could talk about was the climate and the view. Well, the climate may be lacking from time to time, but the view is positively spectacular."

"How much longer must we stay here?"

"Leonardo, there are people who would give their eyeteeth to have a mountain chalet on Graustark. Just relax and enjoy yourself."

"Have you heard from your lawyers yet?" I asked.

"They've still got another government official or two to enrich," he explained. "Everything's coming along beautifully. Another day or two, three at the most, and we can go back to Charlemagne."

"I do not want to go back to Charlemagne."

"Then you can stay here."

"It has been nine days since we left Acheron. I must go back to work."

"We diverted to Graustark because Tai Chong told you to relax for a few days."

"I thought it was because you are hiding from the authorities," I said.

"That is another reason," he agreed wryly. "Still, as long as you're here, why not try to get into the spirit of it?"

"Must we go through all this again?" I asked wearily.

"No, of course not," he said. "But I know you've been feeling morose since you heard from your mother . . ."

"My Pattern Mother," I corrected him.

He shrugged. "Whatever. Why not take a walk with me before it starts snowing again? It's glorious outside!"

"I am more affected by extremes of temperature than you."

"Then dress warmly."

"The paths are narrow and winding, and I would fall."

"All right," he said, staring at me. "I have another suggestion."

"What is it?"

"Why don't you just sit here feeling sorry for yourself?"

"You simply do not understand the enormity of what has happened," I said.

"Your mother's mad at you," he replied. "So what? She'll get over it. Tai Chong has squared things with the police, nobody thinks you're a thief or a kidnapper any longer, you're still working for Claiborne, and you're sitting in a chalet at the most exclusive resort on the most exclusive planet in the Quinellus Cluster."

"I have my work to do."

"For a zillionaire collector who hates the sight of you," said Heath with a smile.

"That cannot be helped."

"Of course it can," said Heath.

"How?"

"Tell him to go to hell. Be a man!"

"I am not a Man," I pointed out.

"That doesn't make you any worse than Abercrombie,"

said Heath. "You really ought to stand up to him."

"He is my employer."

"He's also the most incompetent art collector I've ever heard of," said Heath. "It took him a quarter of a century to find thirty portraits of the Dark Lady, and you found three in the first month you were working for him."

"I had special knowledge about two of them," I replied. "That is why he hired me."

"But you found the third one," continued Heath. "And, more to the point, you found the model."

"Actually, it was you who found her," I pointed out.

"You, me, what's the difference?" he said. "The main thing is that Abercrombie didn't find her. He never once went looking for her. He never even *thought* of looking for her. He sits alone in his house, surrounded by a fabulous collection that he can't begin to properly appreciate, and lets everyone else do his work for him." Heath paused. "I can't for the life of me understand why you're so anxious to go back to work for him when you're sitting by a roaring fire atop the most beautiful mountain in the galaxy!"

"Friend Valentine," I said, slipping into the Dialect of Affinity, for indeed I *felt* affinity toward him, "why don't you simply say what you mean?"

"I don't think I follow you, Friend Leonardo," he replied, though a certain detached amusement in his eyes assured me that he did.

"You think that if you can convince me that Malcolm Abercrombie is a reprehensible example of his species, and that he has received services from me far beyond what he is paying for, I will describe the more valuable pieces of his collection to you and tell you how best to steal them."

Heath grinned. "Then you admit that he's *got* valuable pieces in his collection!"

"I never said otherwise."

"I thought you told me that almost none of the men who painted the Dark Lady were artists."

"That is true," I agreed. "But he has almost four hundred paintings and holograms in his collection, and most of them are not portraits of her."

"Does he have any Moritas?"

"I will not discuss his collection with you, Friend Valentine."

"I'm going to steal something from it whether you help me or not, Friend Leonardo," he promised. "But you could make my life a lot easier by giving me the information I need."

"That would be unethical."

"True," he admitted. "But it could also be profitable. I'd make you a partner."

"I want neither half the profits nor half the guilt," I said.

"No problem at all," responded Heath smoothly. "If you'd prefer to live with a fifth of the guilt, I'll cut you in for twenty percent of the profit."

"No."

"You're absolutely sure?"

"I am absolutely sure."

"Positively?" he persisted.

"Yes!"

"We'll discuss it again later," he said.

"My answer will be the same," I replied.

"You can't possibly feel any loyalty toward him."

"He is my employer," I said.

"Claiborne is your employer."

"And Claiborne says that I am to work for Malcolm Abercrombie," I replied. "I must fulfill my contract to the letter."

"So that you can kill yourself when you've completed it?" he said sharply.

"How did you know that?" I asked, startled.

"Tai Chong told me."

"She had no right to."

"We're old friends," he replied. "We don't have a lot of secrets from each other."

"She is guilty of a breach of confidence," I said.

"Because she doesn't want to see you kill yourself." He paused awkwardly. "Neither do I—especially if you're doing it because of what happened on Charlemagne or Acheron."

"I had spoken to her before I went to Charlemagne.

Although," I added truthfully, "very little has happened since that moment to weaken my resolve."

Heath laughed heartily. "You're a master of understatement, Friend Leonardo."

"It is not necessary for you to call me Friend," I said.

"Why not?" he asked. "We're friends, aren't we?"

"Only until you steal Malcolm Abercrombie's artwork."

He shrugged. "Nothing lasts forever."

"You are wrong, Friend Valentine."

"Oh? What do *you* think lasts forever?"

"The Dark Lady."

He snorted in annoyance. "Forever, hell! She couldn't even last long enough to get back to Far London."

"She is not dead," I said.

"I have a horrible premonition that you're right," he admitted. He paused. "I wonder what race she *really* belongs to?"

"Yours," I said.

He shook his head emphatically. "I keep telling you, Leonardo: She can't be human. She's got to belong to a race that can teleport. That's the only way she could have gotten off the ship."

"And I keep pointing out that the only race of true telepaths are the Dorban, who breathe chlorine and are too large to fit inside your ship."

"Then there must be another race of teleporters that we know nothing about."

"If you say so, Friend Valentine."

"You don't believe it for a second, do you?" he asked.

"No," I said. "Do you?"

He sighed deeply. "Not really." He paused thoughtfully. "Whatever she is, I wish I knew what quality she possesses that makes men who don't know the first thing about art suddenly decide to paint her portrait."

"Even to my inhuman eyes, she is very beautiful," I said. "And yet there is a certain ephemeral quality about her. Possibly they wished to capture her likeness because they knew she would soon be gone."

"Most of them seemed to have died pretty terrible deaths. I wonder if they painted her because they knew *they* would soon be gone?"

"I do not think so," I replied. "A number of them died of natural causes. And it seems to me that if they had a premonition of death, they would hardly take that as a mandate to paint her portrait."

Heath sighed. "I suppose not. Anyway, *I've* seen her and I don't have any urge to take up painting or sculpting." He paused and suddenly stared inquisitively at me. "Well?"

"I have drawn an ink sketch of her," I admitted.

"When?"

"Last night, after you went to sleep."

"Where is it?"

"I am not a very good artist, and it was not a very good rendering," I replied. "I destroyed it." I sighed unhappily. "I was also unable to capture the beauty of the 'Mona Lisa.'"

"The 'Mona Lisa,'" he repeated. "Is that how you got your name?"

"Yes."

"Just out of curiosity, Leonardo, why did you want to draw the Dark Lady?"

"She is the most interesting human I know, and the most beautiful."

"*If* she's human," he said.

"If she is human," I agreed.

"Who was the most interesting and beautiful human you knew before you met her?"

"Tai Chong," I replied promptly.

"Did you ever feel compelled to draw a portrait of Tai Chong?" he asked.

"No."

"Then I come back to my original question: What is it about the Dark Lady that makes people want to sit down and paint her?"

"I do not know," I said. "Perhaps it was because I wanted to preserve my memory of her face."

"But you can see her face whenever you want," Heath

pointed out. "You can have the nearest computer track down some likenesses of her and make prints of them for you."

"That would only show me what others saw," I said. "I wanted to draw what *I* saw."

"Spoken like an artist," he said wryly.

"I am not an artist," I replied. "I wish that I were, but I lack the necessary talent."

"So did Mallachi, but he painted her anyway." Heath frowned. "I just wish I knew why." He got to his feet. "A person could go crazy trying to come up with an answer. I don't know about you, but I'm going out for a walk." He paused at the door. "Are you sure you won't come along?"

"I am sure," I replied. "The paths are very slippery, and I am not well coordinated."

"So what?" he said. "Neither am I."

"You are very graceful," I said.

He snorted contemptuously. "You always wanted to be an artist. Well, I always wanted to be a cat burglar, dressed in black, climbing up the sides of buildings and sneaking into milady's boudoir to steal her jewels." He smiled wryly. "The one time I tried I slipped off a roof, fell onto a balcony, and broke my leg in three places." He shrugged. "So much for graceful—and so much for the romantic life of a cat burglar." He opened the door, and a blast of cold air blew past him. "If I'm not back in an hour, call the authorities and tell them to start looking for my frozen corpse. I'd like a modest funeral: four or five hundred floral wreaths, video coverage, nothing special. And don't tell my family—Heaths die in bed, not falling down mountains."

"I will observe your wishes," I said.

He grimaced.

"That was a joke, Leonardo."

"Oh."

He muttered something that the wind drowned out, and then closed the door behind him.

I waited for a moment, then walked to the desk in the living room and pulled out my stylus and stationery, intent upon finishing the letter I had begun writing earlier in the day.

My Revered Pattern Mother:

Yes, you were right. I have indeed become contaminated by my association with Men. I do not deny it . . . though I am certain that if you would relent and just consent to speak to me, I could explain how the present situation came to pass.

Tai Chong has assured me that I am in no trouble with the human authorities. Although I was an unwitting participant, I neither initiated nor contributed to the theft of the art objects on Charlemagne nor the kidnapping of the Dark Lady. Once I realized what Valentine Heath's intentions were, I did everything within my power to dissuade him. Such is the Rule of Honor; I live by the Rule of Honor.

And yet you tell me that my contamination is such that it cannot be expiated, and that I may not return to Benitarus II. You are my Pattern Mother, and your voice is one with the House of Crsthionn, so I must obey you.

Please know, though, that while my conduct has dishonored the House, I shall nonetheless try to comport myself in a manner that will bring no further discredit upon the race of Bjornn during the few months that remain before my contract with the Claiborne Galleries has been fulfilled.

And yet, I have a terrible premonition that this will not be the simple task that, in my ignorance, I thought it would be when I first left the House. It seems like I have been abroad in the galaxy for a century, though in fact it has been little more than five Galactic Standard months. And the more I associate with Men, the less I understand them.

Tai Chong, for instance, has been in every way a surrogate Pattern Mother to me. She is always considerate of my needs and thoughtful of my comfort, and constantly urges me to follow the moral dictates of my conscience. Yet I have come to believe that she knows full well that some of the paintings she purchases and resells have been illegally obtained, and she neither reports the transgressors to the authorities nor cancels the transactions. Hector Rayburn has always behaved in a cordial manner, yet he assumes that the eventual termination of his employment contract is a foregone conclusion, and the fact seems to amuse rather than horrify him. Valentine Heath is quite the most charming Man I have ever met, and at the same time I cannot conceive of a crime that he would not be willing to perpetrate. Malcolm Abercrombie donates millions of credits to charity, and yet, unbelievably, he has totally rejected the responsibilities of House and Family.

How am I to understand these strange beings, Pattern Mother? How can I purify myself when I must remain constantly in their company? At a time when I need your guidance most, it has been denied to me.

The only course open to me in my situation is ritual suicide, and yet that is the one act explicitly denied me by your insistence that I fulfill the contract between the House of Crsthionn and the Claiborne Galleries. Thus, cast out and isolated from all that I hold dear, I must make my way alone among this almost incomprehensible race in whose company I have been thrust.

Strangest of all is the Dark Lady. In a universe that seems progressively less logical to me, she is the least logical facet of all. I call her human, but in truth she is neither human nor non-human, neither real nor ethereal, neither presence nor manifestation. She is of this time, and yet she lived eight millennia ago. Nor is she a reincarnation, for reincarnations are born and live and die; they do not vanish from an enclosed environment in the vacuum of space.

I have seen her, have met and spoken to her, and still my questions about her continue to mount: Why does she appear when and where she does? What is she? Who is she? What made her beckon her lover to his death? What was her connection to an obscure botanist who lived on distant Earth six thousand years ago? Why do men believe that she haunts a spacemen's graveyard on Peloran VII? What was her relationship to a circus performer who was crippled in a fall from a trapeze three centuries ago?

And what am I to say when Reuben Venzia discovers that I have returned from my mission and offers to exchange information about the Dark Lady with me? If I tell him the truth, he will assume that I am lying; if I do not tell him the truth, I will actually be lying. In either case, I will dishonor the House of Crsthionn. And if I refuse to speak to him after Tai Chong has ordered me to, I will still bring dishonor to the House.

I require ethical guidance, and yet I am forbidden to speak to you, so I shall have to depend upon Tai Chong, who accepts stolen paintings and reveals confidences, to supply me with it. With all contact with my own race forbidden to me, she is the only female I know other than the Dark Lady, and I do not know where to find the Dark Lady. Therefore, Tai Chong will have to serve the function of my Pattern Mother until I fulfill my obligation to the Claiborne Galleries and perform the ritual.

Please believe that I am sorry for the pain I have caused. I truly never intended to

A burst of cold air swept over me, and as I put my stylus down, Heath reentered the room. He stamped his feet until most of the snow had fallen off them, then removed his gloves and blew heavily onto his hands.

"It's really starting to come down," he announced, walking over to me. "I think I'll enjoy the rest of my day's supply of majesty and grandeur through the window, with a drink in my hand." His gaze fell on the letter I had been writing. "May I?"

"If you wish," I said.

He picked up the letter and stared at it. "What the hell is this? I can't read a word of it."

"It is a letter to my Pattern Mother."

"That's the strangest script I've ever seen," he said. "It looks more like a graphics design."

"I have written to her in the Bjornn language, in the Dialect of Regret."

He handed it back to me. "I thought you'd done another drawing of the Dark Lady."

"I am not a good enough artist," I said. "Perhaps someday in the future I will be able to create a rendering worthy of its subject."

"Of course, to do that, you'd probably have to have another look at her, wouldn't you?" asked Heath thoughtfully.

"Perhaps," I agreed. "Although her face was quite memorable. When I close my eyes and remember, I can still see its every detail."

"So can I," acknowledged Heath. "But memory can be deceptive. I think you'd be better able to create your portrait if you saw her again."

"Friend Valentine," I said wearily, "I will not help you to steal Malcolm Abercrombie's art collection."

"Have I suggested it?" he asked innocently.

"Many times."

"You're a very distrusting fellow, Leonardo."

At that instant there was a series of three high-pitched mechanical whines.

"What was that?" I asked, startled.

Heath frowned. "The security system. Someone's approaching the front door."

"Who can it be?"

"Who knows?" said Heath. "I ordered some supplies for the kitchen, but I can't imagine they'd be making deliveries in this weather."

"We are totally isolated here," I said. "What if it is a thief?"

Heath chuckled. "Then we'll invite him in and swap stories."

"Should you not have a weapon at the ready?" I suggested.

"I thought you were the one who abhorred violence," he said, amused.

As I paled to the Hue of Humiliation, I was grateful that my Pattern Mother could not see me, and I realized that her decision was the proper one: I had indeed become contaminated beyond any possibility of exculpation.

"You are quite right, Friend Valentine," I said, stammering in my embarrassment. "It was an immoral suggestion, and I apologize for making it."

"I'll forgive you for making it," he said, pulling a small hand weapon out of his coat pocket, "if you'll forgive me for accepting it."

"You never told me that you owned a weapon," I said.

"You never asked me," he replied with a smile. "And if it will make you feel any better, I've never fired it. I don't even know if it works."

Two chimes sounded.

"Well, at least he isn't trying to gain entrance surreptitiously," commented Heath. "Open."

The door slid into a wall, and Reuben Venzia, covered with snow, his mustache a sheet of frost, entered the room.

"*You*," he said, staring directly at me, "are one goddamned difficult alien to find!"

14.

"**W**HO THE HELL ARE *you*?" demanded Heath.

"Don't worry, Mr. Heath," said Venzia. "I haven't told anyone else where you are."

Suddenly he was looking down the barrel of Heath's weapon.

"Nobody on Graustark knows my real name," said Heath. "I think you'd better tell me who you are and how you found me."

"I'm Reuben Venzia, Tai Chong told me where to find you, and I'm freezing my ass off. If you're not going to shoot me, let me get in out of the cold."

"This is the man you've told me about?" asked Heath.

"Yes, Friend Valentine."

"All right," said Heath, lowering his weapon. "You can come in."

Venzia entered the room, and as the door slid shut behind him he tossed his outer garments onto a nearby chair, cupped his hands in front of his face, and blew onto them.

"I've got a package for you from Tai Chong," he said to

me, "but it's out in the snowcart. I'll get it for you when
the weather lets up."

"You can't get a snowcart up this mountain," said
Heath, suddenly suspicious again.

"I know," responded Venzia. "I left it about a mile and
a half down the road."

"Why did you ride one at all?" asked Heath. "The
village is only two miles away."

"Because no one told me what the approach to this
damned place was like!" snapped Venzia. "Have you got
anything hot to drink?"

"Just coffee," replied Heath.

"Can you put a shot of rum in it?"

"I might, if you'll tell me what you're doing here."

"Looking for Leonardo," said Venzia.

"He, too, is interested in the Dark Lady," I explained to
Heath.

"So you've discovered her name," said Venzia.

"If that *is* her name," replied Heath before I could
answer.

"It's one of them, anyway," said Venzia. "What about
my coffee?"

Heath walked to the nearby kitchen area, poured a cup,
and added a shot of liquor to it. "You're not exactly the
most gracious guest I've ever had, Mr. Venzia."

"I'm freezing to death five thousand light-years from
home," shot back Venzia. "Let me warm up and get my
breath back and I'll find my manners again."

"Fair enough," said Heath, handing him the coffee. "In
the meantime, perhaps you might tell us exactly why
you're five thousand light-years from home."

"Do you mind if I sit down?" asked Venzia, walking
over to a large, tufted chair.

"Certainly not," replied Heath. "I'd be gravely disappointed if your explanation for all this privation you've
undergone was so brief that you could tell it to us while
you were standing."

"I wish Tai Chong had told me how goddamned cold it
was here before I left," muttered Venzia with a shudder.

He took a sip of his coffee, and warmed his hands on the cup.

"Are you feeling any better now?" asked Heath after a brief interval.

Venzia nodded. "I'll be all right in another minute."

"At which time I expect you to tell us exactly what you're doing here," said Heath.

"I'm here to see Leonardo," replied Venzia. "I have to speak to him alone."

"Nobody keeps secrets from me in my own house," said Heath adamantly. "Whatever you have to say can be said to both of us."

"Who are you?" asked Venzia suspiciously.

"Valentine Heath, as you well know."

"But who *is* Valentine Heath?" continued Venzia. "All I know is your name and the fact that you don't want anyone to know you're on Graustark. Why should I be willing to say anything in front of you?"

"Because I am a man of many talents, as well as a myriad of far-ranging interests, not the least of which is the Dark Lady."

"What do you have to do with the Dark Lady?" asked Venzia, eyeing him curiously.

"My interest in her is purely financial," responded Heath.

Venzia looked surprised. "Financial?" he repeated. "How the hell can it be financial?"

Heath smiled. "You asked a question. I answered it. Now I think it's my turn. What is *your* interest in the Dark Lady?"

"That's for Leonardo's ears alone," said Venzia.

"I must remind you once more that you are a guest in my house," said Heath, "and an uninvited one at that. If you continue to abuse my hospitality, I may have to turn you back out into the cold."

Venzia seemed to be weighing his alternatives. Finally he nodded his assent.

"A wise decision," commented Heath. "I think I'll fix myself a drink before we begin."

"I'll have one too," said Venzia.

"You're not through with your coffee yet."

"I will be before you're done," answered Venzia, taking a large swallow and placing the near-empty cup down on a table.

Heath shrugged. "As you wish." He pulled out two glasses and began mixing a blue-tinted concoction. "You still haven't answered my question, Mr. Venzia. What is your interest in the Dark Lady?"

"Simply stated, I want to meet her," said Venzia.

"State it in a more complex way, if you please," said Heath.

"I've got to speak to her," replied Venzia. "She possesses certain information that I must have."

"*What* information?" asked Heath.

"You asked a question, I answered it," said Venzia stubbornly. "Now it's your turn."

Heath finished mixing the drinks, handed one to Venzia, and took his seat again.

"We could go on all night without accomplishing anything if we continue like this," he said. "Therefore, I'm going to be perfectly frank with you, and I will expect you to respond in kind."

"Fair enough," agreed Venzia.

Heath took a sip of his drink, then leaned forward. "I am, due to circumstances totally beyond my control, a professional opportunist."

"What the hell does *that* mean?" demanded Venzia.

"It means that I take advantage of opportunities wherever I chance to find them. Leonardo considers me a thief, but that is a very limiting definition."

"Are you saying you're not a thief?" asked Venzia, confused.

"I most certainly *am* a thief, among other things," replied Heath. "I rank among the very finest, I assure you. In fact, Leonardo and I are currently considering the most practical means of separating Malcolm Abercrombie from his collection."

"That is not true!" I interjected.

"Are you indeed?" asked Venzia, ignoring my statement.

Heath nodded. "I realize that Abercrombie has no items of any significant value, but nonetheless . . ."

"Oh, I wouldn't say that," replied Venzia. "He's got a Skarlos, a Perkins, and three or four Ngonis, a Santini . . ."

"Does he really?" said Heath with an innocent smile. "I must have been misinformed."

"Get to the point," said Venzia.

"The point, Mr. Venzia, is that I am aware of Mr. Abercrombie's obsession with the Dark Lady. It is my intention to deliver her to him, in exchange for certain financial considerations yet to be negotiated."

"Lots of luck," said Venzia.

"You don't think Abercrombie will pay for her company?" asked Heath.

"Getting him to pay should be easy. *Finding* her is the tricky part."

"We found her once. I'm sure we can do it again."

Venzia practically jumped out of his chair. "You've actually *seen* her? In the flesh?"

Heath nodded. "We had her aboard my ship."

"Where is she now?" demanded Venzia intently.

"I have no idea."

"Where did she disembark?"

"You're going to have a difficult time believing this," said Heath, "but she simply vanished while we were *en route* from Acheron to Far London."

Venzia slumped back, dejected. "Then I've missed her again."

"You believe me?" asked Heath, surprised.

"Why shouldn't I?" responded Venzia glumly. "Were you lying?"

"No," said Heath. "But if Leonardo hadn't been along, *I* wouldn't believe me."

Venzia was silent for a long moment. Then he finished his drink in a single gulp.

"Shit!" he muttered.

"You're not surprised that she was able to teleport herself off the ship," said Heath, his face alive with interest. "Why?"

"Nothing that she can do would surprise me," said Venzia.

"I've told you what you wanted to know, Mr. Venzia," said Heath. "Now it's your turn."

Venzia stared searchingly into each of our faces in turn, then sighed again and nodded his head.

"All right," he assented. "Our interests don't coincide."

"I want her, you want her," said Heath. "I'd say they were the same."

"All *I* want to do is speak with her," said Venzia. "*You* want to kidnap her and sell her to Abercrombie."

"I just want to introduce her to him," Heath corrected him. "I am not, after all, a practitioner of white slavery."

"Define it any way you like. It makes no difference." Venzia allowed himself the luxury of a tiny smile. "If I were a betting man, Mr. Heath, I would wager everything I owned that you'll never get the two of them together unless she wants to meet him. You still don't have any idea of what you're dealing with."

"What *am* I dealing with?"

"If I told you outright, you wouldn't believe me."

"Perhaps not, but why don't you tell me and let me make up my own mind?"

Venzia shook his head. "No. For it to make any sense, I'd better begin at the beginning." He took a deep breath, and then continued. "Six years ago I had some business to transact on Pyrex III. Have either of you ever heard of it?"

"Never," said Heath.

"Yes," I said. "There was a major insurrection there against the Oligarchy."

"Right," said Venzia. "It wasn't the native population: I don't think to this day that the Kaarn even understand what the Oligarchy is, or would give a damn if they knew. All they want to do is sit in the sun and create those ridiculous eleven-syllable poems of theirs. But the human colonists were another matter: They thought the Oligarchy was exacting too high a tax on their trade, and they finally declared independence."

"What does all this have to do with the Dark Lady?" asked Heath.

"I'm coming to that," replied Venzia. "I happened to be on Pyrex III when they revolted. There was no way they were ever going to win—the Navy arrived three days later and decimated them—but it was pretty bloody while it lasted. Like most of the other off-worlders, I claimed asylum in one of the embassies and decided to wait it out." His facial muscles began twitching at the memory. "I was in the Sirius V embassy when a bomb hit it. I could feel the structure starting to go, but I thought I had time to help a rescue team move a couple of wounded people out through a window. We'd gotten the first one out, and were just moving the second when the building collapsed and I was buried under a couple of tons of rubble." He paused briefly as he recalled the incident. "I don't know how long I remained unconscious. I remember waking up and trying to dig my way out, and realizing that both of my arms were broken. I could barely breathe, and I began choking on my own blood. I could hear rescue workers calling my name as they dug through the ruins, but I was too weak to answer them. Finally there came a point when I knew I had breathed my last breath and would be dead in another second." He paused again, staring off into space as he must have stared into the darkness on that long-gone day. "And then I saw her."

"Her?" repeated Heath. "You mean the Dark Lady?"

Venzia nodded. "She was standing there, her arms reaching out, beckoning to me. I tried to get up, but I couldn't move."

"Then what happened?" asked Heath.

"I woke up in the hospital," said Venzia, his face still a mask of conflicting emotions. "They must have reached me a minute or two later. They tell me that I wasn't breathing, but that I still had a pulse, and that the paramedics got me going again. I don't remember any of it. All I remember is the Dark Lady, reaching out her hands to me, calling me to join her."

"An hallucination," said Heath.

"That's what I thought," agreed Venzia.

"What changed your mind?" I asked.

"I saw her a year later."

"Where?" asked Heath.

"On Declan IV—my home world. I was still recuperating, and I was getting tired of reading books and watching holovids, so when the circus stopped off for a week, I decided that I was fit enough and bored enough to buy a ticket." He closed his eyes briefly, recalling the experience. "They had an animal tamer there who was absolutely brilliant. This guy worked with Demoncats from Kilarstra, and *nobody's* ever been able to train one of them—and he also had a Blue Dragon in his act."

"A Blue Dragon?" repeated Heath. "I've never heard of it."

"It's a reptile the size of a small house from somewhere out on the Rim—and he actually climbed right into its mouth! I mean, the goddamned thing could have swallowed him whole! I never saw anything like it in my life." He paused for a moment, and opened his eyes again. "When the show was over, I waited around to tell him how much I enjoyed his act. Evidently I wasn't the only one, because the police had cordoned off a walkway for him from the tent to his vehicle, and when he finally came out, he had *her* on his arm."

"The Dark Lady?" asked Heath.

Venzia nodded. "I was flabbergasted. I mean, here was the flesh and blood embodiment of what I had thought was an hallucination. She was identical in every detail."

"Did you speak to her?" I asked.

"The police wouldn't let me get near them." He looked up suddenly. "I'll have another drink now, if you don't mind."

"Now?" demanded Heath, obviously annoyed that Venzia's story had come to a halt.

"Yes, please."

Heath grimaced, got up, walked to the bar, quickly

mixed the drink, and returned with it. The entire process took perhaps forty seconds.

"Okay, go on with it," said Heath. "When did you finally get to speak to her?"

"Never," said Venzia.

"That's it?" exclaimed Heath unbelievingly. "That's the whole story?"

"That's just the beginning," answered Venzia. "I didn't know who or what she was then."

"And now you do?"

"Yes," said Venzia. "I went back the next night in the hope of meeting her. It wasn't romantic or obsessive or anything like that. I just wanted to relate my experience to her." He shrugged helplessly. "I don't even know why."

"So you went back the next night . . ." prompted Heath.

Venzia nodded. "I went back the next night," he repeated, his face twitching again, "and the animal tamer climbed into the Blue Dragon's mouth, and the Blue Dragon closed it, just like he'd done the night before—but this time there was a terrible crunching sound, and when the Dragon opened its mouth again, it was empty." Venzia stopped speaking and drained his glass.

"It sounds horrible!" I said.

"It *was* horrible," he agreed. "I stayed after the show to offer my sympathies to the woman, but I couldn't find her. I asked around the next day, and no one had seen her since the end of the performance." He paused. "She never showed up again, and when the circus left Declan IV, it left without her. I still believed that people didn't just vanish into thin air, and since I knew she hadn't left Declan, I hired a detective agency to find her. They never did."

"*I* believe she vanished from my ship, but *you* shouldn't have," said Heath. "Not based on what you've told us so far. It would have made more sense to assume she simply left the planet before you hired the detective. Declan IV's a pretty busy world; there must be ships coming and going every few minutes."

"That's precisely what I assumed," answered Venzia. "I

thought it was an odd coincidence, and that her disappearance was a little strange, but that was all." He exhaled deeply. "Until I saw a painting of her go up for sale in an estate auction." He turned to me. "Malcolm Abercrombie bought it. It's the one by Justin Craig."

"That must have surprised you," I said.

"Why?" asked Heath sharply.

"Because Justin Craig died in the Battle of Genovaith IV almost thirteen hundred years ago," I replied.

"I found three biographies of him," continued Venzia. "Two made no mention of any woman in his life, but the third one mentioned a dark-haired woman who seemed to be his constant companion during the last two weeks of his life, and vanished mysteriously as soon as he was killed." He paused. "Just as she had done with the animal tamer," he added meaningfully.

"But *he* didn't paint her," noted Heath.

"Why should he?" asked Venzia. "He didn't know the first damned thing about painting."

"Excuse me, Friend Reuben," I said. "But are you telling us that not everyone who has seen her has painted her?"

"Of course they haven't," replied Venzia. "Hell, did everyone who saw her on Acheron run right out and buy a paintbrush and easel?"

"No," I answered, surprised that I had overlooked so obvious a fact. "No, they didn't."

"Anyway, I spent the next two years of my life researching her, tracing her appearances as best I could. She's a very beautiful woman, and many of the men she's known have tried to capture her on canvas or in holograms—but even more of them haven't."

"How did you know that she is called the Dark Lady?" I asked. "Only Sergio Mallachi's painting bears that title, and you have never seen it."

He smiled. "She has many names, some of which I gave to you back on Far London. It just so happens that 'the Dark Lady' is the one that has been used the most often."

"But where?" I persisted. "I know of no other portrait

entitled the Dark Lady."

"In 1827 A.D., Jonas McPherson had her likeness carved on the prow of his whaling vessel, which he named the *Dark Lady*. In 203 G.E., Hans Venable made mention of the Dark Lady in his log, which was jettisoned in a records pod just before his ship was sucked into a black hole that he was charting for the Department of Cartography. In 2822 G.E., she was photographed with a prizefighter named Jimmy McSwain, who told the photographer that she was known as the Dark Lady. Shall I continue?"

"Please do," said Heath, leaning forward.

"All right," said Venzia. "In 3701 G.E., she was holographed in the company of an assassin known only as the Rake when he walked into a police ambush. She survived the attack, but vanished before they could question her. The Rake, with his dying breath, asked to see the Dark Lady once more. Just one year later she was at the side of a bounty hunter named Peacemaker MacDougal; there are no remaining holograms of *him*, but two of *her* survived, and in both of them she is identified as the Dark Lady."

Venzia took a deep breath and then continued. "There is yet another reference to her in 4402 G.E., but while the descriptions match, there are no holograms, photographs, or paintings." He paused for effect. "In every case, she appeared within a month of her companion's death, and without exception she was gone less than a day after it."

"It sounds like the same woman," admitted Heath.

"There's no question about it. I found her under perhaps twenty other names as well, and her appearances always presaged a death."

"And yet *you* didn't die," I pointed out.

"No," replied Venzia. "I didn't die."

"I assume you have an explanation?" said Heath.

"I believe so," said Venzia. He paused, ordering his thoughts. "What I saw was not the Dark Lady herself. I mean, how could it possibly have been her in the flesh? I was buried under tons of rubble. Even if there was enough light for me to see—which there wasn't—how could she have actually appeared beneath all that debris?"

"So we're back to it having been an hallucination," said Heath.

Venzia shook his head vigorously. "No."

"Then what did you see?"

"Call it a vision."

"You call it what you want and I'll call it what I want," said Heath skeptically.

"It was a vision!" insisted Venzia. "And once I realized what it was, I visited a large hospital with a hologram of her that I had duplicated from the police files on the Rake. I received permission to visit the terminal ward, and showed it to every patient that I was allowed to see, asking each if they had ever seen her before."

"And?" said Heath.

"More than three hundred of them responded in the negative. One man thought he remembered her beckoning to him in a dream. He died a week later."

"How many of the other patients died?" I asked.

"Most of them," replied Venzia. "In fact, five of them died the next day." He paused. "I asked a nurse for the details concerning the man who thought he remembered the Dark Lady. He had taken his daughter for a walk, they had stopped to look at a construction site, she had unknowingly walked in front of a robotic bulldozer, and he had managed to shove her to safety, although he himself was terribly mangled in the process. He had actually been legally dead for about ninety seconds before they revived him, and although the hospital kept him alive for another week, they finally lost him."

"Had any of the other patients been pronounced dead and then revived?" I asked.

"Three of them," said Venzia. "Two drowning victims, and a woman who had been electrocuted." He paused. "And in answer to your next question, I have no idea if I was legally dead or not when they found me."

"Then why did he and he alone see her?" asked Heath in frustration. "And what do you and he have in common? You got caught in a cave-in and he was run over by a bulldozer. You were in a war and he was taking his daughter for a walk. You didn't die, and he did. What's the connection?"

As I listened to Heath and considered the problem, Venzia had been staring at me with a curious smile. "I believe Leonardo has figured it out," he said.

"I see the connection," I said. "That is not the same thing."

"That's more than *I* see," complained Heath.

"I see it," I repeated slowly, "but that cannot be the solution."

"Why?" prodded Venzia.

"Because the Dark Lady cannot be Death," I replied. "Otherwise at least three other patients would have seen her."

"I agree," said Venzia.

"Then what is she?" I asked him.

"Will somebody please tell me what's going on here?" demanded Heath.

"Friend Valentine," I said, turning to Heath, "the connection is not the nature of their disasters, but the manner in which the disasters were incurred."

Heath lowered his head in thought. "Venzia was trying to save an injured woman. The patient was trying to save his daughter." He looked up. "She only appears to heroes?" He considered what he had said, then shook his head vigorously. "That *can't* be the answer! Look at Mallachi—there's nothing heroic about getting shot in a bar over a woman."

"It was not that Friend Reuben and the little girl's father were heroic, Friend Valentine," I said. "It was, rather, that each of them courted disaster."

Heath frowned. "What's the difference?"

"In these two instances, nothing," I said. "But there *is* a difference."

"I don't suppose you'd care to explain it?" asked Heath.

"Take the animal tamer," I said. "He was not heroic, and yet he courted disaster every time he performed."

"So she appears to people who court disaster?"

"Let us be more precise," interjected Venzia. "She

appears to people who court death."

"Why does she live with some of them, and just appear for a microsecond to others?" asked Heath.

And suddenly I knew the answer to the riddle of the Dark Lady.

"Some, like Friend Reuben, court death only once, as a completely spontaneous act," I said. "Others, like Mallachi and the Kid and the animal tamer, spend their lives courting death."

"Now you've got it," said Venzia.

"That was the factor I could never determine," I replied. "My original supposition was that each artist had been involved in some military action, but I see now that that was much too narrow a criterion. The circus daredevil, Brian McGinnis in the jungles of Earth, the man who charted black holes—each of them courted death as assiduously as the soldiers and warriors."

"But she's not Death," said Heath, confused. "As you said, if she were, everyone who was about to die would have seen her."

"That's correct," agreed Venzia.

"Then what the hell is she?" asked Heath.

"She is the Dark Lady," answered Venzia.

"*What* is the Dark Lady?"

Venzia sighed heavily. "I don't know."

"This is becoming a very frustrating conversation," complained Heath.

"I don't *know* what she is," repeated Venzia. "All I know is that she has appeared to men for almost eight thousand years. And I mean that literally: She appears only to men, never to women. I know that she takes substance when a man leads a life that continually invites death, and that she never remains after the man is dead. I know that she has occasionally gone a century or more between appearances. I know that she appears as if in a vision to those men who court her just once."

"Court *her* or court *death*?" asked Heath sharply.

"I'm not sure there's a difference," replied Venzia.

"I thought you said she wasn't Death."

"I don't believe she is—but there's no question that she is somehow linked with death. I don't think she actually kills anyone, but she certainly encourages them to take the kinds of chances that result in their deaths."

"*Encourages* them?" repeated Heath dubiously. "Did she encourage *you*?"

"I misspoke myself," said Venzia. "Let's say, rather, that she seems irresistibly drawn to them."

"Does she appear to *everyone* who courts death?" asked Heath.

"I don't know," answered Venzia. "Most of them don't survive the experience."

"What about aliens? Does she appear to them?"

"I can find no record of any alien ever mentioning her or painting her portrait."

"Why didn't she vanish after the Kid was killed on Acheron?"

Venzia considered his answer for a moment. "She has never actually disappeared in front of anyone," he said at last. "Usually, she is simply reported missing." He paused. "Tai Chong told me what happened on Acheron. From her description of the planet, there's no way the Dark Lady could have disappeared from the jail, or even from the planet's surface, without alerting the populace to her abilities."

Heath shook his head. "It's a nice theory, but it doesn't hold water."

"Oh?" said Venzia. "Why not?"

"If she doesn't want anyone to know what she can do, why did she vanish from my ship?"

Venzia smiled. "Because she wasn't revealing any secrets. Leonardo knew who she was."

"Leonardo just figured out who she was five minutes ago!" retorted Heath.

"But I knew that she was called the Dark Lady, Friend Valentine," I said. "And I asked her about Brian McGinnis and Christopher Kilcullen."

"So you did," admitted Heath.

The three of us fell silent for a number of minutes.

Finally Heath uttered a chuckle. "My God," he said. "I've just spent an hour talking about the Dark Lady as if she's really something other than a beautiful woman or a fascinating alien who has mastered the art of teleportation. I'm going to wake up tomorrow and none of this will have happened."

"It is happening right now," said Venzia. "And you know in your heart that she is not an alien."

"What do *you* think she is?" asked Heath.

"I don't know," answered Venzia.

"Leonardo?" asked Heath.

"I am tempted to say that she is the Mother of All Things," I confessed, "but that would be blasphemous."

"Who or what is the Mother of All Things?" asked Venzia.

"She whom we worship, as you worship your God," I replied. "But, while I do not wish to offend you, I cannot believe that the Mother of All Things is a member of an alien race."

"Perhaps she appears to Bjornns in a different form," suggested Heath.

"No Bjornn performs acts that would attract the Dark Lady," I said. "My race cherishes life."

"So does ours, for the most part," said Venzia. "But there she is, nonetheless."

"You revere courage," I pointed out. "We do not. In fact, there is no word for *hero* in the Bjornn language. The concept does not exist among my people."

"Even herd animals are capable of heroism," commented Heath. "Take the herd bull that faces a carnivore while the rest scamper to safety."

"The herd bull acts from blind, unreasoning instinct, not heroism, Friend Valentine," I replied. "Presented with a conscious choice, he would never willingly face a carnivore, and the Dark Lady seems to visit only those men who court her as a matter of choice."

"Just a minute!" said Heath suddenly. "Your people perform ritual suicide. Wouldn't *that* constitute the kind of behavior that would attract her?"

"There is nothing heroic about ending one's own life to avoid continued disgrace, Friend Valentine," I noted.

"We're getting off the subject," interjected Venzia. "She visits *men*. That's enough for us to know."

"All right," said Heath. "We know she visits men. Now what?"

"Now we find her," said Venzia with quiet intensity.

Heath chuckled. "It's a big galaxy, Mr. Venzia—and she might not even be in it."

"Then we figure out where she'll appear next, and we wait for her."

"For what purpose, Friend Reuben?" I asked.

"Poor Leonardo," said Venzia with genuine compassion. "You've put together all the pieces, and you still haven't solved the puzzle."

"I beg your pardon?" I said.

"We sit her down and talk to her," said Venzia.

"Let me get this straight," said Heath. "You've spent six years and God knows how much money trying to find her, and all you want to do is sit down and talk to her?"

"What would *you* do with her, Mr. Heath?" asked Venzia contemptuously.

"You know what I want to do with her," replied Heath. "I'll pay you more for her than Abercrombie will."

"I doubt it," said Heath. "Do you know how much Malcolm Abercrombie is worth?"

"All I want is five minutes of her time," said Venzia. "After that you can sell her to Abercrombie or do anything else you want with her."

"*If* she will let you," I put in.

"One million credits, Mr. Heath," said Venzia, never taking his eyes off the other man.

"A million credits for just five minutes?" replied Heath. "That's right."

"A lot of men have spent considerably more than five minutes with her," said Heath, "and I'll wager that she never told them what you want to know."

"They didn't know who she was," replied Venzia. "*I* do. They probably never asked her the right question." He paused. "*That* is my advantage."

"Assuming that she answers you at all, how will you know if she's telling you the truth?" persisted Heath.

"I'll know," said Venzia confidently.

"Excuse me," I said, "but I truly do not know what you are talking about."

Heath looked amused. "He's got something very important to ask her, Leonardo."

"What is it?"

"What lies beyond?" answered Venzia intently. "She is the only person who knows."

"It may be sacrilegious to know," I cautioned.

"It would be foolhardy not to, if one has the opportunity," replied Venzia. "Is there a true religion? At whose altar should I worship? What traits and habits must I forsake? What must I do to assure my arrival in Paradise? Or if there is nothing beyond this life, then at least I will be free to do whatever I choose."

"You're free now," pointed out Heath.

"Only because I am ignorant of the consequences of my actions," said Venzia. "This way I'll *know*."

Heath smiled. "A heavenly insurance policy."

"If you wish."

"You expect a lot for your money, Mr. Venzia," said Heath.

"I intend to get it," said Venzia earnestly.

15.

Venzia spent the night at the chalet, and in the morning it was decided that the three of us would leave Graustark for Far London.

I not only had my work to do, but now that he had lost the Dark Lady again, Venzia was convinced that sooner or later a new painting of her would come up for sale. In the meantime, he would return with us to Far London where he could keep in frequent contact with me, while he monitored likely heroes and daredevils on the video and programmed his computer to sift through the immense number of printed and electronic media available to it.

As for Heath, I don't think he was fully convinced that the Dark Lady was what Venzia and I claimed her to be, but he had no objection whatsoever to accompanying us to Far London, since that was where he would find Malcolm Abercrombie.

Venzia left the chalet an hour ahead of us, since he had to retrieve his snowcart and return it to the rental agency, and we arranged to meet at Heath's ship, since Venzia had come to Graustark on a spaceliner and had no ship of his own.

"It's going to be a little cramped," observed Venzia, when he had finished carrying his luggage through the entry hatch.

"It wasn't designed to carry three people," replied Heath.

"I can see that," said Venzia. He turned to me. "Here," he said, handing me a square box that was perhaps twelve inches on each side and eight inches deep.

"What is it?" I asked.

He shrugged. "I haven't the slightest idea. Tai Chong told me to deliver it to you."

"A present from Tai Chong?" I mused happily, accepting the box.

"I got the impression that it arrived from Bjornn, and that she was holding it for you," answered Venzia.

"From Benitarus II," I corrected him gently. "Bjornn is the race; Benitarus is the planet."

"Whatever you say," said Venzia, losing interest. He turned to Heath. "I'm hungry. How do I get something to eat?"

Heath nodded. "Just go into the galley and tell it what you want. It's voice-keyed."

"Where do I find its menu?"

"It can make anything you ask for, as long as you don't mind soya products."

"Thanks." Venzia headed off to the galley, and Heath turned to me.

"Well?" he said.

"Well what, Friend Valentine?"

"What's in the package?"

"I do not know."

"Aren't you going to open it?"

"I thought I would do so in the privacy of my compartment," I replied.

"You don't have any privacy in your compartment," responded Heath with a smile. "You're sharing it with Venzia."

"Then I shall open it here and now," I said.

"Excellent idea," said Heath.

I set the package on a flat surface and stared at it without moving.

"What's the problem?" asked Heath.

"I am afraid," I replied.

"You think perhaps someone sent you a bomb?" Heath smiled. "Don't worry, Leonardo; my ship's sensors would have identified anything dangerous."

"It is not a bomb," I said.

"Then what is it?"

I sighed. "I know what it *should* be. I do not know what it is."

"You're not making very much sense, Leonardo," said Heath. He paused. "Would you like me to open it for you?"

"No," I said. "I will open it myself."

"What's all the fuss about?" asked Venzia, carrying his plate in from the galley.

Heath shrugged. "Ask *him*," he said, jerking his head toward me.

"I did not mean to disturb either of you," I apologized.

"Fine," said Venzia. "Then open the damned thing and let's get the hell off the planet."

I turned to Heath. "Perhaps you would prefer to take off first," I said. "The package can wait."

"But *I* can't," he replied. "You've made such a mystery of it that I'm not moving until you open it."

I sighed, and began unwrapping the box. I had to borrow a cutting instrument from the galley to complete the task, but finally the lid was ready for removal.

"Go ahead," urged Heath.

"In a moment," I said.

I paused, took a deep breath, and finally opened the box—and a cry of relief escaped my lips.

"Are you all right?" asked Heath.

"Yes, Friend Valentine," I said happily. "*Now* I am all right."

He peered into the box.

"What's going on here?" he asked. "It's nothing but dirt."

"It is from my Pattern Mother," I answered.

"Why would she send you dirt?" persisted Heath.

"It is soil from the sacred land of the House of Crsthionn," I said.

Venzia seemed to lose interest, and took his meal into the compartment that he was sharing with me.

"I assume that's a good thing to receive," remarked Heath.

"Yes," I said. "I was afraid that the package might contain something else."

"Like what?"

"*Anything* else." I paused. "Each Bjornn celebrates two holy days, Friend Valentine: the day that his House was created, and the day that his own Pattern was accepted by his House. The first occurred while we were in transit from Acheron; the second will happen, in my case, some thirty-two days from now. Now do you understand?"

"Not really," answered Heath. "When *we* have holidays, we exchange presents, not dirt."

"It is *not* dirt," I explained. "It is consecrated ground, from the birthplace of the First Mother of the House of Crsthionn, she whose offspring first bred true to her Pattern."

"Like holy water for a Catholic," commented Heath.

"Holy water is merely symbolic," I replied. "This is the actual soil."

"What do you plan to do with it?" asked Heath.

"First I must borrow your cutting instrument again."

"What for?"

"I must create a flow of my blood, that I may join my flesh with the sacred soil as a sign of my fealty to the House of Crsthionn."

"Are you sure you're not talking about suicide?" he asked suspiciously.

"No, Friend Valentine," I replied. "This is a religious ritual."

"I thought killing yourself was a religious ritual," said Heath.

"This is a more important one."

"All right," he said. "Then what?"

"Then I must cover my body with the soil."

"I suppose there's a reason," he said dryly.

"It further symbolizes my union with the First Mother," I answered. "I must also chant three prayers: one to her, one to the House, and one to the Mother of All Things."

"And that's all there is to it?"

"Then I will remove the soil, after which we must atomize it."

"It seems rather counterproductive to get rid of it, if it's so holy," offered Heath.

"But I will have polluted it by my touch," I explained. "Therefore, it will no longer be sacred, but profane, and by obliterating it, I will have purified myself for another year."

"What did your people do before they had atomizers?" asked Heath.

"That was also before we developed space travel, and we returned the soil to the place from which it came. Even today, those of us who remain on Benitarus II usually choose to perform the ritual at the site of the First Mother's birthplace."

"Do the women of your race also perform this ritual?" Heath asked curiously.

"No," I said. "Why would anyone who is already pure and sacred require such a ritual?"

"They've got you coming and going, don't they?"

"I do not understand."

"Never mind." He paused. "Why were you so worried, Leonardo? What would have happened if the box contained, say, a pair of gloves, or some candy?"

"It would have meant that I was forever denied the sacraments of my race," I said.

"I thought your Pattern Mother already cast you out."

"I have been cast out physically. Had she not sent the sacred soil, I would have been cast out spiritually as well. My soul would have been doomed to wander lost and alone for all eternity."

"Well, at least now I understand your yelp of joy," said Heath. "Has this particular ceremony got a name?"

"The Celebration of the First Mother," I replied.

"And you'll get another box of dirt for your birthday?" he asked.

"It is not my birthday," I replied, "but my Acceptance Day. It is a joyous time."

"How does it differ from the Celebration of the First Mother?"

"When I am at home, there is an enormous feast."

"And that's it?" he asked, surprised.

"Vows of House and Family are repeated in an elaborate ceremony, and my fealty to the House is reaffirmed."

"How is she going to ship *that* in a box?" he asked with a laugh.

"When a Bjornn male is no longer on Benitarus II, the feast becomes the sole symbol of reaffirmation. My Pattern Mother will send me vegetation grown from her own fields, and my act of eating it will seal the bond between us."

"It must be a bit of a letdown compared to what you experienced before you left home," commented Heath.

"It is," I agreed. "But the individual's happiness is meaningless. The House is all."

"If you say so."

"And now may I borrow the cutting instrument, please?" I asked.

He nodded, walked to the galley, and returned with a knife a moment later.

I held my hand over the soil of the First Mother, and then paused before pricking my finger.

"Will the sight of blood distress you, Friend Valentine?" I asked.

"Only my own," he replied easily.

I cut through the flesh, and allowed my blood to trickle onto the sacred soil.

"Purple?" said Heath, frowning.

"Not all blood is red," I replied.

"Do you want a bandage or something?"

"The flow will stop shortly," I assured him, and indeed it did a moment later.

"I suppose you'll want to do the next part in the dryshower," suggested Heath.

"Yes, if you do not mind."

"As a matter of fact, I insist," he replied. "I hate messes."

I thanked him, waited for the ship to leave Graustark and set off on its voyage for Far London, and then completed the Celebration of the First Mother in the privacy of the dryshower.

I had hoped that during the trip Venzia would tell us still more about the Dark Lady, but it turned out that he had already told us everything he knew. This did not, however, keep him from speaking about her incessantly, for he was totally obsessed with meeting her and learning the answer to his question.

Heath remained skeptical. He would join in each discussion, make pertinent observations, and speak of the Dark Lady as if she were precisely what Venzia believed her to be—and yet, between the end of one conversation and the beginning of the next, he would somehow once again become convinced that she was actually an alien, or, at best, a normal woman with the supernormal power of telepathy.

As for myself, I was so relieved that my Pattern Mother had not condemned my soul to eternal exile that even my status as an outcast who could never again return to his home world became bearable. To keep my mind from dwelling on my predicament, I concentrated on our quest for the Dark Lady, trying to force all thoughts of House and Family from my mind.

When the others were asleep, I attempted to capture her likeness again, though once more my meager artistic abilities failed me. One day I even tried to draw her as a Bjornn, her pale skin Patternless, her trappings black, her features perfect, her eyes sad, the Deity Herself set to ink and paper . . . yet when I was done she did not look like the Mother of All Things, but only like a Bjornn female with Patternless skin and perfect features. Somehow I knew then that the Dark Lady, whatever her origin and whatever her quest, came only for Men and not for the Bjornn.

I wrote another letter to my Pattern Mother, thanking her for her gift and telling her what I had learned, but I knew that she would not reply. I also wrote my Pattern Mate, formally divorcing her (though the separation was automatic with my banishment), and wishing her good fortune with the next mate who would be chosen for her. As sorry as I felt for myself, it was nothing compared to the regret I felt for my Pattern Mate, whose life, through no doing of her own, was to be recast at this late date. It could be years before the House found and approved the perfect complementary Pattern, and she would continue to be barren until that day arrived. (Or, worse still, the House in its wisdom could decide that she had wasted enough of her youth and young adulthood, and might pair her with a Pattern that did not properly complement her own. If they did so, sooner or later she might well produce a child with a Pattern that was not acceptable to the House, and thus would be forced to suffer not one but two outcasts in her blameless life.)

It was with such somber thoughts as these on my mind that I sought once again to control my emotions and direct my thoughts back to the Dark Lady. Heath was asleep, but Venzia, who had been quietly reading a book from the computer's electronic library, noticed my agitation and the lightening of my hue.

"Are you all right, Leonardo?" he asked.

"Yes, Friend Reuben," I replied.

"Are you sure? You look distressed."

"I am better now."

"If you say so," he said with a shrug. He paused. "Do you mind if I ask you a question about your friend Mr. Heath?"

"No, Friend Reuben."

"Does he really intend to rob Abercrombie?"

"I am quite certain of it, Friend Reuben."

"Too bad."

"I agree," I said. "Robbery is contrary to moral and civil law."

Venzia smiled. "I meant that we could use him in our search for the Dark Lady, and if he tries to rob Abercrombie he's likely to end up in jail. I understand that Abercrombie's got a state-of-the-art security system in that mansion of his."

"I think Friend Valentine might surprise both you and Mr. Abercrombie," I said.

"Perhaps," said Venzia, dismissing the subject. "I wonder why he remains so skeptical?"

"Possibly because he did not see her under the same circumstances that you did," I suggested.

"Neither did you," he pointed out, "but you seem to have no problem accepting her as she is."

"That is true," I agreed.

"He has the same facts at his disposal that you do," said Venzia, puzzled. "Why can't he come to the same conclusion?"

"Perhaps it is because he has always relied upon his own powers, and has no need for a belief in someone greater than himself."

"And you do?"

"I was raised to believe in and rely upon people greater than myself," I answered.

"I wonder . . ." mused Venzia.

"About what, Friend Reuben?"

"Almost every man she's ever taken up with was totally self-reliant. I wonder what *they* believed in?"

"I suppose we shall have to ask the next one," I replied.

"If we can get to him in time," said Venzia with a grimace.

"You make her sound like a murderer," I said, "and yet we both know she is not."

"I don't care what she is. I'm only interested in what she knows."

I thought of her face again.

"I think that I am more interested in what she wants," I replied.

"What she wants?" he repeated. "Hell, what she wants is death."

"I do not think so, Friend Reuben."

"Why not?"

"If the death of heroic men were what she craved, surely she would be sated by now."

"Some people are never sated," said Venzia.

"I keep remembering her eyes, the sadness of her face, the sense of longing that she radiates," I replied. "I cannot help feeling that she is searching for something, and that she has not yet found it."

"Searching? For what?"

"I do not know," I answered truthfully.

We spoke for a few more minutes in a desultory fashion. Then Venzia went off to our compartment to sleep, and as I remained alone in the cabin, contemplating the Dark Lady, I found myself hoping that someday she would finally find what she sought, and that the ageless sorrow would at last vanish from her face.

16.

AFTER WE REACHED FAR
London, I reported to the Claiborne Galleries, where
Hector Rayburn informed me that Tai Chong had been
arrested the previous weekend while participating in a
nonviolent protest for alien rights on the nearby world of
Kennicott VI. She had refused to pay bail, and was due to
serve two more days before being released.

"I offered to arrange for Claiborne to pay her bail," he
concluded, "but she wouldn't have any part of it. So there
she sits, holding forth to anyone who will listen to her. I
gather she even held a press conference from her cell!" He
seemed vastly amused by her conduct.

"I am very sorry to hear this, Friend Hector," I said.
"She must find confinement in Kennicott's prison very
distressing."

"She's having the time of her life," he said with a laugh.
"Incidentally, don't I still owe you a lunch?"

"It is only ten o'clock in the morning," I pointed out.

"You never heard of an early lunch?"

"I appreciate your offer, Friend Hector, but I truly am
not hungry."

He shrugged. "Well, it's an open invitation. Just give me a day's notice."

"I shall do so," I promised.

"The restaurant I told you about last time has closed," he continued, "but I've heard of one that serves aliens. Maybe I'll check it out today and see if it's any good."

"That is very thoughtful of you, Friend Hector," I replied.

"By the way," he added confidentially, "what's Valentine Heath really like?"

"He is a very charming man," I said. "Why?"

"He's been unloading stolen paintings with us for years," answered Rayburn. "I was just curious about him."

"Why do you accept the paintings if you know they're stolen?"

"Hell, anything that's worth money has been stolen once or twice over the years. At least Heath's paintings are hard to trace."

"How long have you known that Heath trades in stolen artwork?"

"I guessed it when I learned that he never put them up for public auction."

"Does Tai Chong know about it?" I asked, hoping that he would respond in the negative.

"Officially, *nobody* knows about it," answered Rayburn with a knowing smile, "and they would certainly deny all knowledge of it to the authorities if they were questioned." He lowered his voice. "The only reason I'm even discussing it with you is because you're a colleague, and you happen to be on intimate terms with Valentine Heath."

"Knowing Valentine Heath does not make me a thief!" I protested.

"Of course it doesn't," said Rayburn soothingly. "But on the other hand, it doesn't make you as innocent as a newborn babe either, does it?"

"I have never stolen anything, Friend Hector!"

He smiled. "I'm not making any moral judgments, Leonardo."

"But you are," I insisted. "You are saying that I have been corrupted by my association with Valentine Heath."

"Well, the police *did* contact Tai Chong about you when you left Charlemagne," he said.

"It was a misunderstanding," I said. "I was not responsible for any wrongdoing."

"Okay," he said, still smiling. "I believe you."

"I think that you do not."

"Look, I seem to have upset you, and I certainly didn't mean to. We were talking about Heath."

"We were talking about whether Tai Chong knew that the paintings Heath sold her were stolen," I corrected him.

"Would you rather that she didn't know and didn't stand on picket lines to get you people your rights?"

"I was unaware that she had campaigned for Bjornn rights," I said, grateful for the change in subject.

"Bjornn, Canphorite, Rabolian—what's the difference? You guys are all fighting for equality, aren't you?"

"The Bjornn do not fight," I replied.

"You know what I mean," he said awkwardly.

"Yes, Friend Hector," I replied. "I know what you mean."

"Well," he said, walking to the door, "I'm off. See you this afternoon."

"You must be anticipating a very large lunch," I commented.

He grinned. "And a little something to wash it down with." He paused. "You're sure you don't want to come along? Five-hour lunch breaks aren't going to be so popular once Tai Chong gets back."

"No, thank you, Friend Hector."

He shrugged, waved to me, and walked out onto the street.

Since I had been given no explicit assignment, and my two immediate superiors were unavailable, I spent the rest of the morning methodically going through the previous two weeks' auction catalogs, hunting without success for any representations of the Dark Lady. In the afternoon I searched the listings of private offerings, with the same result.

I was just about to leave the gallery for the night when Malcolm Abercrombie called me on the vidphone.

"I heard you were back," he said when the connection was completed and he could see my face.

"I arrived this morning," I responded.

"Did you bring the Mallachi painting with you?"

"Yes."

"Then why the hell haven't you brought it out?" he demanded.

"I was under the impression that you and Tai Chong had not yet negotiated a price for it," I said.

"So what? She'll try to rob me, I'll counteroffer, and we'll haggle for a few hours, but we all know I'm going to buy it in the end."

"I shall have to ask Tai Chong for guidance in this matter," I said.

"Your boss is cooling her heels in a Kennicott jail, in case you hadn't heard."

"I am aware of that."

"Then you must also be aware of the fact that she isn't due out for a couple of more days," continued Abercrombie. He glared at me. "I'm not prepared to wait that long. I want it *now*!"

"I do not have the authority to give it to you," I said apologetically. "In the absence of Tai Chong, that decision must be made by Hector Rayburn."

"Where is he?"

"I do not know."

"Will he be at the gallery tomorrow?"

"Yes, he will."

"Get his permission the second he walks in the door," said Abercrombie, "and then come directly over to my place with the painting. Is that clear?"

"Yes, Mr. Abercrombie," I said. "It is perfectly clear."

"Tomorrow morning," he said ominously, and broke the connection.

I went back to my room for the night, and, after getting Rayburn's consent, delivered the painting to Abercrombie the next morning as he had ordered.

The next two days passed uneventfully as I continued searching unsuccessfully for representations of the Dark Lady.

On the morning that Tai Chong was due to return, Heath stopped in at the gallery and sought me out.

"Hello, Friend Valentine," I said, looking up from my desk computer. "I trust you have been well."

He nodded. "And you?"

"Quite well," I said, wondering why he had come to the gallery.

"Have you been in touch with Venzia since you landed?"

"I speak with him every night, Friend Valentine."

"Interesting man," said Heath.

"Yes, he is," I agreed. "Is there something I can do for you, Friend Valentine?"

"As a matter of fact, there is," he replied. "I heard from my attorneys again last night. Most of the charges have been dropped, but my funds are still frozen." He paused. "*All* my funds, not just those on Charlemagne." He shook his head in wonderment. "They even found that account I had on Spica II."

"I regret that I cannot lend you any money, Friend Valentine," I said. "But all of my salary is sent to the House of Crsthionn. Even my room and meals are billed to Claiborne, which deducts them before forwarding payment to my Pattern Mother."

"I don't want a loan," said Heath irritably. "I need *money*, not favors."

"I do not understand," I said, though of course I did.

"Do I have to spell it out for you?" he said. "I want you to help me beat Abercrombie's security system."

"I cannot help you, Friend Valentine," I said. "Perhaps Reuben Venzia can find work for you."

"Heaths don't *work*," he said disdainfully. "They *spend*."

"I am very sorry for you, Friend Valentine," I replied, "but I cannot be a party to robbery."

"I thought we were friends."

"Friends do not encourage friends to break the law," I pointed out. "I will not allow my ethical code to be eroded by my association with you. The fact that I like you does not imply that I am willing to help you commit a crime against a man whom I dislike."

"Spare me your lectures," said Heath with an expression of distaste.

"Then allow me to make a practical observation, Friend Valentine," I said. "Even if you were to rob Malcolm Abercrombie, you would still not have any money. You would have only his paintings."

"Which I would then convert into money."

"How? They are insured."

"Tai Chong has handled delicate problems like this for me in the past."

"Not with paintings that were stolen from her own clients," I replied.

"You'd be surprised."

"Possibly I would be," I said unhappily. "But I will not help you."

He sighed. "All right, Leonardo. I'll just have to do it alone."

"You will be apprehended and incarcerated."

"Not necessarily. I've cracked tougher systems before."

"If you thought you could steal the paintings without my help, you wouldn't have asked me for it," I said.

"Your help would have made it much easier," he said. "That doesn't mean it's impossible." He paused. "The house itself shouldn't present too much of a problem; I've probably seen every safeguard he's got. But crossing the grounds will be difficult, since I'll be out in the open. It'll take me a few days to figure out a safe approach, and I'll have to plot an escape route, but it can be done." He looked at me sharply. "But one question remains."

"What is that, Friend Valentine?"

"If I pull it off, will you report me to the police?"

"I would prefer that you did not make the attempt."

"I know what you prefer, Leonardo. Please answer my question."

"I truly do not know," I said.

Suddenly he smiled. "Cheer up," he said. "If his security system's as good as you think, you may not have to make the decision." He patted my shoulder. "I'll be in touch."

He turned and walked out before I could think of a reply, leaving me to contemplate the question he had asked. I was still lost in thought when Tai Chong entered.

"Welcome back, Leonardo," she said.

"And to you, Great Lady," I replied, getting to my feet. "I trust you are well?"

"As well as can be expected," she answered. "The cuisine and decor at the Kennicott jail leave a little something to be desired." She paused. "Did I make the news on Far London?"

"Hector Rayburn tells me that you did," I said. "I returned only three days ago."

She smiled triumphantly. "I *knew* I would! Did they run my hologram?"

"I do not know."

She shrugged. "No matter. At least we focused the public's attention on the plight of Kennicott's aliens."

"Have any reforms been made, Great Lady?" I inquired.

She seemed surprised by the question. "I really don't know, Leonardo," she said. "But I'm sure it's just a matter of time." She smiled again. "But enough about me. Did Reuben Venzia find you?"

"Yes, he did."

"And he gave you the package from your Pattern Mother?"

"Yes."

"Good. I wouldn't have told him where you were, but I thought the package might be important."

"It was, Great Lady. I thank you for your concern." I
paused. "I should like to explain what actually happened
on Charlemagne."

"It's not necessary. Your message was quite complete,
and the problem has been dealt with to everyone's satisfaction."

"Not to Valentine Heath's, I am afraid."

"Is he on Far London?"

"Yes, Great Lady. His assets are still frozen."

"That's too bad," she said.

"I fear that he is contemplating an illegal act to replen-
ish his funds."

"Oh?" she said, arching an eyebrow. "Do you know
what particular illegal act he has in mind?"

"Robbery," I said.

"Money?"

"Artwork, Great Lady."

She frowned. "On Far London?"

"Yes, Great Lady."

"Stupid," she muttered.

"I agree," I said. "Can you convince him not to do it?"

"Perhaps," she said. "Do you know where he is?"

"No, Great Lady—but I saw him this morning, and he
promised to contact me again in the near future."

"When he does, tell him that I want to talk to him."

"You will dissuade him?"

"I'll do my best," she said reassuringly.

"Thank you, Great Lady," I said. "I have become very
fond of him. I would not like to see him incarcerated."

"Neither would I," she said earnestly. She looked directly at me. "Has he actually seen Abercrombie's collection yet?"

"How did you know he planned to rob Malcolm
Abercrombie?" I asked, startled.

She smiled. "I know Valentine's tastes."

"In artwork?"

"In everything *but* artwork—and Mr. Abercrombie's
collection is the only one on the planet valuable enough
for him to indulge those tastes." She walked to her office

door, then turned to me. "You *will* tell him to get in touch with me first?"

"First?" I repeated, puzzled.

"Before he does anything he might regret."

"Yes, Great Lady," I promised her.

"Good. I hate to be rude, but I've got a lot of work to catch up on . . ."

"I understand," I said. "I am glad that you are back, Great Lady."

"Thank you very much, Leonardo," she said, and entered her office.

I spent the remainder of the day in another fruitless search for paintings or holograms of the Dark Lady. On my way home I stopped at my usual restaurant and found Venzia waiting for me.

"Any luck yet?" were his opening words.

"No," I responded. "And you, Friend Reuben?"

He shook his head. "I must have gone through two thousand newstapes," he said. "Not a sign of her. Tomorrow I start on the magazines." He grimaced. "I hate to think of how many of *them* I've got to wade through."

"I have examined every brochure and catalog that we have received within the past two weeks," I said. "None of them list any portraits of her for sale."

"Why only two weeks?" he asked.

"Because she was on Acheron less than three weeks ago," I replied, "and while there is always a possibility that an older portrait of her might be offered for sale, your findings have convinced me that the artist will almost certainly be dead. We must find the man she met *after* vanishing from Friend Valentine's ship."

"*If* she's reappeared yet," said Venzia glumly. "There have been periods where she's simply vanished for years, even centuries."

"Possibly," I said. "But is it not also possible that she did not vanish, but rather that you have been unable as yet to determine her whereabouts during those periods?"

"It's possible," he admitted wearily. He yawned. "God, I'm tired! I think I'm going to take the rest of the night off." He sighed deeply. "I've been spending twenty hours a day on those goddamned newstapes. If she's appeared again, I sure as hell don't know where."

"Rest well, Friend Reuben," I said.

"Thanks," he replied. "Maybe we *both* ought to knock off for the night. You can't be feeling too fresh yourself."

"I think I shall go to the library," I said. "I still have work to do."

"For Claiborne?" he asked.

"No—for us. You have suggested a most interesting line of inquiry."

"*I* have?" he said, surprised.

"Yes," I replied. "I shall eat dinner here, and then I will pursue it."

"You'll let me know if you come up with anything promising?" he said.

"Certainly, Friend Reuben," I said.

We parted, I ate a light meal, and then I walked to the library, trying to order my thoughts before speaking to the computer.

17.

I SAT AT MY CUBICLE IN THE library, watching the computer come to life.

"Good evening," it said at last. "How may I help you?"

"I am Leonardo of Benitarus II, and we have spoken before."

"I regret to inform you that I have found no other portraits of the subject you seek."

"I know," I said. "I seek other information this evening."

An enormous list began scrolling on the screen. "I have been instructed by Reuben Venzia to inform you at such time as you came here that he has viewed these tapes and magazines without success."

"I am not interested in viewing tapes or other electronic media," I said.

The screen went blank.

"I await your command."

"Who is the greatest human hero currently living?"

"I am incapable of making the subjective judgment required to answer your question."

"Then can you tell me which living member of the

human military has received the most decorations for valor?"

"Admiral Evangeline Waugh."

"A woman?" I asked, disappointed.

"Yes."

"Which living man is the most decorated?"

"Sugi Yamisata."

"What is his rank?"

"He has none."

"Is he retired?" I asked.

"He is currently in military prison for killing a fellow soldier while under the influence of illegal stimulants."

"Has he been in prison for more than three weeks?"

"He is currently serving the fifth year of a thirteen-year sentence," answered the computer.

I quickly decided that Yamisata could not be the man the Dark Lady would visit next. He had not courted her for at least five years, and was in no position to attract her attention for another eight.

"How long will it take you to produce a list of all human males whose jobs require them to enter life-threatening situations?" I asked.

"That cannot be done," replied the computer.

"Why not?"

"There are currently more than twenty billion men serving in jobs that require them to enter life-threatening situations. By the time I finished listing them, the list would be invalid."

"Twenty *billion*?" I repeated, surprised. "How many are in the military?"

"Thirteen billion."

"What are some of the other professions?"

"Law enforcement, four billion; fire departments, one billion; toxic waste disposal—"

"Stop," I said.

The computer was instantly silent.

"How may I determine the identity of the one living human male who has courted death more assiduously than any of the others?" I asked.

"The courting of death is an inexact term, and hence calls for a subjective judgment that I am not qualified to make."

"Then I will need your input on how best to structure my questions," I said. "The subject of the portraits you have been searching for is a woman known as the Dark Lady. Over the millennia she has appeared in the company of numerous men, and invariably she has been attracted to men who relish life-threatening situations. The last two men she visited were a bounty hunter and an outlaw. Is there any way to predict where she will appear next?"

"There are several internal contradictions in your statement," said the computer.

"Please elaborate," I replied.

"*Lady* is a term applied to human women. The longest-lived human woman on record died at age 156. You claim that the Dark Lady has been alive for many millennia. Either she is not a human being and hence not a lady, or else you are in error concerning her age."

"I do not believe that she is a normal human being," I said.

"No sentient, carbon-based, oxygen-breathing life form has a life span of several millennia."

"You must accept as a given that she exists, and that she is not an alien life form."

"This is contrary to my programming."

"Then consider her to be hypothetical," I said. "*If* this hypothetical woman exists, is there any way to predict where she will next appear?"

"Even granting her existence for the purpose of this exercise, you still possess internal contradictions in your initial premise," answered the computer. "There is no factual data proving that either bounty hunters or criminals relish life-threatening situations."

"I see."

"And since those terms imply entire classes, unlike the Dark Lady, which implies a specific individual, I cannot allow you to hypothesize that all bounty hunters and criminals relish life-threatening situations, for I possess data to the contrary."

"I understand," I said. "If you will grant the Dark Lady's existence for the purpose of this hypothesis, can you recommend the most efficient means of predicting her next appearance?"

"I possess insufficient data about the Dark Lady," answered the computer.

"May I give you more?"

"Yes."

"The Dark Lady seems to be attracted to men—human males—who knowingly and voluntarily place themselves in life-threatening situations." I paused for a moment, half-expecting the computer to interrupt with a reason why that statement was invalid, but it remained silent. "As a limiting factor, I believe that this would eliminate those military personnel and law enforcement officials, both paid and voluntary, who are thrust into battle on direct orders, as opposed to those who exceed the scope of their orders by performing acts of individual heroism."

"Contradiction," announced the computer. "Acts of individual heroism are frequently committed in compliance with direct orders, such as a soldier who is told to hold a position in the face of overwhelming enemy strength without being told how."

"Thank you," I said. "Please ignore my qualification."

"Registered."

"It is possible that she may be attracted to a military man," I continued, trying to order my thoughts more carefully, "but since war is a series of brief engagements punctuated by nonengagements of indeterminate length, I believe that it is impossible to predict her appearance in a pitched battle, simply because the time and location of the battle is itself impossible to predict. I also believe that the same principle holds true in regard to law enforcement officials and any others who are charged with maintaining public safety."

"Agreed."

"Therefore, while she may indeed appear next in the

company of a military man or a police officer or a bounty hunter, if we are to have any chance of predicting where she will eventually appear, we must look elsewhere."

I waited for the computer to tell me why I was mistaken, but it remained silent.

"I therefore suggest that we search for a man who possesses a job that is neither military nor involved with public safety, but which nevertheless requires him to put himself in life-threatening situations on a regular basis."

"Contradiction. This eliminates from consideration all men who put themselves into life-threatening situations for some reason other than employment."

"That is a very interesting concept," I said. "In fact, a man who invites death with no hope of financial gain might very well be more attractive to the Dark Lady than, say, a circus daredevil. Do you agree?"

"I have no opinion, since the Dark Lady is *your* hypothetical creation."

"Then, for the purpose of this exercise, please consider as a given the fact that she would find such a man more attractive." I paused. "Let us next consider what categories this group would include: mountain climbers, amateur athletes who practice martial arts . . ." I sighed dejectedly as dozens of similar interests and hobbies occurred to me. "The list is endless."

"The two examples you named are both avocations," noted the computer. "You must, by your definition, also include mentally and emotionally unstable men who possess a death wish."

"No," I replied. "Such men do not voluntarily place themselves in life-threatening situations. They are psychologically compelled to do so."

"Are not all men who willingly place themselves in life-threatening situations psychologically compelled to do so?" asked the computer.

"It is possible," I admitted. "Nevertheless, we must draw the line somewhere. I wish to consider only those men who are clinically sane."

"Registered," said the computer. "Have you some reason for choosing this criterion?"

"I do not believe that the Dark Lady, who is sane, would be attracted to a madman."

The computer did not contradict me, and I realized with a sense of growing excitement that I had taken yet another step, however small, toward identifying the man I sought.

"So we have narrowed down our list to those sane men who voluntarily risk their lives without thought of remuneration," I said. "Now, among these men, who must number in the hundreds of millions, there must be risks of greater and lesser magnitude. After all, a father who enters the room of a child that possesses a contagious disease is voluntarily risking his life with no thought of financial reward, yet the act itself is of a lesser magnitude than the man who hunts dangerous game with primitive weapons for the love of sport and excitement. Are you capable of making such distinctions?"

"Not without more data than can be provided by any source to which I have access."

"Including the Central Census Bureau on Deluros VIII?" I asked.

"That is correct."

"All right," I said. "Do you recall that I once asked you what the various artists who had painted the subject known as the Dark Lady had in common?"

"They possessed no common link," said the computer.

"But there *is* a common personality profile, is there not?"

"Yes," responded the computer. "It is a very broad profile, but it exists."

"Then we shall eliminate all those men who do not fall into the parameters of that profile."

"Registered."

"Next, eliminate all drug addicts, who almost certainly risk their lives every time they indulge in their addictions, but are frequently incapable of comprehending the risk they are taking, or at least do not consider it to be a life-threatening risk."

"Registered."

There were probably still tens of millions of possibilities
. . . but I had begun with billions. It was yet another step.

"Furthermore," I stated, "the Dark Lady has never, to
my knowledge, appeared to a child, so we will declare an
arbitrary minimum age of sixteen years."

"Registered."

"And the man must still be active."

"I am unclear on this point," said the computer. "Must
he be physically active, or active in a death-inviting
manner?"

"What is the difference?"

"A man in a wheelchair can still risk his life, just as a
healthy, vigorous man can decide to stop risking his life."

"He must still enter life-threatening situations with
regularity," I replied.

"Registered."

"He need not be handsome or physically attractive," I
added, for many of the men who had known her were
unattractive by any known standards."

"Registered."

"She does not take physical form for those who risk
their lives only once or twice, so let us further assume that
the man we seek has been placing himself in life-
threatening situations for a considerable period of time."

"'A considerable period of time' is too inexact," said
the computer.

I tried to imagine how long the Kid, who was one of the
youngest of her known consorts, had been an outlaw.

"Let us say a minimum of five years," I said, hoping that
I hadn't overestimated the length of his lawless career.

"Registered."

I tried to think of further limiting criteria, but my mind
was a blank.

"Based on the data I have given you," I said at last,
"how many men still possess the requisite qualifications?"

"I must access the Census Bureau on Deluros VIII to
answer your question."

"Please do so."

"Whenever I access an off-world computer for data, there is a cost involved. To whose account should it be billed?"

It was a difficult question. Obviously I could not pass the cost along to Claiborne or Malcolm Abercrombie, since this had nothing to do with them. On the other hand, I myself could not pay for it, since all my salary was deposited in a House of Crsthionn account.

"Please charge the cost to Reuben Venzia," I said after some consideration.

"I have no authorization to make such a billing. Please stand by while I access his personal computer." There was a moment's silence. "Reuben Venzia has agreed to accept all charges. I am now accessing Deluros VIII. I estimate that it will take thirty to forty minutes for me to complete my survey. I can continue speaking to you during the interim, or if you wish to use any of the library's other facilities, I can summon you when I am ready."

"I think I will leave for a few minutes," I said.

The computer went dark, and I left the cubicle, expecting to feel the usual flood of warmth and security that I experienced whenever I entered a crowd of sentient beings. As I walked to the center of the room, surrounded by some twenty non-humans, I did indeed feel an immediate sense of well-being, but it did not begin to compare to the surge of emotion I had felt each time I further narrowed down the Dark Lady's field of potential suitors. Ordinarily this would have troubled me deeply, but I was so intent on deducing the identity of the man who would be the next to entice her across the barrier between spirit and flesh that I scarcely noticed it at all.

I remained in the company of my fellow beings for half an hour, feeling more and more anxious with each passing minute. Finally I returned to the cubicle and simply stared at the blank screen until the computer came to life again a few moments later.

"Summoning Leonardo of Benitarus II," it said over the library's public address system.

"I am right here," I replied. "Do you have the information I seek?"

"Based on the records of the Central Census Bureau on Deluros VIII, which may be incomplete, 7,213,482 men fulfill your criteria."

"Are you still tied in to Deluros?" I asked.

"No, but I have temporarily retained all the pertinent data in my memory banks," answered the computer. "I will erase it when you have completed your inquiry."

"Based on the data you have accumulated, can you see any obvious means of narrowing the list even further?"

"Yes," replied the computer. "If the Dark Lady is to visit the man you seek, I suggest the elimination of all married men."

"But Christopher Kilcullen was married," I pointed out.

"He was divorced from his fourth wife at the time he painted the portrait of the Dark Lady."

"I had forgotten that," I admitted. "How many of the men are married?"

"4,302,198 are married."

"Eliminate them," I ordered.

"Done."

"How many remain on the list?"

"2,911,284 men remain," responded the computer.

"We can't check out almost three million men," I murmured. "We must reduce the number still further."

"Waiting . . ."

"Let us assume that if someone has been courting the Dark Lady assiduously for more than twenty years, she would have already appeared to him," I suggested.

"Nothing in the data you have given me would imply that this is true."

"I know, but I must try to narrow the list. How many men will this criterion eliminate?"

"1,033,102 men will be eliminated."

"And how many remain?"

"1,878,182 men remain."

"Eliminate those men who have voluntarily entered life-threatening situations on less than twenty occasions."

"682,646 men will be eliminated."

"Now eliminate those men who have voluntarily entered life-threatening situations on less than fifty occasions."

"1,121,400 men will be eliminated."

"How many remain?"

"74,136 men remain."

"Now eliminate those men who have voluntarily entered life-threatening situations on less than one hundred occasions," I said, trying without success to think of yet another limiting factor.

"72,877 men will be eliminated."

"How many remain?"

"1,259 men remain."

"Now eliminate those men who have voluntarily entered life-threatening situations on less than two hundred occasions."

"1,252 men will be eliminated."

"So we're down to seven men."

"*If* you are using a valid criterion," cautioned the computer.

"If I am, we might as well follow it through to the end. How many of these men have voluntarily entered life-threatening situations on less than 250 occasions?"

"All seven men will be eliminated."

"Then I shall need another criterion," I said.

"The next logical step is to determine which man has risked his life more frequently than the other six."

"Perhaps," I said. "But there is very little difference between them. Each seems to live in continual mortal danger." I paused. "Still, for the record, I suppose you should give me the name of the man who heads the list."

"Gottfried Schenke of Tumiga III."

"In what manner does he continually face death?" I asked.

"He collects the mollusks that live in the largest ocean of Tumiga III."

"Why is that dangerous?"

"The waters are inhabited by numerous carnivorous fish and animals. Schenke has been hospitalized four times in the last nine years as a result of their attacks."

"But hundreds of millions of people swim in carnivore-infested waters all across the galaxy," I protested. "Surely tens of millions of them have entered the water more than 250 times!"

"That is true."

"Then why is only Schenke on the list?"

"Because your criterion specified that each man must knowingly and voluntarily enter a life-threatening situation. All but the smallest handful of swimmers do not know or believe that they are entering such a situation, and would not enter it if they were aware of the dangers or felt personally threatened by them."

"I see," I replied. Suddenly another criterion occurred to me. "Now eliminate from that list of seven men those who are homosexuals."

"Three men are eliminated. Four men remain, including Gottfried Schenke."

"Who are the other three?"

"Wilfred Kramer of Hallmark, a big-game hunter in the jungles of Hallmark, Alsatia IV, and Karobus XIII." The computer paused. "Eric Nkwana of New Zimbabwe, who holds seventeen mount-diving records."

"What is mount-diving?" I asked.

"A sport in which the participant dives from a mountaintop into a rushing river."

I shuddered at the thought of it.

"Who is the other?" I asked.

"Vladimir Kobrynski of Saltmarsh. He has been a prizefighter, a skydiver, a test animal, a—"

"A test animal?" I interrupted. "Please explain."

"He volunteered to receive injections of virulent diseases for which cures were being sought."

"Is that not contrary to our nonbenevolence criterion?"

"I do not believe so," responded the computer. "At the time he was serving a prison sentence for the crime of manslaughter, resulting from the altercation on Altair III. He volunteered for the injections in exchange for a reduction of his sentence. Shall I continue?"

"Please do."

"He has also been a hunter and an explorer, and he is currently an artist."

"What is life-threatening about being an artist?" I asked, mystified.

"He has created a new art form called plasma painting, a highly dangerous procedure whereby hard radiation is illuminated and manipulated into a glowing work of cosmic art which dissipates in less than a minute."

"He certainly seems to have courted her vigorously," I mused.

"He has actually entered life-threatening situations on seventeen fewer occasions than Gottfried Schenke," said the computer.

"But Schenke may simply be a devoted collector," I said. "This man seems to have structured his entire life in pursuit of the Dark Lady."

"Have you any further questions?"

"I cannot think of any," I replied with an exhausted sigh. "I just wish I knew whether or not this entire evening was simply an exercise in futility."

"I cannot answer that."

"I know," I said wearily. "I don't suppose any of the four men on our final list has painted a portrait of the Dark Lady within the past two weeks?"

"No," answered the computer. "In fact, only one of them has ever evinced any interest in her portrait."

"Explain!" I commanded sharply.

"Two years ago, through one of his agents, Malcolm Abercrombie purchased a portrait of the subject whom you refer to as the Dark Lady. The auction was held on Beta Santori V."

"Continue," I said expectantly.

"The underbidder was Vladimir Kobrynski. I realize that this has nothing to do with the hypothetical problem that you posed this evening, but there is only a .0000037 percent probability that his name would occur in both contexts unless there were a connection."

"May I have a hard-copy printout of any data you possess about him that is available for public access?"

"Printing . . ."

A sheet of paper emerged from the machine.

"And have you a hologram of him in your memory banks?"

"I have not yet erased it. Please observe the screen."

The holographic screen shimmered to life, and for the first time I saw the harsh, craggy face of Vladimir Kobrynski.

18.

THE DARK LADY STOOD BE-
fore me, her arms outstretched, beckoning me to follow
her. I took a tentative step forward, then another.

"Come, Leonardo," she crooned. "Come see such
things as you have only dreamed about. Come cross the
barrier with me. Come learn the eternal mysteries of Life
and Death."

I took another, less tentative step.

"Come," she whispered. "Come with me and learn the
sublime secrets of the Other Side. Come!"

I sat upright on my sleeping cot, my hands shaking, my
hue fluctuating wildly. Finally, as I realized that it had just
been a dream, I became calmer.

Or *had* it been a dream? I rarely dreamed, and when I
did, I could not remember the details upon awakening
—and yet I recalled *this* dream with perfect clarity.

The more I thought about it, the more I wondered if it
was not a dream but a vision, a manifestation of the
Mother of All Things. It seemed presumptuous to think
that she would visit *me*—let alone any Bjornn male—yet
every detail of the experience remained fresh and clear in
my mind.

"Lights!" I ordered hoarsely.

The room was instantly illuminated, and I began pacing back and forth, pondering the meaning of what had happened. I had gone directly to Venzia's hotel from the library to tell him what I had discovered. He had become extraordinarily agitated, and told me that he planned to depart for Saltmarsh, Kobrynski's home planet, within the hour. He offered to take me with him, but I felt that I could not leave Far London without Tai Chong's permission, and although I had asked him to postpone his journey until the morning, he had refused, his face glowing with a fanatical zeal.

So I had come back to my room, distressed that my part in the Dark Lady's saga had come to an end, and had gone directly to bed. Since she was prominent in my thoughts all evening, it was logical to assume that I had simply dreamed about her, subconsciously working out my frustration at being left behind.

That was the logical explanation—but was it the *right* one? Did the Dark Lady merely visit human males, or had she also appeared to *me*? And if she had appeared to me, was she indeed the Mother of All Things? Was it blasphemous even to consider the possibility, or was it sacrilegious *not* to follow her when she had beckoned me?

I didn't know, and the more I thought about it, the more confused I became. I was still considering all the ramifications of the problem when day dawned and I left my room to go to the gallery.

As I entered the small, sparsely furnished lobby of my hotel, Valentine Heath was waiting for me, totally oblivious to the curious glances from the residents and the hostile glares from the humans who looked in while walking past.

"Good morning, Leonardo," he said. "You look awful."

"I did not sleep well, Friend Valentine," I replied.

"I'm sorry to hear it."

"How did you know that I lived here?" I asked. "I never told you."

"It's not very difficult to trace an alien on Far London," he replied with a smile. Suddenly the smile vanished. "You really should move out," he continued. "The carpeting is threadbare, the wallpaper is peeling, and the hired help keeps staring at me in a surly manner."

"It is the best hotel available to non-humans," I responded.

"I don't believe it!"

"Neither did I, until I visited some of the others," I said. I turned slightly so that I would not see the desk clerk, a Canphorite who was staring fixedly at Heath and myself with an expression of distaste. "Now that you have found me, what do you want of me?"

"The same thing I wanted yesterday," said Heath. He paused uncomfortably. "I owe the Far London Towers seventeen thousand credits. They've demanded payment by tomorrow morning."

"We have only been on Far London for four days," I said in amazement. "How did you manage to spend so much money?"

"I told you: I have expensive tastes. The Presidential Suite costs twenty-five hundred credits a night exclusive of meals, and since I came here without any extra clothes, I ordered a new wardrobe from the hotel's tailor."

"That was unwise, Friend Valentine. You should have stayed at a less expensive hotel."

"What's the difference?" he responded with a smile. "Given my current circumstances, I can't afford any of them until my funds are unfrozen."

"But why the Presidential Suite?" I said. "Surely you do not need such spaciousness."

"I require my little luxuries," he replied defensively. "Besides, that's neither here nor there. I absolutely *must* raise some money or they'll arrest me tomorrow morning."

"Perhaps you should leave the planet," I suggested.

"I can't afford fuel for my ship, or even pay the hangar fee on it." He paused again. "I went to Venzia's hotel late last night to see if I could borrow some money, but he had checked out an hour before I got there."

"I know."

"Where is he?"

"He is on his way to Saltmarsh."

"Saltmarsh?" repeated Heath. "I've never heard of it."

"It is a small planet in the Albion Cluster."

"Why has he gone there?"

"To meet the Dark Lady," I replied.

"How does he know she's there?"

"I told him."

"All right: How did *you* know?"

"I deduced it, with the help of the library's computer," I answered.

"Are you certain you're right?"

"I believe so."

"Then why didn't you go with Venzia?" he asked.

"I have other obligations."

"To Claiborne?"

"I thought they were more important when I spoke to Friend Reuben last night," I said. "Now I do not know."

"What's changed?"

"You will laugh if I tell you," I said.

"Not even if I want to," he replied reassuringly. "What happened, Leonardo?"

"The Dark Lady may have come to me in a vision."

"*May* have?" he repeated with a frown.

"It may have only been a dream," I answered truthfully. "I do not know." I paused for a moment, then continued. "But if it *was* a vision, then I must see her again."

"How important is this to you, Leonardo?" asked Heath.

"If it was a vision, it may be the most important thing in my life," I replied with a dejected sigh. "But I cannot afford passage to Saltmarsh, so I will never know."

"Don't be so sure of that," he said.

"What do you mean?" I asked suspiciously.

"If you tell me what I need to know about Abercrombie's security system, by tomorrow morning I'll not only have enough money to fuel my ship, but I'll have to leave Far London in rather a hurry." He paused meaningfully. "I see no reason why I shouldn't go into hiding on Saltmarsh, and take you along with me."

"I will not be blackmailed," I said adamantly.

"This isn't blackmail," he replied. "It's an even trade. If

you don't give me what I need, I *can't* give you what you
need. It's as simple as that."

"I cannot do what you ask, Friend Valentine."

"I wish you'd change your mind, Leonardo," he said.
"But even if you don't, I've got to go after his collection
tonight. I simply can't wait any longer." He paused. "If
you change your mind, you can contact me at my hotel
until midnight."

"I will not change my mind."

He extended his hand. "Then wish me luck."

I shook his hand, but made no comment, and after a
moment he turned and went out the door. I watched him
until he was lost in the rush-hour crowd, and then began
walking to the Claiborne Galleries, the image of the Dark
Lady still vivid in my mind.

When I arrived I went directly to my desk and began to
write a letter.

Dear Tai Chong:

I find myself in a painful moral dilemma. There is a
possibility that the Dark Lady visited me in a vision,
and if this is so, I must find her and determine exactly
who she is and what it is that she wants of me—but in
order to do so, I must help a friend commit a criminal
act, and I myself must enjoy the fruits of that crime.

Yet if I do not help him, I will not be able to visit the
world where she will make her next appearance, and if
she is indeed who I suspect she is, this may literally
constitute an act of heresy.

There is also a possibility that I am wrong, that she
did not contact me at all, and that she indeed has no
interest whatsoever in non-humans. But I cannot know
this until I speak to her, and I cannot speak to her
unless I help my friend. Therefore, if I am wrong, if
indeed she did not visit me, then I will have helped my
friend commit this criminal act for no higher purpose
than financial gain, and I will share his guilt.

I require moral and ethical guidance, and there is no
one else to whom I can turn. Therefore, I entreat you
to

I felt a hand on my shoulder and sat upright, startled.

"The boss wants to see you," said Hector Rayburn.

"Right now?" I asked.

"That's what she says."

"Thank you, Friend Hector," I said.

I instructed my computer to store the letter in its memory, then got to my feet and walked to Tai Chong's office.

"Come in, Leonardo," she said with a pleasant smile.

"Yes, Great Lady," I said, entering the room. I noticed immediately that a new hologram had been added to those that showed her winning awards and posing with various artists: This one depicted her being led to the Kennicott jail by two burly policemen, a triumphant expression on her face.

"Interesting, isn't it?" she said, following my gaze.

"It is frightening, Great Lady," I said truthfully. "The policemen look very powerful and very angry."

"They were," she said happily. "I think I am prouder of that hologram than any of the others."

I did not know what to reply to a person who took such obvious delight at being arrested for breaking the law, so I made no reply.

After a moment she cleared her throat and spoke again: "I was wondering if you've heard from Valentine Heath yet?"

"I spoke to him this morning, Great Lady."

"And?"

"He is still determined to rob Malcolm Abercrombie."

"Did you tell him that I wanted to see him?"

My hue deepened in humiliation.

"I forgot, Great Lady."

"Well, no matter," she said. "But please remember to tell him the next time you see him."

"I will not see him again, Great Lady."

"Oh? Why not?"

"Because he intends to rob Malcolm Abercrombie to-night, and he will almost certainly be apprehended." I paused. "He is staying at the Far London Towers, Great Lady. Possibly *you* can dissuade him."

"Perhaps," she said. "What makes you so sure that he will be caught? He's a very clever man."

"Because he has never been inside Malcolm Abercrombie's house, and he is unfamiliar with the security system. He has asked for my help, but I refused."

"I see."

I shifted my weight uneasily. "I have a request to make, Great Lady."

"What is it?"

"Does Claiborne have a branch on Saltmarsh?"

"That's in the Albion Cluster, isn't it?"

"Yes, Great Lady."

"I believe we do have a small outlet there," she said. "Why?"

"I desire an immediate transfer to Saltmarsh."

She frowned. "Why? Are you unhappy here?"

"No, Great Lady!" I exclaimed. "Quite the contrary: I love my work and I am happy with my surroundings. But I believe that the Dark Lady will soon be on Saltmarsh, and it is imperative that I speak to her."

"Why?"

"There is a possibility—not a certainty, but a possibility—that she may have enormous religious significance for the race of Bjornn," I replied. "I realize that it sounds ludicrous when I say it, but I must see her again to determine the truth."

"Why didn't you mention this to me yesterday?" she asked.

"I only found out last night," I replied. "I had hoped to take a leave of absence and go to Saltmarsh with Reuben Venzia, but he has already departed without me." I paused. "You are my only hope."

She stared at me thoughtfully. "What about Heath?" she asked at last. "You *are* friends, are you not?"

"He lacks the money even to fuel his ship," I said. "That is why he is so intent on robbing Malcolm Abercrombie."

"Has *he* any interest in the Dark Lady?" she asked, drawing meaningless little patterns on a pad of paper as she spoke.

"He is interested in her only as a piece of property that he can sell to Malcolm Abercrombie," I said.

"How vulgar," she replied. She seemed lost in thought for a moment, and then she suddenly stood up. "I wish I could help you, Leonardo," she said sympathetically, "but the fact of the matter is that I simply cannot send you to our Saltmarsh branch."

"Is it because of the problems on Charlemagne?" I asked.

"No," she replied. "You have been completely exonerated of all wrongdoing." She paused. "But your contract is with the Far London branch of the Claiborne Galleries. The Saltmarsh branch has no authority to employ you."

"Cannot an exception be made?" I asked. "This may be a matter of vital importance."

She shook her head. "I'm afraid not, Leonardo. If you had the means of getting there, I could conceivably grant you a brief leave of absence—but I must justify all my actions to my superiors, and I can't justify transferring you to Saltmarsh merely for your personal convenience."

"I understand, Great Lady," I said unhappily, my hue reflecting my disappointment. "I am sorry to have bothered you."

"It was no bother, Leonardo," she said soothingly. "I'm just sorry that I couldn't be of more help to you."

I left her office, returned to my desk, sat perfectly still, and analyzed my conversation with Tai Chong. There was a time when I would have accepted it verbatim, but my continued association with Men had taught me to question every statement and every motive—and as I questioned her statements and motives, I began to realize that, far from wishing to stop Valentine Heath from robbing Malcolm Abercrombie, Tai Chong actually wanted him to succeed. That was why she wished to speak to him: to tell him which paintings she could place without any embarrassing questions being asked. And that was why she had refused to transfer me to Saltmarsh: to eliminate any possibility of my meeting the Dark Lady again unless I helped Heath.

Or could I be mistaken? I knew that Tai Chong was not

unwilling to deal in art of questionable ownership, but could such an intelligent and compassionate woman truly be willing to stand by and allow one of her clients to be robbed? And even if that were true, would she actually try to manipulate events to guarantee the success of the robbery?

I did not know, but experience had taught me that if a human being acted from one of two possible motives, the more selfish motive was probably valid. With a sigh, I instructed my computer to erase the letter I had been writing her.

I worked until lunchtime and then, instead of going to my usual restaurant, I walked to the most affluent section of the city and came at last to the Far London Towers.

I received a number of hostile stares as I walked through the lobby, but no one tried to stop me as I summoned an elevator and entered it. I did not know the number of the Presidential Suite, but I reasoned that it had to be on the top floor, and so I directed the elevator to take me there.

I emerged into an opulent corridor, filled with exquisite sculptures from all across the galaxy, and finally came to a large hand-carved door of Doradusian hardwood.

"Who's there?" demanded Heath's voice as the security system informed him of my presence.

"It is Leonardo," I answered.

An instant later the door slid silently into the wall, and I entered a lavishly furnished room. Heath got up from a form-fitting chair and walked across the plush carpeting.

"You look even worse than you did this morning," he commented. "Come in and sit down."

"Thank you," I said, walking over to a sofa that hovered a few inches above the floor.

"Are you all right?" he asked solicitously. "Your color keeps darkening."

"It is the Hue of Shame."

"Oh?"

I nodded. "I have come to tell you what you want to know," I said.

PART 4

The Man Who Got It All

19.

$\mathbf{M}$Y CRAVING FOR FOOD WAS greater than it had ever been in my life.

Gradually, as consciousness returned to me, I remembered that I was inside the Deepsleep chamber. I opened my eyes, winced as the light struck them, winced again from the pain of movement, and lay perfectly motionless as I silently counted to three hundred. Then, stiff but no longer in agony, I sat up, clumsily swung my legs over the side of the module, and carefully stood up.

Heath was sitting on the edge of the other module, his usually well-groomed hair wild and unkempt, a disoriented expression on his face. He flexed his arms tentatively, then lowered his feet gently to the floor.

"Good morning, Leonardo," he said, noticing me for the first time. "How are you feeling?"

"Hungry," I replied.

"Not without cause," he replied. "You haven't eaten for thirty days."

"And how are you, Friend Valentine?" I inquired.

"Starving!"

Heath headed off toward the gallery, groaning when his muscles didn't respond as he wanted them to, and I fell into step behind him, trying to ignore the shooting pains in my limbs.

"Oh, am I stiff!" he complained.

We reached the galley and ordered our food, then sat down at the tiny table and proceeded to eat voraciously and silently for the next few minutes. Finally Heath leaned back on his chair and sighed contentedly.

"God, that was good!" he said devoutly. "I'm so full I may just go back into Deepsleep and take a little nap while I digest it all."

"That is not necessary, Friend Valentine," I said. "The human body digests its food in—"

"That was a joke, Leonardo," he interrupted.

"Oh," I said. Then, because I did not wish to hurt his feelings, I added, "It was very funny."

"Thanks," he said wryly.

"You are most welcome, Friend Valentine."

"You know," said Heath, "I used to wonder why someone didn't just deposit one hundred credits in a bank at eight or nine percent—or even two percent, for that matter—and then go into Deepsleep for a few centuries. He'd wake up the richest man alive." Heath grimaced. "Then I went into the chamber for a month or two, and I realized that you could die of starvation in less than a year. There's a big difference between shutting down your systems completely and just slowing them down to a crawl."

"Also, the Oligarchy has decreed that no investment shall accrue interest while the investor is in Deepsleep," I pointed out. "That is why the Deepsleep process is a government monopoly: so that each chamber can be programmed to report the duration of each being's Deepsleep experience to the Treasury computer at Deluros."

"But that's a relatively recent ruling," he replied. "It didn't exist during the Republic or the Democracy, and Deepsleep's been around almost twenty-five hundred years. No, I'm convinced that more than one man must have tried it and starved to death before coming out of Deepsleep."

There was a momentary silence.

"Where are we now, Friend Valentine?" I asked at last.

He shrugged. "We should have reached the Albion Cluster about two days ago," he responded. "I can check our exact position with the computer." He activated the computer with a voice command. "Computer, please give me our present position."

"We are in the Albion Cluster, and will pass the Maximus system at a distance of three light-years in approximately seventy-nine minutes."

"Right on schedule," said Heath with a smug smile. "We must be a couple of days ahead of Venzia."

"But he left almost thirty-six hours before we did," I said.

Heath smiled confidently. "There aren't too many ships around that are as fast as this one—and Venzia doesn't strike me as the kind of man who'd own one of them." He ordered a glass of wine from the galley, then asked the computer if it had recorded any messages while we were in Deepsleep.

"Yes," replied the computer. "I have stored three messages in my memory banks."

"Give them to me in the order you received them," said Heath.

"The first is from Louis Nittermeier," announced the computer.

"My lawyer," explained Heath.

"Valentine? Valentine?" said a man's high-pitched voice. "Damn! Why are you always in Deepsleep when I want you?" There was a momentary pause. "All right —let's see what I've got. All charges against you have been dropped, and you're free to return to Charlemagne. They confiscated about half your artwork—everything that wasn't registered with your insurance company—but we're negotiating to get it back. I think half a million credits will do it; there's one more guy I've got to see at police headquarters, but I've been told on reasonably good authority that he's not unwilling to bargain. What else?" Another pause. "Oh, yes—you lost your apartment on the west side of town, the one you rent under one of your aliases. Evidently you've neglected to pay your rent for the past four months. I've managed to tie it up in court so nobody else can move in; if you want it back, send me forty thousand credits for your back rent and maybe another ten thousand for a security deposit. And don't forget to pay your hard-working attorney. End of message."

"It wasn't much of an apartment anyway," said Heath with an eloquent shrug. "Computer, play the next message."

"Valentine," said Louis Nittermeier, sounding terribly agitated, "what the hell did you do on Far London? The police have been in touch with me three times today." A pause. "Some guy named Abercrombie is screaming bloody murder, and from the little I've been able to find out about him, he doesn't seem to be the kind of man who can be bought off. I'm sure you're as innocent as a newborn babe . . . but just in case you aren't, you'd better not get within five hundred light-years of Far London until you get yourself a good lawyer there—and I emphasize the word *good*. I'm not licensed to practice out there, and I wouldn't know what buttons to push even if they let me in." Another pause. "Just between old friends, don't you ever get *tired* of this? I mean, does every toothpick you own have to be made of gold—and twenty-four-karat gold at that? One of these days you're going to bite off more than you can chew, and they're going to land on you so hard that you never get up. For all I know, it's already happened with this Abercrombie." A weary sigh. "Well, good luck, and don't forget to pay your faithful attorney. Out."

"How could he have known it was *me*?" asked Heath, frowning. "I've never met the man in my life."

"He knows that you were the seller of the Mallachi painting, and that you returned to Far London with me," I replied.

He shook his head. "*Lots* of people come to Far London every day. Why me? As far as he knows, I'm a legitimate dealer who sold him the piece he wanted." He seemed to lose interest in the subject. "Computer, play the final message."

"This is Tai Chong," said a familiar voice. "We seem to have a major problem here." She paused for a moment and then continued in a carefully neutral tone. "It seems that someone stole four valuable paintings from the home of Malcolm Abercrombie three nights ago. I have absolutely no idea who committed this heinous crime, but for some reason Mr. Abercrombie has the obviously mistaken notion that you are responsible, Valentine. He's gotten the police to issue an arrest warrant, and, while I have no idea where you are, if this message chances to reach you, I thought I should apprise you of the situation and urge you to turn yourself in to the authorities so that you can clear your good name."

Heath grinned at her suggestion.

"If you are with him, Leonardo, I regret to inform you that Mr. Abercrombie has charged you with complicity in this crime, and that you are now a fugitive from justice."

She paused again, and Heath turned to me.

"You'll notice that she didn't tell *you* to surrender to the authorities," he said in amused tones.

"Why not?" I asked, sincerely puzzled.

"Because she knows you'd do it."

"I am certain that I can smooth things over and get the charges against you dropped, Leonardo," continued Tai Chong's voice, "but in the meantime, although I find this course of action repugnant, I have no choice but to suspend you without pay. My hands are tied in the matter; it is company policy to dissociate ourselves from anyone convicted of a felony—and while you most certainly have not been convicted of anything and will not be, the fact remains that this is the second felony warrant issued against you in the past two months."

I sat stunned as she continued speaking.

"Your Pattern Mother contacted me when your weekly salary was not deposited in the House of Crsthionn account, and I had no alternative but to explain the situation to her. I regret to inform you that she knows the police are searching for you in connection with the theft. I will not rest until I have convinced her that you were in no way responsible for this unfortunate incident," she added hastily. "I feel terrible about this, Leonardo, and I give you my word that I'll do everything in my power to see that you do not suffer unduly. You have always been loyal to me, and I will be loyal to you. Even if this thing drags on interminably, as now seems likely, there is a possibility that I will be able to use you as a free-lance consultant."

"My Pattern Mother knows?" I repeated, horror-stricken.

"I have no idea where the two of you are, and of course I can have no idea of your destination—but if this message reaches you, Valentine, I am counting on you to surrender to the nearest authority, and also to convince Leonardo to do what is right for him. Good luck and Godspeed."

"That's a classy lady," said Heath admiringly. "I'll bet she had six policemen in her office when she sent the message."

"But I thought I was doing what she *wanted*," I said, totally devastated.

"You were," answered Heath. "She never thought Abercrombie would suspect a Bjornn of collaborating with *anyone* to break the law." He shook his head. "He's either brighter than I thought, or very paranoid."

"What will become of me?"

"You weren't listening very carefully, were you?" said Heath easily.

"I don't know what you mean."

"She promised that she'd take care of you. She'll keep her word."

"How?" I asked uncomprehendingly.

"The same way she takes care of *me*," said Heath. He smiled. " 'Free-lance consultant' is a euphemism for procurer of stolen artwork. I guarantee that you'll make more this way than you ever would as an employee, or even as an art dealer on Bjornn."

"Benitarus II," I corrected him automatically.

"Wherever."

"But I cannot become a thief!" I protested.

"What else can you be?" responded Heath seriously. "Your Pattern Mother won't talk to you and Claiborne has suspended you."

"I can perform the ritual of suicide," I said.

He shook his head. "Claiborne didn't *fire* you. If Tai Chong gets the police to drop their charges, you still have to work off the rest of your contract."

"I owe nothing to a woman who manipulated me into helping you commit a crime, and now wants me to become a thief."

"You have an interesting concept of honor, Leonardo."

"I do not understand what you mean," I said.

"Are you honor-bound only to meet those commitments you make to people who live up to your high moral standards?" asked Heath. "You're saying that you're letting *her* morality determine your own." He paused. "*I've* been living by that particular code for years—but then, I've never pretended to be a man of honor."

"But how am I to honor my contract when Tai Chong obviously prefers that I steal paintings for her?" I asked helplessly.

"I don't know," said Heath. "You'll have to figure that out for yourself."

"I cannot!" I protested. "I must seek ethical guidance."

"From me?" he asked with an amused laugh.

"No, not from you."

"Your Pattern Mother won't help you, and you don't want Tai Chong's advice," he said, "so who can you ask?"

"I do not know," I replied. "I will find someone."

"In the meantime, you're on your own, and we've got a living to make."

"I will not steal artwork," I said adamantly.

"Have I suggested it?" asked Heath innocently.

"Yes."

"Well, forget it—for the moment, at least. I think there's a much easier way to turn a profit." He leaned forward intently. "We're going to beat Venzia to Saltmarsh, which means we'll find the Dark Lady before he does. It's my guess that he'll pay a considerable amount of money for five minutes of her time."

"If you can find her on Saltmarsh, so can he," I said.

Heath smiled confidently. "We'll wait for him at the spaceport and tell him we've kidnapped her."

"Why should he believe you?"

"Because it makes sense," said Heath. "Why would I lie to him?"

"Because you are Valentine Heath."

"But *he* doesn't know Valentine Heath as well as you do."

"He knows that the Dark Lady will vanish before you can force her to do anything against her will," I pointed out.

"But from everything you and Venzia have told me, she's never done it in front of anyone who isn't aware of her true nature. We'll just keep her in a crowd."

"Keep her in a crowd?" I repeated.

"That's right. The more people there are, the less likely she is to pull her disappearing act."

"I thought you were going to *lie* to Friend Reuben," I said.

"If I have to," responded Heath. "It makes more sense to actually deliver the goods—but if we can't, then we should certainly have an alternate plan in mind."

"And all you plan to do is detain her until Venzia arrives?" I asked.

"That's right," he replied.

"Have you nothing to ask her yourself?" I continued.

"Such as?"

"The answer to Venzia's question."

Heath shook his head. "Absolutely not. What fun would life be without some mystery?"

"But if there is an afterlife, do you not want to know?"

"I'll know soon enough," he replied.

"But—"

"Look," he said. "I've never been the kind of person who reads the last chapter of a mystery novel first. It's cheating. Well, this is the same thing."

"Since when did cheating bother you?"

"Touché," he said.

There was a brief silence.

"You have not answered my question," I said at last.

"Leonardo," he began with a sigh, "one of the reasons I prefer to think that when we die everything we are dies with us is that if there are any ground rules for getting into heaven, any at all, then I'm condemned to eternal damnation. The Dark Lady can tell me only two things: that there *is* an afterlife, or that there *isn't*. If there isn't, nothing I believe in has changed; and if there is, I'd rather not know about it. Does that answer your question?"

"Yes, Friend Valentine."

"Do *you* plan to ask her anything?"

"Possibly," I replied.

"What?"

"I am not sure yet."

"Well, you'd better make up your mind soon; we'll be landing on Saltmarsh in about five hours." Heath paused thoughtfully. "You know," he said, "Saltmarsh is only about four days from Benitarus II. Maybe when we're done, I'll take you home and you can try to patch up your troubles with your Pattern Mother."

"I thank you for the thought, Friend Valentine," I said. "But I have been forbidden to set foot on Benitarus II."

"Maybe she'll change her mind if she knows we're practically on her doorstep."

"She will not."

"You never know," he replied.

"*I* know," I replied. "My Acceptance Day passed while we were in Deepsleep, yet she left no message and sent no gift of food."

He laughed. "We're fugitives from the law, Leonardo! Nobody except Tai Chong knows where we're going, and we haven't broken radio silence for close to thirty days. How would your Pattern Mother know where to send a message?"

"That is true," I answered.

"And as for a present, we've been traveling at light

speeds for a month. Even if she knew how to find us, how do you think she could deliver it?"

"Thank you for your observations, Friend Valentine," I said sincerely. "I find them most comforting."

"Then do you want to visit her when we're through here?" he asked again.

"I will never be allowed to see her again," I explained patiently. "Furthermore, I will probably perform the ritual of suicide within the next few days."

"Again?" he demanded. "Don't you have any other topic of conversation?"

"Yes, but none is as important. I may be morally compelled to—"

"Spare me your compulsions," he interrupted. "I want you to give me your word that you won't take your life, or talk about taking your life, until Tai Chong has a chance to get the police to exonerate us."

"I give you my word that I will not talk about taking my life until Tai Chong has a chance to exonerate us," I said carefully.

He threw up his hands in exasperation. "You're a very difficult person to talk to, do you know that?"

"You have said so before."

"Well, I'm saying so again!"

"I am sorry if I have offended you, Friend Valentine," I said.

"And stop being so damned apologetic for everything!" he said irritably. "If you're going to be a successful criminal, that's the very first thing you've got to change!"

"I am not going to be a successful criminal," I replied.

"Then you're going to be a damned hungry one."

He stalked off to his cabin, while I remained in the galley, chewing absently on some soya by-products and wondering what advice my Pattern Mother could give me that might help me prepare myself for a life of crime.

20.

$\mathbf{H}$EATH PUT THE SHIP INTO orbit around Saltmarsh, then contacted the planet's only spaceport.

"This is the *Pablo Picasso*, Charlemagne registry, thirty-one days out of Far London, Valentine Heath, race of Man, commanding. We require landing coordinates."

"Please state the nature of your business on Saltmarsh," replied a feminine voice.

"Commerce."

"What type of commerce?"

"I buy and sell artwork."

"The Saltmarsh economy is based on the New Kampala shilling. Will you require local currency?"

"Are credits accepted?"

"We *are* a member world of the Oligarchy," the voice replied archly.

"Then I won't need to convert any money," said Heath.

"Our atmosphere contains 16.23 percent oxygen and 79 percent nitrogen, and our gravity is .932 Deluros VIII Standard. Will either of these conditions present a health hazard?"

"Not to me," replied Heath. "Are there any trace

elements that would prove harmful to a Bjornn?"

There was a brief pause.

"Have you any members of an alien race aboard your ship?"

"Yes."

"Please inform them that they are not allowed to disembark."

"That doesn't make any sense," protested Heath. "My business associate is a member of the Bjornn race from Benitarus II. If you'll check your records, you'll find that Benitarus has a Most Favored Planet trading status with the worlds of the Oligarchy, and has always enjoyed cordial relations with the race of Man."

"Under no circumstance is *any* alien permitted to set foot on Saltmarsh. There are no exceptions."

"May I speak to your superior, please?" requested Heath.

He spoke to the woman's department head, and to the Immigration Bureau, and to the minuscule Department of Alien Affairs, but after half an hour it was obvious that the government of Saltmarsh was unwilling to make any exceptions in its racial policy.

Finally Heath turned to me.

"That's it, Leonardo. I can't go any higher unless they let me speak to the governor, and we know what his answer will be."

"I agree, Friend Valentine," I replied.

"Well," he continued, "do I go looking for Kobrynski alone, or do we leave? It's up to you."

"I must find the Dark Lady," I said. "You will have to go alone."

"All right," he said. "What if I find Kobrynski and she's not there?"

"Then you must wait for her."

"For how long—a day, a week, a year? At what point do we conclude that you were mistaken about her next consort?"

"Sooner or later she will join him, and I will see her again," I said confidently.

"Unless what you think was a vision was actually a meaningless dream."

"If that is what you believe, why did you take me here?" I asked.

"Because it's halfway across the galaxy from Far London," he replied. "And if you've guessed right, there's a small fortune to be made if I can keep her from disappearing." He paused. "But don't forget that my ship's registration number is now in the Saltmarsh computer, and that we're still wanted by the police. Every hour we remain here gives them that much more time to find us."

"I know—but I must find out if she is who I hope she is."

"All right," said Heath. "I just want to be sure that you understand the precariousness of our present situation." He paused and sighed. "The first step is to find Kobrynski. If she's with him, I'll come back here and we'll plan our next step; if she's not, maybe I can convince him to come back to the ship with me and let you explain the situation to him. It'll be a lot easier than trying to smuggle you onto the planet."

"You will not be able to convince him to do anything against his will," I said.

"I can be pretty persuasive," said Heath.

"If he were a man who could be persuaded, she would have no interest in him."

"We'll see," replied Heath skeptically. He activated his radio again and contacted the spaceport. "This is Valentine Heath. Your conditions for landing are understood, and we shall abide by them."

"Very well, *Pablo Picasso*: You are cleared for landing. I have just fed the coordinates into your ship's computer."

"Thank you," said Heath.

Twenty minutes later we touched down, and he left the ship while a pair of armed guards took up positions just outside the hatch, presumably to stop me from polluting Saltmarsh's soil by stepping on it.

I watched Heath until he disappeared from view, then activated the computer and began writing.

To the Dark Lady:

I do not know how to address you, nor even how to deliver this letter into your hands, but my Pattern Mother has disowned me and Tai Chong has manipulated me into becoming a criminal, and of all the females I know, only you are left to provide me with ethical guidance.

And yet, if you are truly the Mother of All Things, you not only know of my shame and dishonor, but have yourself authored them in the Book of Fate for reasons that I cannot fathom.

I do not know why you visited me, or what you want from me. I have been taught to honor the House and the Family, and yet the House has cast me out and the Family is forbidden to speak my name. I have been taught to obey the law, and yet I am now a thief, and the only hope for my continued survival is to become an adept thief. I have been told by the Priestess and the Holy Writings that the Mother of All Things made the Bjornn in Her own image, and yet you have taken the shape of an alien race. I have been instructed to cherish life, and yet you, who gave me life, love only death.

I cannot judge you, but I must learn to understand you. Is everything I have lived for wrong? Do you want me to die in a blaze of glory, as Men wish to do? If the House is mistaken, if the Family is deluded in its beliefs, why have you never corrected them? Why do you only manifest yourself to Man?

Or am *I* mistaken about your true nature? Was my vision in fact only a dream?

I must know the answer, for if it was only a dream, then I am truly the villain my Pattern Mother believes me to be. I made the decision to help Valentine Heath steal Malcolm Abercrombie's artwork, and if I did not do so at your request, then my soul shall wander, condemned and alone, through the great void for all eternity.

This is why I must know who you are, and what you

want of me. Have I passed beyond the ken of all decent beings, or is this part of your plan for me? I do not feel evil, but I have done evil things.

This is the crux of the matter: the evil that I have done. My employment was terminated by Malcolm Abercrombie before I knew of your existence, yet I was grateful when Tai Chong pressured him into taking me back into his employ. I knew that Valentine Heath was a thief before I was aware of your existence, but I did not report him to the authorities. I knew the Kid was being lured to his death before I was cognizant of your true nature, yet I did nothing to warn him. I saw Valentine Heath bribe the mayor of Acheron, and I did not protest his actions.

I think back on the events of the past few months, and I am faced with an inescapable conclusion:

I did not do these evil deeds for you.

Therefore, I must have done them for *me*.

And still I do not feel evil. Am I so deeply immersed in immorality and degeneracy that I can no longer tell the difference between good and evil?

Or have you forsaken your Bjornn shape and become a woman for a reason? Is it possible that the humans are right and we are wrong, that Valentine Heath more closely approximates your ideal of virtue than does my Pattern Mother?

I cannot speak of these things to anyone else, but I cannot continue to live with the uncertainty. My profession—my former profession—has taught me to deal with color and line, but my upbringing tells me that life is not art: It must be black or white—and even at this late date, even with the police searching for me, even as I plan ways to break the law of still another world by finding some covert means of visiting you, if indeed you are here, even now I do not know if I am doing your bidding or simply multiplying my villainies.

I must know: Are you merely Death made flesh, seeking your lovers wherever you can find them—or are you truly the Mother of All Things?

I must know what you are, or I shall never know
what I am.

A sign, Greatest of Ladies. I beg of you: a sign.

Your devoted

And here I stopped. Her devoted what? Son? Worshipper? Servant? Or villain?

I sighed and stared at the screen, amazed at my audacity. Some beings pray to the Mother of All Things; others ignore her; but no one else would dare to write her a list of demands.

I ordered the computer to erase the letter and delete it from its memory bank, then stared morosely at the viewscreen, absently watching the two guards as they stood motionless in the hot Saltmarsh sun, their backs stiff and straight, their uniforms immaculate, eyes forward, weapons at the ready, prepared to defend the sanctity of their planet from all the alien defilers. I found myself wondering what *they* would do in my place.

Most likely they would stride boldly through the hatch and defy anyone to stop them. Humans had that way about them, that ability to act first and justify their actions later. I had always been taught that such an approach was irrational and irresponsible—and yet they stood upon half a million worlds, and the Bjornns lived on one island continent. For better or worse, while we had lived lives of ethical purity, they had swarmed out to the stars by the billions, exploring, conquering, plundering, ruling, never asking for quarter, never giving it, never apologizing, never looking back. They had expanded too quickly during the Republic, antagonized too many of their neighboring races, and they had been forced to fall back and regroup—but the Republic had nonetheless lasted for two millennia. They had begun the era of the Democracy as one race among many, but before long they had achieved primacy once again—and the Democracy had lasted for almost three millennia. Now there was the Oligarchy, a council of seven that ruled the vast, sprawling galaxy as completely as it could be ruled, and in the four centuries of its existence no non-human had ever sat upon an Oligarch's chair.

Could a Bjornn have filled such a chair, I wondered—or would she have crushed it with the weight of her ethical baggage? Had the Mother of All Things studied Her handiwork and decided that pragmatism was the missing element? Did the Dark Lady cherish all that was best in Man, or did she call to the grave all that was worst in him?

It was an interesting thought, that last. Was there a meeting ground somewhere between the two races, a point of proper balance between the Yin and the Yang? Was she moving Man closer to that point by eliminating those men who most typified the extreme? And if so, was I also part of that plan, a prototype of the new Bjornn race, a thief and fugitive who dared speak directly to his deity?

Or had I merely learned to rationalize, to blame my sins and my shortcomings on a mysterious woman who neither knew nor cared about the Bjornns *or* Vladimir Kobrynski, who might be tens of thousands of light-years away at this very minute, or might never become flesh again?

I sat morosely, with such thoughts occupying my mind, for the better part of two hours. Then the hatch opened, and Heath, a large package tucked firmly under one arm, entered the ship.

"Did you find her?" I asked eagerly.

He shook his head. "I didn't even find *him*—but at least I know where he is now."

"Where?"

"An uninhabited little world called Solitaire. It's the only planet circling Beta Sybaris." He paused. "Evidently plasma painting is even more dangerous than we thought. I gather it can wipe out an entire planetary population if they don't take the proper precautions—and the government of Saltmarsh couldn't see any reason why they should go to the trouble and expense of protecting their citizens from Kobrynski's latest hobby. So," he concluded, "they invited him to leave, and now Friend Vladimir is off creating masterpieces on Solitaire, where he can't kill anyone except himself."

"How far away is it?" I asked.

"We can make it in just under two days," replied Heath. He placed the box down on a counter. "By the way, I've got a little present for you." He watched me for my reaction. "It's from your Pattern Mother."

"It cannot be," I said morosely. "She does not know I am here."

"Tai Chong must have told her, because she sent it to the local Claiborne branch, and they turned it over to Customs on the assumption that we'd show up sooner or later. I just hope she didn't tell anyone else." He paused. "Stop looking so suspicious, Leonardo. The Benitarus system is only a week away from Saltmarsh. She had plenty of time to send it and still have it arrive ahead of us."

"That is true," I admitted, allowing hope to rise within me. "She *did* have time."

"See?" said Heath with satisfaction. "I *told* you she wouldn't forget your Acceptance Day."

"I must confess that I had feared she would never contact me again, Friend Valentine," I said, beginning to unwrap the package. "Especially when I was told that she knew I was being sought by the Far London police." My fingers tugged awkwardly at the tapes and sealers. "If I have been denied only the Celebration of the First Mother, there is still a possibility that I may someday be allowed to return to my Family."

"You look very excited," remarked Heath. "You're practically glowing."

"I *am* excited, Friend Valentine," I replied, finally working my way through the wrapping material and opening the box. "This is more than I had dared to hope for, and—"

Suddenly I stopped speaking, and simply stared into the box.

"What is it?" demanded Heath. "What's wrong?"

"I asked the Dark Lady for a sign," I said dully. "She has given me one."

I reached in and withdrew a small, dead rodent, holding it up by its tail.

"I have been cast out for all eternity," I continued. "All Bjornns will be instructed to shun me whenever and wherever they may encounter me, and my name will be removed from the Book of the Family."

"You might be wrong," said Heath. "If she was truly cutting you loose, she wouldn't have bothered sending anything at all."

"That would have been preferable," I said.

"I don't understand."

"The climax of Acceptance Day is the feast," I explained, my hue fluctuating wildly as I attempted to regain control of my emotions.

"That's why I think you're mistaken," replied Heath. "This thing couldn't have been sent for your Acceptance Day. Bjornns are vegetarians."

"This is my Pattern Mother's way of telling me that I am not only disgraced, but that I am no longer even a Bjornn."

"What does she think you are?" he asked, staring at the rodent.

"An eater of flesh."

"An eater of flesh?" he repeated curiously.

"A Man," I said.

21.

Vladimir Kobrynski did not look like the popular conception of a daredevil.

His tanned face was heavily lined, his hair was thin and receding, his nose was oversized, he was missing a portion of his left earlobe, and his teeth were crooked and miscolored. Though naturally burly and muscular, he nonetheless carried about twenty-five excess pounds, and his belly hung over his belt. The color of his arms didn't match: The right one was brown from exposure to the suns of many worlds, while the left one was quite pale, leading me to conclude that it was artificial. He walked, not with a limp, but with a certain stiffness, as if an old injury was constantly bothering him.

It had taken us fifty-three hours to reach Solitaire, and another half hour to pinpoint Kobrynski's location, for the planet was heavily pockmarked with mountains and craters. He had erected a portocabin at the base of an extinct volcano, and Heath, after alerting him to our presence and identifying ourselves via ship-to-surface radio, had carefully maneuvered our ship down next to his.

He was waiting for us when we emerged from the hatch,

an expression of open curiosity on his face.

"You're Heath?" he said, staring at Valentine.

"That's right."

"Welcome to Solitaire. I'm always grateful for company." He turned to me. "You must be Leonardo. Funny name for an alien."

"I am sorry if it offends you," I said.

"It takes a lot more than that to offend me," he replied easily. Then he paused, looking from one of us to the other. "Okay," he said at last. "I know you're not from Saltmarsh, and I know I've never met either of you before—so suppose you tell me what you're doing here and why I've suddenly become so popular." He smiled. "I'm not enough of an egomaniac to think it's because you want to see my plasma paintings."

"You make it sound like we're not your only visitors," said Heath carefully.

"I got a radio message from someone named Venzia," answered Kobrynski. "He ought to be here in a couple of hours. All of a sudden everyone wants to talk to me. Why?"

"Venzia?" repeated Heath, puzzled. "How could he have caught up with us so quickly?"

It was Kobrynski's turn to look puzzled. "You guys were having a race to see who could reach me first?"

"In a manner of speaking," replied Heath.

"Why?"

"Because we think that you're a very important man, Mr. Kobrynski," said Heath, "and we have some questions we'd like to ask you."

"Why am I so important?"

"That's one of the things we'd like to speak to you about," said Heath.

Kobrynski shrugged. "Why not? I've got nothing to hide." He paused. "It's too hot out here. Come on into the cabin." He turned to me. "You, too."

We followed him into the portocabin, a large structure that was filled with numerous very sophisticated computers, as well as various other machines that I could not identify. Mounted on the walls were several animal heads, each more fearsome than the last.

"Very impressive," said Heath.

"The equipment or the animals?" asked Kobrynski.

"Both," said Heath. He pointed to one of the heads, a hideous, snarling reptile with six-inch fangs. "Isn't that a Thunder Lizard? I think I saw one once in a zoo on Lodin XI."

Kobrynski nodded. "It's a Thunder Lizard, all right —but you must have seen it in a museum. They've never been able to capture one alive."

"Where do they come from?" I asked.

"Gamma Scuti IV."

"Thunder Lizards look very savage," I observed.

"They are," agreed Kobrynski. He gave the head a fond pat. "Especially this one. He was gnawing away on my left foot when I finally killed him."

"Is that how you lost your arm, too?" I asked.

He shook his head. "That was about fifteen years ago, in a skydiving accident." He flexed his artificial left arm. "No great loss. This one works better than my real one." He paused. "Anyone care for a drink?"

"Yes, thanks," said Heath.

Kobrynski reached into a cabinet, withdrew a bottle of Altairian rum, and tossed it to Heath. "How about you?" he asked me.

"I do not partake of stimulants," I replied. "But I thank you for the offer."

"Suit yourself," he said, sitting down on the edge of an unmade bed and motioning us to seat ourselves on a pair of metal stools. "Okay. Start asking your questions. I think I'm as interested in them as you are in the answers."

"Are you alone here?" asked Heath.

"Is that a question, or the prelude to a robbery?" asked Kobrynski in a tone that boded ill for any potential burglar.

"It is a question of the utmost importance," I said.

"I'm alone."

"There's no woman with you?" persisted Heath.

Kobrynski waved his real arm in a sweeping gesture that encompassed most of the planet. "Do you see one?" He paused. "What's all this about a woman? Venzia asked me the same damned thing."

"We are seeking a certain woman," I said. "I have reason to believe that she will appear here before too much longer."

"On Solitaire?" he said with a sardonic laugh. "What could possibly make a woman come out to a hot, ugly, lifeless world like this?"

"*You* could, Mr. Kobrynski," I replied.

He looked surprised. "Me?"

"That is correct."

"Maybe you didn't get a good look at me in the sunlight," he said. "I haven't exactly got the kind of face that would make a woman follow me around the galaxy."

"*This* woman will," I said.

"Keep talking," said Kobrynski, his face alive with interest.

I turned to Heath. "May I be permitted to conduct the interview, Friend Valentine?"

Heath smiled. "You took it over a couple of minutes ago."

"I apologize for my poor manners," I said.

"There's no need to," said Heath. "After all, you're the expert."

"Thank you," I said, turning back to our host. "Mr. Kobrynski, two years ago you were the underbidder on a painting that was sold on Beta Santori V."

"How did you know that?"

"It is a matter of public record," I replied. "Do you recall the painting?"

"Of course I do. It was the only piece of art I ever tried to buy, and some rich bastard from Near London or Old London wound up with it."

"Far London," I corrected him.

"Do you know him?" asked Kobrynski. "He never showed up at the auction himself; he had an agent do his bidding for him."

"His name is Malcolm Abercrombie," I replied. "He was my employer until quite recently."

"He must be loaded."

"He is quite wealthy," I agreed. "May I ask what it was about that particular painting that interested you? I have seen it, and in all candor, it is not a very well-executed portrait."

"Are you here to ask me about paintings or about some woman you're looking for?"

"Both," I replied. "Would you please answer my question? I assure you that it is quite important."

Kobrynski shrugged. "I didn't give a damn about how good a painting it was," he said. "I told you: I don't collect artwork."

"But you tried to purchase *that* painting," I continued. "Why?"

"Because of the subject matter."

"The woman who was depicted?"

He nodded. "That's right."

"Have you ever seen her?" I asked.

"Almost every night for close to twenty years," replied Kobrynski.

"That's impossible!" interjected Heath.

"I'd be very careful who I called a liar, Mr. Heath," said Kobrynski ominously.

"Have you ever been to Acheron?" asked Heath.

"I've never even heard of it."

"I know for a fact that she was on Acheron for at least a month," said Heath. "How could she possibly have been with you at the same time?"

"I didn't say I'd *met* her," answered Kobrynski. "I said I've *seen* her." He tapped his head. "In here."

"I don't understand you, Mr. Kobrynski," said Heath.

"She keeps appearing to me in my dreams," replied Kobrynski. "I used to think that I had invented her. Then I saw the painting." He paused. "I guess I must have seen it once before, and carried the memory of her face around in my subconscious."

"You can think of no other explanation?" I asked.

"I sure as hell can't have *met* her," he replied. "The painting was six centuries old."

"Why did you attempt to purchase it?" I asked.

Suddenly his eyes narrowed. "Look," he said harshly. "If it's been stolen, and your boss is thinking of blaming *me* for it, just because I bid on the damned thing . . ."

"I assure you that it has not been stolen," I said, "nor is Malcolm Abercrombie still my employer."

"Then why do you care why I tried to buy it?"

"Please believe that it is important to me."

"Well, it's embarrassing to me," he replied. Finally he shrugged again. "What the hell. You've come all this way; you might as well have your answer." He paused. "I tried to buy it because I thought it was a way of putting my demons to rest."

"I do not understand."

"It's going to seem crazy to you," he said, "but even though I'd never met the woman in the painting, somehow I started to believe that she was real, that someday I would meet her." He shifted uncomfortably. "I suppose I was even a little bit in love with her."

"It does not seem crazy to me," I said. "Please continue."

"Well, it seems crazy to *me* when I say it," he replied uneasily. "You know, every time I climbed into a ring or faced a charging animal, I felt that I was proving myself to her, and that if I could just win enough fights and face enough animals, somehow she'd know what I had done." He grimaced. "So here I sit, a certifiable romantic talking to two strangers about his infatuation with a phantom. Maybe we'd better get back to your flesh and blood woman."

"I find phantoms more interesting," I responded. "Could we talk about her a bit longer?"

He sighed. "Why not? I don't suppose I can say anything that will make me feel any more foolish than I feel right at this moment."

"Do you still dream about her?" I asked.

"Every night."

"Does she ever smile in your dreams?"

He stared at me curiously for a long moment. "No, she never does," he said, obviously surprised at my question. "She always has this sad expression on her face, like . . ." His voice trailed off.

"Like what?"

"Like she's searching for something. Something important to her."

"Has she ever appeared to you when you were awake?"

"I told you," he said irritably, "she's just an image of some woman who lived centuries ago. No, not even that; she's my memory of an artist's conception of her." He stared curiously at me. "Why are you so interested in her?"

"She is alive," I replied.

"She can't be!"

"She is alive," I repeated. "And I believe that she will soon appear on Solitaire."

"It can't be the same woman," said Kobrynski firmly.

"It is."

He laughed suddenly. "You're crazier than I am."

"I am not crazy," I said. "I believe she will appear here soon—and when she does it is imperative that I be allowed to speak to her."

"You've actually seen her?"

"We have," interjected Heath.

"It must be someone who looks like her," said Kobrynski. "She'd be more than six hundred years old."

"More than eight thousand years, actually," I said.

"Then it can't be the same woman," repeated Kobrynski.

"She's not exactly a normal woman," said Heath wryly.

"No alien ever looked like that," said Kobrynski.

"She's not an alien, either," said Heath.

"So she's not a woman and she's not an alien," said Kobrynski. "What is she?"

"I don't know," admitted Heath.

Kobrynski turned to me. "What do *you* think she is?"

"A phantom," I replied.

"A phantom?" he repeated.

"She has appeared to many men over the millennia," I explained. "She is drawn to those who court her. The library computer on Far London has confirmed that you will be the next man that she visits."

"Then your library computer is missing a couple of chips," said Kobrynski. "I've never met her. How the hell could I court her?"

"By continually entering life-threatening situations," I replied.

"Then you've come to the wrong place. They're fighting wars all over the galaxy; there are soldiers who are risking their lives ten times a day."

"She is drawn to men who voluntarily risk their lives with no thought of profit," I continued. "A soldier does not risk his life unless he is ordered to do so."

"How can she know whether I've risked my life or not?"

"You told me earlier that you thought she somehow would know if you did so," I replied. "You were correct."

"But if she's never seen me . . ." he began, confused.

"She is not a woman," I said.

"Why are *you* so interested in her?" asked Kobrynski suddenly.

"There are certain things I must ask her."

"If there's any truth to this half-baked story of yours, just risk your life and she'll come to you."

"In eight millennia, she has never been observed in the company of a non-human."

"Then I repeat: Why are you interested in her?"

"It is very difficult to explain," I said.

"Good. It's time someone besides me felt awkward."

"She appeared to me in a vision," I said. "I must find out why."

"A vision?" he repeated. "You mean, like a religious visitation?"

"Perhaps."

"Perhaps?" he repeated. "What does *that* mean?"

"It may have been a dream. If it was a vision, I must discover why she has singled me out among all non-humans, and what she wants of me."

"And if it was a dream?"

"Then I will know she did not contact me, and I will be free to perform a religious ritual that has been too long postponed."

"What ritual?" asked Kobrynski suspiciously.

"Suicide," I said.

Kobrynski blinked his eyes. "I stand by my first statement: You guys are crazy."

"I am sorry that you should think so," I said.

"Look," said Heath, leaning forward. "I don't know what she is: a woman, an alien, a teleporter, or Leonardo's Mother of All Things. But I *do* know that she was on my ship less than two months ago, and that there are more than forty paintings, holograms, and sculptures of her dating back more than eight thousand years. That much, at least, is a fact."

"You've actually *met* her?" asked Kobrynski.

"Both of us have," replied Heath.

"Why didn't you ask her what you wanted to know then?"

"*I* don't have any questions for her," said Heath. "And Leonardo didn't know what she was—or what he *thinks* she is—at the time."

"Okay," said Kobrynski. "I know what *his* interest in her is. What's *yours*?"

A mask of impassivity suddenly covered Heath's face. "I'm just helping Leonardo find her."

Kobrynski looked from Heath to me and back again. "You're lying," he said at last. Then he turned to me. "You're telling the truth—but you're crazy." He paused. "What about this Venzia? What does *he* want from her?"

"He wants to know what lies beyond this life," I replied.

"And he thinks she can tell him?"

"Yes."

Kobrynski frowned. "What did they do—empty all the asylums in the Oligarchy and give all the inmates my name?"

"It is not necessary for you to believe us," I said.

"Good—because I don't."

"All we ask," I continued, "is your permission to remain on Solitaire until she appears."

"She's not going to appear," said Kobrynski.

"I hope you are right," I said.

"I thought you wanted to talk to her."

"I *have* to talk to her," I responded. "No one *wants* to confront his god."

"So now she's a god instead of a lonely woman who likes men that take chances?"

"I do not know," I said. "That is what I must find out. May we have your permission to stay on Solitaire?"

"It's not mine to give," said Kobrynski. "Stay or go as you please."

"Thank you."

"No need to; I always humor madmen." He paused. "When do you think she's going to show up?"

"I do not know."

"Well, if it's anytime after tonight, she'd damned well better be a goddess."

"Why?" asked Heath.

"Because I've been toying with a new variation of my plasma painting," replied Kobrynski. "I'm going to test it out tonight—and when I do, this whole damned planet's going to be radioactive for the next seventy or eighty years."

"What do you mean?" I asked.

"Do you know what's involved in plasma painting?" he asked.

"I was given a brief description of it by the library computer on Far London."

"Well, it's an interesting process, but it always seemed a bit *limited*," said Kobrynski. "Now that I've got an unpopulated planet to play with, I'm going to use unstable atoms to create controlled explosions for artistic emphasis."

"Have you tried it yet?" asked Heath.

Kobrynski smiled. "If I had, you'd have received a lethal dose of radiation the instant you left your ship." He paused. "But I've run it through the computer, and it tells me that it should work."

"Is it safe for us to stay on the planet while you're creating your plasma painting?" asked Heath.

Kobrynski nodded. "The cabin is shielded against radiation." He paused again. "If you've got protective suits in your ship, it might be a good idea to get them and bring them here to the cabin. I can dig up something for *you*—but I wouldn't know how to go about fitting *him*," he added, gesturing toward me.

"I might as well get them right now," said Heath, walking out the door.

Kobrynski and I sat in silence for a few moments. Finally he sighed deeply.

"For what it's worth," he said, "I wish you *weren't* crazy."

"Oh?"

"I've been lonely all my life."

"I thought humans did not mind being alone," I said.

"Don't you believe it, Leonardo," he replied.

"Then, if I may ask a personal question—"

"Just what do you think you've *been* asking?"

"I apologize if I have offended you."

"I'm not offended, just embarrassed," said Kobrynski. "And since it was my own answers that embarrassed me, I've got no one to blame but myself. Go ahead and ask your question."

"If you dislike being alone, why have you spent so much of your adult life in lonely pursuits?"

He considered his answer for a moment.

"I'll be damned if I know," he said at last.

He fell silent again, and a moment later Heath returned with our protective suits.

"It's getting awfully hot out there. It must be close to 120 degrees."

"It's a dry heat, though," said Kobrynski. "No humidity to speak of."

"Wet or dry, cooked meat is cooked meat," said Heath.

Kobrynski chuckled. "You should have been with me

when I was hunting Horndemons on Ansard V. *Then* you'd appreciate a dry heat."

"I think I'll just take your word for it," said Heath, pulling out a handkerchief and wiping the perspiration from his face.

"What subject are you going to paint tonight?" I asked.

"I haven't decided," replied Kobrynski. "I've done the preliminary work on half a dozen of them."

"Preliminary work?" I said.

He smiled. "You've never seen a plasma painting, have you?"

"No, I have not."

"You cast it into the sky, perhaps two miles above the ground," he said. "On a cloudless planet like Solitaire, you can go as high as five miles, and fill the sky from horizon to horizon." He paused. "With a celestial canvas that large, you can't paint the details piecemeal. You create the preliminary painting on that computer"—he pointed to one of his machines—"and then, when you're satisfied with it, *that* one"—he indicated a different computer—"analyzes it and determines how best to irradiate the atmosphere to create the effect you want. The other machines do the actual work."

"What colors can you produce?" asked Heath.

"Everything from the ultraviolet into the infrared," answered Kobrynski. "They're not opaque, mind you —you'd burn the world to a crisp. Besides, I like to see the stars shining through my creation."

"How long does it last?" inquired Heath.

"It takes form in about a minute, and takes another ninety seconds to dissipate. It can maintain its complete integrity for perhaps thirty seconds."

"Forgive me for saying it," said Heath, "but it seems to me that you're going to a lot of expense and trouble for an effect that lasts half a minute."

"No more than you're going to find a phantom," replied Kobrynski. "And for the half minute that it lasts, I've done something proud, something no one else has done."

"May we see the subjects that are under consideration

for this evening?" I asked.

He shrugged. "Why not?"

He activated the first computer with his voice, then ordered it to cast a hologram of his first subject in the air in front of us.

It was an eerie alien landscape, with a blood-red river that lapped at the shores of a desolate bank, while skeletal, leafless trees leaned across the water at impossible angles.

"Larabee IV," said Kobrynski.

"I've not heard of it," said Heath.

"It's out past the Quinellus Cluster. Strangest planet I've ever seen. There are only two colors: deep red and dark purple. Everything—rocks, water, vegetation—is either one or the other."

"Are there any animals?" I asked.

"The Pioneer Corps' survey says there are, but I never saw any. Next!"

We saw, in quick succession, a Doradusian mountain range, an abstract representation of a laser rifle, a still life of Binder X fruits, and a naturalistic impression of a Thunder Lizard.

"I'm almost ashamed to show you the last one," said Kobrynski.

"Why?"

"Because it looks like a direct steal from a painting you've already seen."

"The Dark Lady?" I asked.

"Is that what you call her?"

"That is what she calls herself," I replied. "May we see the preliminary painting, please?"

"Next," ordered Kobrynski—and an instant later the Dark Lady's face appeared almost within my reach, her sad eyes staring directly into mine.

"It's *her*, all right," said Heath.

"It is indeed an excellent likeness," I agreed. "How long have you been working on it?"

"Three years," said Kobrynski uncomfortably, as if he were ashamed that he had not been able to create it in an evening.

"Where would you create the explosions?" I asked.

"Probably in her eyes," he said. "It would give them life."

I nodded in approval. "It might even make her look less unhappy."

"Maybe the earlobes, too," suggested Heath. "I can't remember now—did she wear earrings or not?"

"She wore no jewelry at all, Friend Valentine," I replied.

"Computer—deactivate," commanded Kobrynski.

The image disappeared—and just as it vanished, Reuben Venzia opened the door and entered the cabin.

"Who are you?" demanded Kobrynski.

"He is Reuben Venzia," I said.

"Well, well," said Heath with a wry smile. "The gang's all here."

22.

"**S**HE IS NOT HERE YET, Friend Reuben," I said as Venzia mopped the sweat from his face.

"But thanks for waiting for us, just the same," added Heath sarcastically.

"I just couldn't take the chance," replied Venzia. "It was too important to get here before *she* did. Besides, I never had any agreement with you; I was under no obligation to take you here or anywhere. You just want to sell her to Abercrombie."

"Just a minute," interrupted Kobrynski. He turned to Heath. "You never *did* say why you were interested in her. I think it's about time you told me."

"Why?" responded Heath. "You don't believe in her anyway."

"If she exists, I'm not letting you sell her to *anyone*."

"She can take care of herself," said Venzia. "Or didn't Heath tell you what happened the last time he decided to sell her?"

"Well?" said Kobrynski, staring at Heath.

"She vanished."

"What do you mean, vanished?"

"I mean," said Heath, "that she disappeared from inside a sealed spaceship."

Kobrynski shook his head in disgust. "You're *all* crazy."

"*I* didn't say it," Venzia pointed out.

"No, but you believe it."

"Yes, I do."

"By the way," said Heath to Venzia, "how the devil did you get here so quickly? I would have sworn we'd reach Saltmarsh three days ahead of you."

"I stayed in Deepsleep for two weeks, and when I woke up I radioed ahead, found out that Kobrynski was on Solitaire, and changed course."

"I should have thought of that myself," admitted Heath.

"Some master thief!" snorted Venzia contemptuously.

"Well, no matter," replied Heath with a shrug. "We beat *her* here, and that's all that counts." He paused. "By the way, you're not the only person with a question for her when she shows up."

"What are you talking about?"

"Friend Leonardo had a nocturnal visitation from the Dark Lady."

"She actually appeared to you?" demanded Venzia, turning to me.

"I am not certain, Friend Reuben," I replied. "That is what I must ask her."

Venzia seemed about to make a comment, then pursed his lips and emitted a short sigh. "So now we wait," he said.

"Now we wait," I agreed.

"Excuse me for interrupting," said Kobrynski sardonically, "but this cabin doesn't sleep four; as a matter of fact, it doesn't even sleep two. I'm happy to have three madmen provide me with a little diversion during the day, but when you get ready to sleep, you go back to your ships."

"Do you wish us to leave now?" I asked.

"It's up to you—but you can't see the full effect of a plasma painting through a ship's viewscreen."

"When will you begin?" I asked.

"It'll be dark in another twenty minutes or so," he said. "I think I'll start in about an hour."

"Then, if you don't mind," said Heath, "Leonardo and I will stay here until you're finished."

"I'm staying too," added Venzia.

"It's fine by me," said Kobrynski. "But I ought to warn you that I've only got enough food for me. If you guys are hungry, this would be a good time to go to your ships and grab some dinner."

"You've only got enough food for one meal?" asked Venzia with open disbelief.

"I'm leaving tomorrow," replied Kobrynski.

"Where are you going?"

"I don't know," he answered. "If I'm not pleased with my painting, I'll probably hunt up another deserted planet and try it again."

"And if you *are* pleased?"

He shrugged. "There's no sense doing it again if I do it right the first time. There's a new Murderball league forming out on the Rim; maybe I'll take a crack at it."

"Murderball?" repeated Heath curiously.

Kobrynski nodded. "It's a combination of an ancient game called rugby and something they used to call Bikes and Spikes."

"Bikes and Spikes?" echoed Heath. "Didn't they outlaw that a couple of centuries ago?"

"In the Oligarchy," answered Kobrynski. "They still play it on the Outer Frontier."

"They lost a lot of people in Bikes and Spikes," said Heath. "What's the fatality rate for Murderball?"

"Twenty-eight percent, in a ten-game season," said Kobrynski. "It sounds exciting."

"It sounds frightening," I said with a shudder.

Kobrynski looked at me for a moment. "Do you know what sounds really frightening? Sitting alone in a hospital bed, waiting to die." He looked out a window. "If you guys are going to eat, you'd better get moving."

"How long does it take you to set this plasma painting up?" asked Heath.

1 "Maybe half an hour."

"Then I think I'll look at the painting before I eat. Nothing ruins a good meal like haste."

"It's up to you," said Kobrynski with no show of interest.

"I will remain here," I said. "I wish to see how a plasma painting is created."

"What about you?" Kobrynski asked Venzia.

"It's too damned hot out there," muttered Venzia. "My ship is a couple of miles away. I'll wait until it cools down."

"What subject have you chosen to paint?" I asked.

"As long as the three of you are here, I suppose I might as well paint the Dark Lady," answered Kobrynski. He grimaced. "I really hadn't planned to do her for another few months, until I've got every detail absolutely right."

"She looked perfect in the hologram," offered Heath.

Kobrynski shook his head. "I haven't got the mouth right yet."

"It looked fine to me," said Heath.

"No," said Kobrynski. "She always seems to be just on the verge of saying something, like she's just a hundredth of a second from moving her lips. I still don't have that feeling when I look at the hologram." He shrugged. "What the hell. I could work on it another fifty years and still not get it right. I might as well go with what I've got."

There was a brief period of twilight, and then the sky darkened with surprising suddenness.

Kobrynski waited a few more minutes, until the last light of the sun had vanished from the distant mountains, and then began issuing commands to his machines. Gradually they began to hum and glow, virtually throbbing with energy.

"Are they supposed to do that?" asked Heath uneasily.

Kobrynski nodded. "They're just acting as a conduit, from the pile to the canvas."

"The canvas?"

"The sky, Mr. Heath," replied Kobrynski with an amused smile. "The sky."

He continued giving orders, making minute adjustments, altering instructions, juggling vectors and angles, for another twenty minutes. Finally he stepped back from his equipment and turned to us.

"It's just about ready," he announced.

"Where do we look?" asked Heath.

"All of the windows have been treated," replied Kobrynski. "You can watch through any of them." He paused. "There's no danger as long as you don't leave the cabin, but you should probably climb into your protective suits, just to be on the safe side."

"What protective suits?" demanded Venzia.

"That's right: You weren't here when I mentioned it. The whole planet's going to get a lethal dose of radiation when the explosions start." He paused. "You'll be safe here."

"But how will I get back to my ship?"

"I've got a spare suit packed away somewhere. We'll dig it out when you're ready to leave."

"Maybe I should go to my ship right now and get my own suit," said Venzia.

Kobrynski shrugged. "It's up to you. Can you find it in the dark? Solitaire doesn't have any moons."

Venzia looked momentarily surprised. "I'm not sure," he admitted. "I think I'll stay here after all, and accept the loan of your suit when it's time to leave."

"Fine."

Heath and I had finished donning our shielded outfits when I noticed that Kobrynski had not yet donned his gloves, and I mentioned the oversight to him.

"The gloves are awkward to manipulate," he replied, "and sometimes I've got to make some last-second adjustments manually."

He turned back to the computers and began issuing still more orders, all of them expressed as mathematical formulae and totally incomprehensible to me.

"Soon now," he said, not looking up from his equipment.

The three of us moved closer to a window and watched the still night sky.

"One more adjustment," he murmured, reciting one last equation. "Now, on my mark—go!"

I peered intently through the window. At first nothing seemed to be happening. Then, slowly, gradually, the air seemed to become perceptibly *thicker*, and I could see swirling patterns starting to form, molecular motion made visible.

A bolt of lightning flashed, but unlike every other lightning bolt I had ever seen, this one did not dissipate, but remained in the sky, twisting itself into a curved line of flame. Another flash of lightning, and another line was added to the painting. A swirl of electrical energy for texture, glowing ionized molecules for color, more streaks of lightning, and suddenly the Dark Lady began taking shape before my astounded eyes.

In another moment her face covered the heavens, her sad eyes glowed with the light of distant nebulas, her teeth were white with starlight, her hair was a billowing mass of dark clouds, dotted here and there with pinpoints of stardust. Then the explosions started, highlighting her with an unimaginable release of energy.

"It is fabulous!" I exclaimed.

"I've never seen anything like it!" added Heath in awed tones.

"The mouth is still wrong," said Kobrynski. He turned back to his machines. "If I can just capture her lips in the instant before she speaks . . ."

He began making manual adjustments.

"How long does it last?" asked Venzia.

"It should start losing its integrity in about ten more seconds," said Kobrynski, pushing keys and plotting vectors. "Damn! It's still not right, and I'm going to lose it! I can't make the adjustments fast enough!"

"It's not breaking up at all," noted Heath.

"It will."

We all watched the image intently.

"If anything, I'd say it's getting brighter," observed Heath.

Kobrynski walked back to the window and stared at his creation, frowning in confusion.

"I don't understand it," he said. "She should be fading out of existence."

"But she's not," said Heath.

"Then maybe I've got a chance to fix those lips!" said Kobrynski excitedly. He quickly returned to the machines, pressing still more keys.

"That's it!" he cried triumphantly, joining us at the window once more.

And indeed it was now a perfect representation of the Dark Lady, rendered in glowing detail across a cosmic tapestry. She seemed so real that I found myself listening for the words that seemed about to issue from her mouth.

And then, so naturally that it took me a few seconds to realize what was happening, her lips began to move.

"Vladimir," she whispered across the sky as mountains shook. *"Come to me."*

"Did you hear that?" demanded Kobrynski, his eyes wild with excitement.

"Come, Vladimir," she crooned as the cabin trembled and the machines whined in protest.

"Then it *was* a dream, after all," I mumbled, stunned by the realization that she was calling only for Kobrynski.

Kobrynski walked to the door as if hypnotized, and Venzia grabbed his arm.

"No!" he yelled. "Not until I ask my question!"

Kobrynski merely shrugged his arm, and sent Venzia flying across the room.

"Where do you think you're going?" demanded Heath.

"To *her*," said Kobrynski tranquilly.

"Open that door and Venzia will die—and so will you, if you don't put some gloves on."

"She won't harm me," replied Kobrynski.

"She's not even there!" snapped Heath. "You're walking into a radioactive furnace!"

"Vladimir," whispered the Dark Lady.

"She's calling me."

"Leonardo, say something to him!"

"She is not the Mother of All Things," I said dully, feeling slightly disoriented. "She is only the Dark Lady."

"What are you talking about?" snapped Heath.

I turned to him. "Then what does she want of me?" I said, confused. "I do not understand."

"Come to me, Vladimir," whispered the Dark Lady.

Kobrynski opened the door.

"No!" cried Heath, diving toward him in a vain attempt to stop him. He was too late, and an instant later the force of the storm had slammed the door shut again.

We both raced to the window to watch, and Venzia, an ugly bruise on his forehead, joined us.

Kobrynski stopped some fifty yards away from the cabin and reached his hands to the sky in a gesture of supplication—and, just before her image was dispersed, the Dark Lady's hauntingly sad expression vanished, to be replaced by a smile. I looked back to where Kobrynski had been standing, but there was no sign of him.

"Where is he?" I asked, puzzled.

"He vanished," said Heath. He paused, frowning in confusion. "At least, I *think* he vanished."

"NO!" screamed Venzia, running to the door and opening it. "You can't leave yet! I have to talk to you!"

"Do not leave, Friend Reuben!" I shouted after him. "You have already been exposed to radiation when Kobrynski opened the door, and you are not wearing any protection. You will die!"

"Don't try to stop me!" snarled Venzia, twisting free and racing outside to the spot where Kobrynski had vanished. "Please!" he yelled at the top of his lungs. "I've got to know!"

"We must bring him back inside!" I said urgently.

"Let him yell for his answer," replied Heath wearily. "He's dead already."

"But—"

There was a final violent explosion overhead, and then the sky returned to normal.

"Activate the radiation meter at the top of your faceplate, Leonardo," said Heath. "If the force of that last blast didn't kill him, he'll be burnt to a crisp in another ten seconds. His brain's already fried."

"I should have stopped him," I said, running out of the cabin. "I *must* help him!"

"He's beyond help," replied Heath, but he nonetheless came with me.

Venzia had collapsed by the time we reached him. His face was covered with black blisters, and his hair was singed and smoking, but he was still alive, and we finally managed to carry him back into the cabin and lay him down on Kobrynski's cot.

"We might just as well have left him outside," remarked Heath. "You can't open the door to a nuclear furnace and expect your quarters to remain uncontaminated."

I checked my radiation meter, and the reading confirmed his statement.

Venzia murmured something through his burnt lips.

"I think he wants water," said Heath.

"But the water is contaminated," I said.

"Give it to him anyway. What's the difference?"

I poured some water into a small metal cup and held it to Venzia's lips.

"Thanks," he muttered. His head fell back onto the cot. "Where is she?" he managed to rasp.

"She is gone," I said as the full import of what had happened dawned upon me. "She is not the Mother of All Things. She came for Kobrynski, not for me."

"And now I will never know what lies beyond," whispered Venzia.

"You will know very soon, Friend Reuben," I said gently.

Suddenly he tensed, his eyes staring blindly into space.

"What is the matter, Friend Reuben?" I asked.

"I see her!" he rasped.

"Is she beckoning to you?"

He frowned. "No. She's with *him*."

"With Kobrynski?"

"Yes."

"What is she doing?" I asked.

"She's smiling." He collapsed back onto the bed. "She's finally smiling," he whispered, and died.

I sat motionless beside Venzia's body for a few moments. Then I felt Heath's hand on my shoulder.

"I think it's time to leave, Leonardo," he said.

"Yes," I said. "It is time."

"We'll have to leave his body here. We can't risk taking it onto the ship."

"I know," I replied, getting to my feet and following him to the door.

"You know," he said thoughtfully as we walked slowly to the ship, "I'm still not quite sure what I saw."

"*I* am."

"I wonder where she'll show up next?" he mused.

"She will never appear again," I replied.

Epilogue

This, then, is the chronicle of the Dark Lady.

But it is also the chronicle of Leonardo, who continues to wander the galaxy shunned and alone, whose name may never again be uttered by any member of his House or Family, and whose sins are beyond number.

Many times after I left Solitaire in the company of Valentine Heath I considered performing the ritual of suicide, but always I was ethically compelled to await the end of my suspension from Claiborne and the fulfillment of my contract. And when the day finally came that my employment was officially terminated, I realized that if I was no longer a Bjornn, I was no longer required to abide by Bjornn customs.

Heath and I moved from planet to planet for three years, always one step ahead of the police, while I apprenticed myself to the only trade for which I was qualified. It was during this time—more from the boredom of travel on his small ship than for any other reason, or so I thought—that I began drawing a series of sketches of the Dark Lady, trying but never quite succeeding in capturing her elusive beauty.

Then one day Heath was apprehended, and I found myself totally alone. It was then that I realized what my true mission in life was, why events had conspired to place me on Solitaire on that fatal day, why she had appeared to me in a vision, and what it was that she wanted of me.

There have been many portraits of her, and always she has been portrayed with a hauntingly sad expression on her face. With Kobrynski and Venzia dead and Heath in prison, only *I* can paint her as she last appeared, and as she will appear for the rest of Time.

It will take me many attempts and many years, for I am as clumsy in my painting as I am in all other things. But someday I shall succeed—for only then, with the completion of the last portrait of the Dark Lady and its juxtaposition to all the others, will both of our odysseys finally be complete.

A Selection of Legend Titles

☐ Eon	Greg Bear	£4.95
☐ The Infinity Concerto	Greg Bear	£3.50
☐ Wolf in Shadow	David Gemmell	£3.50
☐ Wyrms	Orson Scott Card	£2.95
☐ Speaker for the Dead	Orson Scott Card	£2.95
☐ The Misplaced Legion	Harry Turtledove	£2.95
☐ An Emperor For the Legion	Harry Turtledove	£2.99
☐ Falcon's of Narabedla	Marion Zimmer Bradley	£2.50
☐ Dark Lady	Mike Resnick	£2.99
☐ Golden Sunlands	Christopher Rowley	£2.99
☐ This is the Way the World Ends	James Morrow	£5.50
☐ Emprise	Michael Kube-McDowell	£3.50

Prices and other details are liable to change

ARROW BOOKS, BOOKSERVICE BY POST, PO BOX 29. DOUGLAS, ISLE OF MAN, BRITISH ISLES

NAME..

ADDRESS..

....

....

Please enclose a cheque or postal order made out to Arrow Books Ltd. for the amount due and allow the following for postage and packing.

U.K. CUSTOMERS: Please allow 22p per book to a maximum of £3.00.

B.F.P.O. & EIRE: Please allow 22p per book to a maximum of £3.00

OVERSEAS CUSTOMERS: Please allow 22p per book.

Whilst every effort is made to keep prices low it is sometimes necessary to increase cover prices at short notice. Arrow Books reserve the right to show new retail prices on covers which may differ from those previously advertised in the text or elsewhere.